SAFE WITH YOU

A SMALL TOWN MILITARY ROMANCE

VETERANS OF SILVER RIDGE
BOOK 2

CLAIRE CAIN

This book is especially dedicated to the readers who will most identify with Winnie. You are magic, friends, and you are loved.

CHAPTER ONE

Winnie

I had a super special set of skills I'd acquired over the years. Sadly, they weren't Liam Neeson's from *Taken*—because that would've been too amazing and useful—but I would like to think they allowed me to stay calm in the face of stress or danger. They gave me a certain edge.

How, one might ask? I'm an expert people pleaser.

Oh, sure, it might not sound like a skill any person would even want, let alone call a skill, and I could see how that might be a perspective shared by many. But I wouldn't have survived the last thirteen years if I hadn't developed an incredible ability to internalize any upsetting emotions and lock them down tight in order to do what needed to be done.

That was why I hadn't *accidentally-on-purpose* missed the flight from Wichita, Kansas, to Salt Lake City, Utah, this morning like I had the one weeks ago. That first flight would've been simple—come out to Utah and get married, then head right back home, and I'd chickened out. Was all this really necessary? It would involve someone else—someone with no stakes in my crisis. How could I drag them into this cesspool and live with myself being so self-centered?

But things had escalated in the meantime, and now, I'd used the very bold inner version of me, the one I'd summoned from the depths and dusted off, to keep me from bailing on this whole scenario.

The plan was to save the family business and dig my brother out of debt while keeping his mess of a life from my parents. Nothing else really mattered at this point.

That's why seeing a man I'd always been a little bit in love with for the first time ever in real life didn't make me nervous.

Not at all nervous about it, nope!

So completely not nervous.

My hands weren't shaking, and my mouth hadn't dried out the second I deplaned. That had to be because of the Utah air, and never mind the fact that I came from Kansas, where the air is also dry. My body didn't feel like I might've been sweating through the layers of winter clothing I'd donned hours ago, and I hadn't been mentally spiraling out about the many, many ways every single step of this ill-conceived plan could go wrong.

I wasn't freaked out that my brother had gotten so deep in debt that he had loan sharks stalking *me* for money even after he'd paid them a huge sum. I was completely fine with the fact that my father, who'd had a heart attack less than two years ago, had decided to retire and sell off part of the business just so my jerk of a brother could liquidate his half and "follow his dreams" aka gamble his inheritance away and pretend he'd invested it *and* the trust money he'd blown through in record time.

Also absolutely not a concern that the actual bad guys my brother owed insane amounts of money to had decided to target me, or that I'd decided even before I realized how bad things were for Jeremy that I'd call in the promise Tristan had once made me, even though guilt had flooded me so intensely I'd almost gotten ill.

I felt totally fine marrying the soldier I'd been writing emails and letters to since I was sixteen like it was a normal, acceptable course of action and not a desperate move to get the trust from my grandfather two years early in hopes of saving the family farm and ideally, keeping my parents from realizing just how messed up their only remaining son was.

I definitely hadn't spent the last fourteen-ish years dreaming about meeting Tristan Donnelly, only to have him find out about my idiot brother's issues and end up burdening the man I'd been enamored with for what felt like ever with my problems.

Oh. Wait.

With a giant exhale, I worked to steady myself mentally and physically. Heading into a downward tailspin I did everything to avoid? I couldn't let it happen. No one wanted to come to the airport to pick up a friend, only to find a mess of nerves and overthinking in her place. And while what exactly lay ahead for me and Tristan was unclear, we were at least and most certainly friends.

The fact that I'd wanted this descriptor to change a half dozen (or more) times over the years didn't enter the scenario at this point. We had strictly lived in the Friend Zone and—

"Winnie?"

My heart shot through the roof, and I sucked in a

breath. I had talked to him on the phone exactly five times in our fourteen years of friendship. Each and every word of those conversations were written on my heart and etched into my memory, and I'd know that voice anywhere.

I spun on my heel, awkwardly jerking my giant suitcase around, and grinned before my eyes hit him.

"Tristan?" I knew it would be him, and good thing the name had made it off my tongue, because once I finally saw him...

My heart may have stopped beating altogether. Maybe it just skipped. Whatever the case, when it restarted, any effort at pretending to feel calm because of some silly set of failings I liked to pretend were superpowers had evaporated in the face of him.

He was... gorgeous.

Brown hair tucked under a ballcap, brim pulled down low enough I couldn't quite see what I knew would be hazel eyes. He'd told me that once—how he had the same eyes as his mother, and at the time, I'd never wanted anything more than to see him.

I took in the rest of him. A beard trimmed close. Full lips. Shoulders broad, with a general presence formidable enough to startle you if you happened upon him on the street. And yet, also a stillness about him that set me completely at ease.

Well, at ease on the one hand. Because this was Tristan. I knew him better than I knew anyone else in this world, but he was still very much a mystery to me.

And on the other hand, not at all at ease, because he was so deeply and desperately attractive, far more than I had even imagined, and I was practically vibrating with nervous awareness. Funny how we'd communicated all this time and never jumped on a video call. There'd been a certain mystique to faceless letters on paper, emails on screen, and a precious few voice calls on phones. In the early days when he was deployed, video calls wouldn't have worked. And since we'd started that way, we just... kept going like that. Oddly, we never exchanged pictures either, like pen pals would.

"You get all your bags?" he asked, his head dipping.

I imagined if I could see his eyebrows, they would've dipped with the question. Clearly, he could see I had my bags, but he made no move to touch me or approach me, almost like he could tell I wasn't fully functioning.

Then he did touch me, a hand on my arm with a quick squeeze and release, and another, quieter question.

"You okay, Winn?"

His voice startled me—how had I spaced out when I'd been longing for this moment? Probably the surreal feeling and the jumble of relief and overwhelm pummeling me, but still. Tristan was here! *Right* here!

"I—yeah. Sorry. Hi. I'm so sorry. I'm good. I have my bags. I'm good. Sorry."

A tiny, perplexed smile hit his lips, and I got a sneak peek of that mouth curved just so and no longer felt the burgeoning embarrassment from my babbling response because he'd stolen any other thought from my brain. I was more flustered than I could ever recall being when actual danger wasn't a factor, and yet here I was, my brain nearly melting out of my ears from his proximity and my cuckoo response to him.

Not really how I'd planned for this to go. Then again, what did go to plan in my life?

He nodded once though, mercifully not asking if I was really okay, because we both knew I wasn't. "Good. Ready to go?"

My smile reflexively arrived, and I started walking. "Absolutely."

In a few minutes, we reached the parking deck and found his car, a nice-looking black truck with dirt all over it. The snowstorm didn't cause flights to cancel this morning, but it seemed to be intensifying, and from what he'd said in our texts earlier, it'd take a while to drive to his small town.

He hoisted my suitcase into the back seat as though it weighed far less than the fifty-three pounds it clocked in at during check-in, then hustled around to open the door. And then he held out a hand to help me into the truck.

The absurd thing was, I hadn't mentally prepared to touch him. How that could be, I couldn't say, but I did know very clearly that taking his warm large hand in front of me sent me into an internal tizzy.

He watched me as I stared at his palm, all the while my body coming to grips with the more obvious plan to enter the truck and get out of the cold and eventually let go of said hand. Small fireworks exploded internally as I slid my palm onto his, but I was fairly certain the expression on my face mirrored something like consternation. And I couldn't read his expression because I was still locked on our hands—mine in his. His holding mine.

Tristan Donnelly in real life, holding my hand.

Once I was in, he stepped back, and the absence of his warmth against my palm felt patently wrong. Working to find my bearings, I settled into the seat as I watched him round the front of the vehicle. I could swear I saw his hand press between the sides of his jacket against his chest for a heartbeat, but then he swatted at the brim of his hat as though to knock the bill down even lower over his eyes, and he loaded into the driver's seat.

He started up the truck and fiddled with the vents,

adjusting them all to point toward me. "I don't want you to be cold on the drive, so just let me know what you need."

"Okay," I said, my voice practically scraping out.

And afterward, he just... drove. Neither of us spoke, and I ended up staring out the window at the mountains rising up on our right, then the canyon walls as we headed into their depths.

I begged my brain to come up with something to say—maybe one of the hundred things I'd always wanted to say to him when I saw him in person. But none of them would come because this wasn't how I'd imagined this meeting.

We were supposed to smile and hug and greet each other like old friends. I was supposed to keep my head on straight and not lose all ability to speak because he was even better in person than in our emails.

But now, it was all ruined.

Because he hadn't chosen to be here, meeting me in person. Not really. This all came from the mess back home and the reason why I came here—to fix it. Not to meet him.

Knowing this, the least I could do was stay calm and let him focus on driving. I knew him to be quiet and used to his space, so I wouldn't invade it. He had been a good friend all these years, and the only thing I could do to thank him for what he was doing was keep it simple and not let all my feelings come seeping out.

I'd do what I did best. I'd tuck them away and make sure he stayed as happy as possible given the circumstances.

But now that I'd thought of them, there was no blockade high enough to stop my mind from running those anxious trails leading to *what if*. And the low hum of the road wasn't enough ambient noise to cover the clanging of my brain.

So without doing any of the things I'd promised myself I'd do, I burst out, "So. We're getting married."

EMAIL

Fourteen years ago

To: Tristan Donnelly
     From: Winniechickendinny

Hello there, Tristan Donnelly,

I'm Winnie Delmonico, the youngest of the Delmonico family and your newest Adopt a Soldier program matchup. I hope you'll tell us how we can support you. My parents are great, and my older brothers might write too, but this whole thing was kind of my idea so you'll hear from me most.

I'm a sophomore in high school and hit the big one-six in a few months. I have a little over two years left until I graduate, and then I'm definitely heading out of state for college. I love my family, but it'd be nice to have my own experiences.

As the youngest and only girl in my family, I take on the role of peacemaker. My older brothers Thomas and Jeremy are decent human beings, and it seems like the further out from high school they get, the better. Or at least I assume this will happen for Jeremy when he graduates in the spring... time will tell, Tristan. Time will tell. Do you have siblings?

I absolutely love animals, but sadly, my parents are allergic to anything that thinks about having fur, so that's a no go. Ironically, we have a few horses on our farm, and don't ask me how I know, but I'm allergic to them. I've tried to point out this cosmic imbalance but have been told that since horses don't live inside the house, my allergy is manageable. Thus, I am a dog person without a dog, a cat lover without a cat. Do you like animals? Have any pets?

Okay, that's probably enough from me this time. I'm not sure what you'd prefer—more talking about my life? I'd love to know about yours, but I'm sure you're busy. I can't imagine what it's like to be deployed and living in... well, I have no idea what your living conditions are like, so fill me in there if you want. Anyway, I hope you liked this email, and I'll try to send a package soon if you'll tell me what you want or need.

Stay safe, Tristan.

Winnie

CHAPTER TWO

Tristan

I steadfastly kept my eyes on the road despite everything in me wanting to look at her and get a read on her expression now that she'd said those words.

Something hid in her tone—disbelief? Amazement? Dread? I didn't know because we'd only talked on the phone a small handful of times over the years, and I couldn't interpret her yet.

"We're getting married," I confirmed, because I hadn't quite registered the reality either.

This woman I'd been connected to since she was a teen, this person who'd been a cornerstone in my life and yet whom I had never met in real life let alone touched until I set a hand on her wrist an hour ago... she would be my wife.

A garbled laugh filled the space between us as I made the final turn to my house. Purchasing it was the first thing I'd done upon moving here about nine months ago, and the closer I got to the small cabin, inching down the long gravel driveway, the more at ease I became.

"This is beautiful. I—I love the trees. And the house. And the rocks."

Her gaze tracked from one side of the truck to the other, and I followed it as I parked, the tension slipping from my shoulders and neck with the simple act. I knew she got chatty when she was nervous, because she'd shared stories of such instances over the years, but seeing it in person was something else. Warmth and fondness snaked through me— all these years imagining her nervous babble coming to life right here.

My small log cabin–style home sat nestled into a space between massive pine trees with a stretch of pasture between. They stood out most now since they hadn't dropped their needles, but in summer, the oak and maple and even a ways back, aspen, showed out well, too.

"Thank you. It feels like home." Or as close as I could ever get.

My home during my years on active duty had changed with every move until I settled into my unit in North Carolina, and then I'd lived in the same house for ten years. But life there had been so busy and demanding, I'd hardly allowed myself to settle in. I'd always known that when I retired, then I'd truly find my space, and maybe recapture something of what I'd felt when I'd lived with my parents. I'd never get that back, exactly, but here in this little house with my dog and my quiet life, it didn't feel empty, at least.

I glanced at her then, our eyes meeting for the first time since the airport—colliding more like. They were a punch to the gut landed with plenty of impact and no bracing on my end because she was so completely beautiful and there was no denying it.

I'd done my best not to fully register this—to focus on the drive and what lay ahead instead of the reality that this woman—*this* woman—was the same one I'd been writing letters and emails to for over a decade. For the majority of my adult life.

There you are.

A pit yawned the instant the thought shot through my mind like a dying star. *No. No.* I wasn't having a moment with my heart staggering around in my chest with this woman's name etched into it. This was my friend, the only real constant I'd had in a lifetime of change and unpredictability.

No.

"I'm so glad, Tristan."

Something sweet and hot twisted through me at the sound of my name on her lips and the genuine, warm tone in her voice. I'd only heard it a few times, but this was twice today. It came like another hit, another moment in time I doubted I'd ever forget, and it drove home how wrong all of this was.

Winnie Delmonico was one of the warmest, sweetest people I'd ever encountered, yet so far, she'd been a clammed-up stranger. I couldn't blame her. All of this felt foreign and unwieldy. But I hoped she'd relax a bit and we'd recover some of the usual rapport and connection we'd built over the years.

We were friends—always had been. I hoped she'd let this notion take over at some point.

I cleared my throat and nodded, tearing my eyes from hers and exiting the car. Sitting and gazing at her wasn't going to help her get comfortable with me or help me handle... whatever it was happening inside me.

She'd already opened the door by the time I reached her

side, so I grabbed her suitcase from the back seat and noticed she'd worn jeans tucked into boots. Somehow, in the flurry of finding her, recognizing her long, dark hair from behind, and actually speaking to her, I hadn't recalled she'd come prepared for the weather. But of course she had.

"Is she inside?" she asked, trudging along next to me.

The snow wasn't high yet—most of it that'd come down in the last storm had melted off the walk and only clung to the rocks and grass now, but there was a layer accumulating and I hated the thought of her slipping around just getting to the house.

"She is. She'll be very happy to meet you." *Understatement.* I unlocked the door and instantly, Juniper's nose was sniffing and seeking the new scent. "Hey, buddy girl, back up for me. Back up."

She commenced her tornado dance, swirling around in circles and jumping, almost bucking, as I entered. Even if it were just me, I'd get this part. She was joy and enthusiasm bottled up and injected into a furry package, and her greeting never failed to lighten my mood.

"Oh my gosh, oh my gosh, you're so gorgeous," Winnie said as she entered.

I shut the door behind her as she offered her hands to Junie to sniff, then slid her palms over her soft head.

"Oh, you're a sweet girl, aren't you? I'm so happy to meet you!"

I set her suitcase aside and allowed myself to take in this meeting between my two best friends. It was no surprise Junie had already taken a seat and offered her paw to Winnie, but seeing her with Winnie...

She was an easy dog to love. A yellow Labrador was the kind of dog people innately and automatically liked if they didn't hate dogs, and I already knew Winnie was a dog person without a dog and a cat lover without a cat. She'd never gotten to have animals, and it was one more thing she'd kept herself from for someone else's sake. But the way she dropped to her knees and was talking to Juniper like she knew her, like she already loved her, did something to me.

"You're so sweet, aren't you? Just like your daddy. You are the world's best dog because of course you are, and you are—oh my gosh you're precious."

Winnie's eyes shifted to find mine, and without looking, I already knew what'd happened. Juniper had given her a hug.

Yes, my ridiculous sweetie of a dog gave hugs. She put one paw up on a shoulder and rested her head on the other one, effectively hugging the lucky recipient with her warmth and overflow of love.

"Is she hugging me right now?" Winnie asked in a whisper, like she didn't want to scare her away.

I stifled a chuckle because the idea she'd end it before Winnie did was of no concern, but I crossed my arms and looked on. If a quick flash of jealousy that my dog was receiving a hug before I ever did flared up, I buried it. "She is."

Winnie melted. Her shoulders drooped, and she rested her head more fully on Juniper's side and closed her eyes, soaking in the contact.

Guilt and frustration warred in me, and a deep sense of *wrong* hit. Not that I didn't want her hugging my dog, but because it wasn't *me* comforting her.

What a useless thought because Juniper was the best and there was nothing amiss with Winnie loving her instantly, but she'd been off since she'd arrived, and I'd anticipated it yet failed to help her.

An obnoxious strumming ringtone rang out, and I

pulled my phone from my pocket to turn off the alarm. "Sorry. We've got about an hour until our appointment."

She released Juniper and pulled back, then rose to her feet. "Do you have—"

"You can go—"

We exchanged awkward smiles, and I gestured for her to go ahead.

"Do you have somewhere I can freshen up?"

Her eyes cut away from mine to focus back on the grinning dog nuzzling her hand.

"Of course. Your bedroom's down the hall, and there's a bathroom inside, too. I'll be out here when you're ready."

Suitcase in tow, she made her way to the bedroom and closed the door while I busied myself dealing with anything that would distract me from Winnie being in my bedroom. Since this place was small and there was only one main bedroom and a room I usually used for workouts when I didn't make it into town for sparring with the guys or a workout at Grit, she'd take my room and I'd borrowed an air mattress from Bruce. It'd be fine.

Fifteen minutes later, Winnie emerged. Foolishly, I hadn't braced for it, but she walked out looking exactly as gorgeous as she had earlier, and I had no defenses up.

She'd changed into a soft-looking cream-colored dress with long sleeves that fit her close and tall brown boots. She'd added to or refreshed or *somethinged* her makeup, so her lips were a pretty pink color and her eyes accentuated by whatever magic she'd wrought.

I swallowed hard, taking in the soft waves in her dark hair cascading over her shoulders and the way her hands twisted together in front of her.

Those gorgeous eyes pinned me, and I couldn't move or breathe and certainly couldn't speak. She'd been beautiful in jeans and a coat and snow boots, and now, she was a mesmerizing combination of comfortable and sexy—I wasn't sure I'd ever encountered the pairing, but it instantly became my new favorite.

Pretty sure everything about Winnie was my favorite. Also pretty sure reacting this strongly to someone I'd just met made no sense.

You didn't just meet her…

My mind, that same one trying to make cosmic connections without my permission, needed to stop pushing me toward her. My relationship with Winnie was already under incredible stress now that we were standing in the same room after so long being separated by time and space and computer or phone lines—I didn't need to complicate it further.

"Hey, can we, uh… you know, I was just thinking maybe we could…" She cleared her throat. "You know, um, just…"

She glanced around like she was seeing the living room for the first time, her gaze flitting from the worn leather chair by the fireplace to the tattered couch next to it. A TV mounted on the wall straight ahead was the newest feature to the room, and Juniper's bed took up a decent portion of the far corner between the fireplace and the TV.

I might not've been able to read the nuance in her expression, but I saw something I didn't like there, the very thing I'd been worried about since before she'd arrived—she felt lost.

I crossed to her. "You can say anything you need to say, Winnie. You're safe here."

I could've gone on, but I wouldn't… not yet.

Her lashes fluttered, and she finally met my gaze. "I'm wondering if we can start over. I feel like this has been so weird and it's not what I planned, but my mind has been going a mile a minute and I just want a do-over."

A small huff of a laugh snuck out, maybe in relief. "Of course. Whatever you want."

She bit her lip, inspecting me for a moment before dropping her hands and squaring her shoulders. "Okay, so here goes…"

I nodded, charmed and admittedly curious. I wanted to know what she'd planned as much as she seemed to want to recreate the moment, so why not?

She smiled—bright and pretty and genuinely happy.

"Hey, Tristan, I'm so glad to see you here at the airport." She glanced around like a goof, pretending to see the airport around her. "Thank you for coming to pick me up."

I laughed low and bowed slightly. "My pleasure, truly. I hope your flight was okay."

Her brows pinched a bit and she inhaled, those dark eyes skewering me. "It was fine. Can I… can I hug you?"

"Of course," I said, then stepped forward with arms open, and she did, too.

Relief and satisfaction and a dangerous longing burst in my chest hard enough to steal my breath.

We fit together like fingers in a fist, neatly aligned and natural. We interlocked, my arms high over her shoulders and hers low around my back, a perfect pressure and hold. I'd known she was short, but this close contact drove it home as my chin brushed the top of her head and she tucked herself tight against my chest.

There you are.

My eyes shut and I breathed in the contact, the peace, that came from having her right here with me instead of miles away and in danger. I hadn't realized how on edge I'd been since she missed her flight weeks ago, before the holidays, and she'd rescheduled for today. I'd chopped enough wood to power my house and Saint Security's grid for months.

That's all this was—relief she was here safe. Relief to finally see her in person, even though I'd agonized a fair bit about what this might do to how things had always been between us.

"It feels silly to say I missed you, but I have," she said, her voice quiet, just for me.

Was it silly? *Call me the court jester, then*

"I'm glad you're here."

I pulled back a bit, and she did the same, though I hadn't intended to release her. It made sense that we wouldn't linger in the embrace because a hug like that was intimate. And though we had a deep friendship, we'd never done this before. It felt good—right, even.

"Right" is the new understatement of the year.

Unfortunately, we couldn't stay there all day, but I needed her to know one thing. "We're going to get this part over with and you're going to be okay."

She nodded like my saying so actually reassured her. I hoped with everything in me it did.

"I hope you're right."

More than anything I'd ever wanted in my life, I hoped so, too.

EMAIL

Fourteen years ago

To: Winniechickendinny
    From: Tristan Donnelly

Winnie,

Thanks for writing. It's cool you guys signed up to do this. Do you have any military in the family? Sounds like maybe not. This is a nice way to stay connected. I'm an only child.

Right now, I live in a tent, though it's bigger than a camping tent. I won't be deployed much longer, thankfully. I'm more than halfway done, and then I'm going to train up for an assessment for a different kind of job. We'll see how it goes.

Oh and I love dogs especially, but cats can be decent. I'm gone too much to have a dog these days but definitely someday.

You can send me anything you feel like. I'm all set on

the basics. Maybe your favorite candy? A good book you've read lately? Times between missions can drag, so anything to pass the time is great.

Thanks for writing,
Tristan

CHAPTER THREE

Winnie

The courthouse in Silverton was a beautiful little building about twenty minutes from Tristan's house and, from what I gathered, only a short walk to the main downtown area. I looked forward to wandering the quaint streets and learning more about this place. I might not end up being here long, but I hoped I could enjoy this fleeting glimpse at a life outside the one I'd gotten stuck in.

The plan had been to come here, get married, then head back to Kansas. It's what would've happened the day I missed my flight on purpose. Today, though, I wouldn't be heading back. Not yet, anyway. Which meant I'd be in Silverton for a short but indefinite while.

Tristan managed to exit his side and make it to mine before I'd even unbuckled, so when he offered me his large hand to climb down from the truck, I couldn't not take it.

Not that I wouldn't want to. It's just... the hug back at the cabin.

My stomach flipped just thinking about the comfort and calm that washed over me when his arms had been around me. Such a strange reality because at the same time, my heart had been pounding so hard, I was surprised he hadn't noticed. Being near him like that had sent such a flood of emotion through me, I'd nearly choked on tears and happiness and overwhelm.

I stepped down, and he let go of my hand. The urge to snatch his back up and hold it like a lifeline nearly overpowered me, but we didn't have this kind of relationship. How could we, when we'd just met in person?

But saying we'd just met didn't compute because Tristan Donnelly was braided into my fabric by now. I wasn't sure how I would've survived the years since my family had adopted him as our soldier, but I didn't have to, because he'd been there. Many times closer than any other, he'd been a constant for me and I for him.

There were parts of me he didn't know, but there were also parts of me *only* he knew. For all the danger and turmoil I'd been in lately, without a doubt, he was a safe place.

He definitely was.

"Bruce and his girlfriend will be here. I wanted you to have someone to be your witness and she won't tell anyone, I guarantee it."

My pulse jumped at the thought of meeting Bruce, a man I knew to be one of Tristan's best friends, and Nikki. I'd heard a little about her over the last few months since she'd worked for Saint Security, where Tristan spent his days.

"Okay. I guess they know this is... uh, you know, for a reason?"

I didn't want to say fake because it wouldn't be. It would be legal and real and an important shield against the people coming after me as well as a key to unlock the trust from my grandfather, but not anything like I'd dreamed my wedding would be. I'd packed this cream sweaterdress both because it was warm and cute and because I hated the idea of getting married without at least feeling decent. I'd debated picking up something prettier and more flattering—more like a wedding dress—but I'd run out of time, and since I was watching my budget carefully, it hadn't made sense to splurge.

"They do. Bruce helped me run all of this by a friend of his who's a lawyer, and he asked if he could tell Nikki. I hope it's okay."

His earnest expression sent a wave of calm through me, though nerves crashed right back again as we stepped inside the building.

An astonishingly good-looking man stepped up with a hand extended. "You must be Winnie. It's great to meet you. Welcome to Silverton."

I took his hand, unable to keep from returning the smile he gave me. "Thank you, Bruce. I've heard a lot about you over the years."

"Likewise. And this is Nikki Hastings. She moved here not too long ago. Wanted to make sure you had a few friendly faces around."

His gaze at his girlfriend was open and so affectionate, a pang of longing nudged at me.

Nikki extended her hand. "Nice to meet you, Winnie. Please let me know if you need anything—I know these are unique circumstances."

My cheeks flushed, suddenly embarrassed by the reality that I was getting married to Tristan because I *had* to.

Technically, I didn't have to. I could've waited another two years and watched my family's business fade while my brother sank deeper into debt and danger. I could've gone to the police, maybe, but that likely would've ended up with my brother in jail—I wasn't certain just how bad the guys he'd gotten involved with were, but the way they'd talked to me hadn't made me feel any better about the situation.

It was possible the eventuality of Jeremy going to jail wouldn't kill my dad outright, but I couldn't imagine it would be *good* for him. My parents knew Jeremy had gotten himself into a tight spot, and they also knew he owed a huge sum and the collectors wanted to come after me and maybe even the farm for more money. Legally, they didn't have a leg to stand on, but Jer had done an amazingly convincing job at manipulating our parents to believe it wasn't his fault and these guys weren't criminal, just persistent.

It all ended up with me marrying Tristan. After my oldest brother Thomas passed, my grandfather had put money into trusts for me and Jeremy, accessible at age thirty-two *or* upon marriage. Jeremy had gotten access to his in the last year and blown through it so quickly, all of it was gone now. Learning just how deep in he was and that even the smaller version of the family business was in danger of failing... it clicked.

I could help the family business and my parents' legacy —I could try to protect them from just how awful things had gotten for Jeremy and hopefully stave off the stress and negative effects all this would have on their health. And though I hadn't realized it when I'd first brought up this arrangement, it let me put distance between me and the men pursuing Jeremy and now me—Calvin and his henchmen, as I'd started thinking of them.

I shivered recalling those jerks. They'd scared me in a way I had never experienced. So much so, I'd emailed Tristan words I'd never imagined saying. *"Remember when you said you'd do anything to help me? I may need you now."*

That had been during our fourth phone call ever. He'd responded to the email and simply written, "Winnie, please call me." His number had been right there, the same one it'd always been, and I'd called it without a second thought.

He'd told me to tell him what I needed and he'd do it. He knew a little about what had happened, and I didn't mention the increasing pressure *I* was feeling thanks to Jeremy's issues. And Tristan?

His response had been immediate and hadn't wavered for a second. "I'll do it. Anything you need, Winnie—I've always meant that and nothing's changed."

Tristan was a man who did what he said he'd do. I doubted he ever imagined I'd come to him asking him to marry me, but if he ever questioned it, he never revealed it to me.

Fast forward a few months and here I stood, blushing with embarrassment over this mess—over being the one to clean up after my brother and try to protect my parents and ask this wonderful human to sacrifice *for me.*

"It's a decent plan, Win. It'll be okay."

Tristan's hand rose like he might set it on my back—*yes, please*—but he let it drop back by his side.

"I know. I mean, it's ridiculous, obviously." I flashed a self-deprecating smile at Bruce and Nikki. "But it should release the trust to me, hopefully soon, and gets me away from... everything."

The threats. The possibility of another physical attack. The horrible reality that my brother had turned into a man I didn't recognize and was possibly willing to trade *me* for what he wanted.

Actually, that last one was inescapable, but there was no point in dwelling on all of it right now. And Tristan didn't know about that part yet... not the extent of it.

"It's unconventional, but not unheard of. We know a guy who married a girl to get her out of a bad situation and it really helped her. If this helps you, there's no one better than Tristan." Bruce patted Tristan's shoulder.

I made a mental note to find out more about the guy who'd married the girl to save her, because just the mention of such a scenario existing outside of right here and now gave me a sense of... what? Not normalcy, but maybe like this wasn't as wild an idea as it felt like.

"We ready, folks?" A stylish Black woman in a crisp navy pantsuit peeked her head out the door of what must've been one of the courtrooms.

"Yes, ma'am. We'll be right there," Bruce said with a kind wave, then turned to me. "You two take a minute. We'll meet you in there."

Hand in hand, he and Nikki walked inside the room, and I watched them go until the door swung shut. Anxiety pulsed through me as though it'd liquified and filled my veins. I'd have a monster headache after this no matter what.

Tristan's hand on my arm brought me back to myself.

"We don't have to do this," he said, head dipped so he was looking right in my eyes.

I swallowed hard. "We do. I really think we do. I mean, unless you want to not do it. And then I truly understand. I don't want you to feel stuck or like you can't—"

Both of his hands squeezed mine, and he pinned me with his gaze.

"No. I'm good. I want to do what I can to help you, so all I need now is for you to tell me what you want. If you want to get married right now, we'll do it. If you want to leave here and figure out some other solution, we'll do that. I will find a way."

Tears welled in my eyes, and I sucked in a breath. I'd known Tristan was the best of men for years, but here he stood proving it all over again. He'd done so a million times over, but this moment solidified it once more.

"I don't think there's anything else to do that won't have fallout." That wouldn't end up with my brother in jail and my dad back in the hospital, at best, not to mention the family business crashing and burning after thirty years of thriving.

His chest rose with a large inhale, and he looked like he wanted to say something. His lips thinned a touch, as though he were displeased, and my heart sank yet again. He didn't want to do this, and I couldn't blame him. I didn't either—not really. This was not how I'd imagined my wedding day, even if the groom wasn't all wrong.

"Really, Tristan, if you have any second thoughts about this, I want you to tell me and to know I will never ever fault you for not going through with this. I—"

"What I want is not important, Winn. I'm here for you. What I do need is for you to know that you don't have to fix everything. You can let Jeremy get the consequences he's brought on himself. He's failed you and himself and your parents, and he's going to have to learn. It's not your job—"

"I appreciate you saying that."

My voice cut through the space between us, and his jaw flexed as he bit back whatever else he was going to say.

He'd tried to tell me there were other ways, and I wasn't so stubborn that I couldn't hear him. But he didn't understand how fragile my parents were or how callous Jeremy was. He hadn't watched both of those dynamics intensify over the last few years, and he didn't see how I was the only piece of the puzzle with enough flexibility to do something. I was the only one with access to a lump sum and time to recover if I lost it all to helping the farm. My parents couldn't afford to lose the farm income at this point—yes, they'd retired and my father was no longer the one on the tractor or combine sowing wheat and soy beans, but they'd still be making an income off the business they owned... unless it failed.

Tristan didn't know just how dark it'd gotten before I left.

He had wanted me to come here for a break from Kansas no matter what but didn't want me to have to marry him, like I was the one getting the raw deal. Like this beautiful man wasn't making yet another sacrifice after a lifetime of them.

"Let's just get it done," I said. What a romantic notion for a wedding, right? But what other choice did I have?

If there were any, I didn't see them. I only hoped Tristan would forgive me for all of this someday.

CHAPTER FOUR

Tristan

The county clerk glanced back and forth between us, an expectant expression on her face. "Well, then, by the authority given to me by the great state of Utah, I now pronounce you husband and wife."

Winnie's eyes found mine, and my chest pinched. She looked like she might be sick, and the ashen quality to her face hit me in the ribs. If I didn't understand how backed into a corner she was, even if I didn't agree with her refusing the one thing that could fix much of this, I might've been a little hurt.

If it'd been a wedding she'd chosen—we'd both chosen—then all of this would've been different. If we'd been entering into this marriage with our hearts leading instead of habitual problem-solving and fear.

I'd never planned on marriage, let alone marriage to Winnie. She'd always been this... paragon. She'd been someone safe and special and whole, a beautiful part of my life I'd never touch and mess up, and therefore, I'd never lose. But now, all of that had changed, and I wasn't exactly resisting it. At least not the part where she was here and things had changed... but I couldn't let it get too far out of the norm.

Knowing she wouldn't be here if circumstances were different made it worse than not having her here at all.

I would protect Winnie from anything. What I wasn't sure she understood was that I would've done so whether we married or not. Granted, we both hoped the marriage would alleviate the financial strain on her family's business and create one more barrier to the guys trying to get to Jeremy through her. I would've helped in any other way possible, too.

"Congratulations," Bruce said as he patted my shoulder and drew me in for a quick hug.

Nikki was grinning at Winnie, and gratitude filled me for both of them.

"Thank you for being here."

It wasn't enough. Bruce had consulted with a lawyer on my behalf but in a way that wouldn't lead back to me so no one would know about the situation between me and Winnie. He'd cut me slack when I'd been distracted the last few months and kept me busy when I needed something other than Winnie to think about through the holidays while I waited for this day.

Waited for. Dreaded. Dreamed of. Tried to convince myself this wouldn't change everything.

"Wouldn't miss it. And you know we're here. Anything you need."

His dark brown eyes were filled with sincerity, and like I'd always been able to, I knew I could count on him.

"Thank you."

We'd slowly walked back down the aisle and exited the courtroom. We'd booked the last appointment of the day so there were few others here to witness, though we'd gotten a handful of curious glances. Courthouse weddings weren't unheard of here by any means, but it was a small enough community so Bruce and I were both fairly recognizable as members of Saint Security. It'd be a matter of days before the whole town knew I'd gotten married to a woman no one had ever seen before.

But how could they when even I hadn't set eyes on her until today?

Her small hand folded into mine as we exited the room, and a lick of heat traveled from my palm to my wrist and higher.

No.

"We'll have to introduce you to everyone sometime soon. Any chance you'll think about joining us on Friday?" Bruce said, his gaze cutting to mine, then back to Winnie.

I frowned but didn't speak, because Winnie could speak for herself. It was a luxury she hadn't had much of, and I wasn't about to be the jerk who talked over her and acted like I knew what she wanted.

"Oh, that's so kind. Can I, uh, see how I'm getting settled in? I've got to figure out my remote work, and I'm not sure how that'll look. And obviously, I don't want to crowd into Tristan's life and smother him or anything."

She chuckled this odd, mildly unhinged sound that pulled my eyes to her to make sure she was okay.

"No pressure at all. Offer stands indefinitely."

Bruce grinned, then bid us farewell. Nikki waved and maybe even winked at Winnie, and then we were standing there, hands linked.

Holding her hand felt good—better than good. It felt like they were made to be fitted together, but that wasn't the kind of thoughts I should be having right now.

"Ready to go home?" I asked, and with a somber nod from her, we headed out.

"I'm sure you're tired. Please get some good sleep and maybe... maybe we can talk a bit tomorrow?"

I hated the tentative sound to my voice. I wasn't someone who typically had any trouble verbalizing my thoughts, though I rarely did so. I'd been communicating with Winnie for years, and having her here didn't change my comfort level.

But she seemed stifled, almost muted. She'd grown quiet on the way home, and aside from a few sounds of mild interest as I pointed out my favorite places in the quaint downtown of Silverton as well as the Saint Security building and a few other landmarks, she'd hardly spoken. We'd picked up takeout from Guac on the way back and ate the delicious Mexican food in virtual silence.

Even for me, an introverted man who valued alone time and quiet, I struggled to navigate whether to strike up conversation or just let her be. In the end, I talked a bit but refrained from asking her questions. I didn't want her to flip into fixer or people-pleasing mode, and she seemed so far inside her head, who was I to drag her out?

From everything I knew about her life, she'd been simultaneously smothered with expectations from and undervalued by her family. My goal was to give her space to think and safety to be whoever she wanted to be.

"Thank you. Truly. I know I'll never be able to thank you enough." Her words caught, and she averted her gaze, emotion clear on her face and in her voice.

"You'll have to find a way to stop thanking me at some point."

Those beautiful, dark eyes flicked up to meet mine and she shook her head, but there was a faint grin on her lips.

"We'll see."

I nodded. "Night, Winnie. Let me know if you need anything."

I could swear there was something she wanted to say or something she did need, but instead of saying anything else, she offered me a saccharine smile and slipped into the bedroom.

I hoped she'd sleep well and wake feeling rested. I hoped she'd feel safe here—in this space, with me and Juniper, and with the plan we were living out now.

I hoped she didn't regret what we'd done or whatever we would encounter as we dealt with the fallout in the days to come.

Twelve and a half years ago

To: Tristan Donnelly
     From: Winniechickendinny

Tristan,

Prom is next week. The guy who asked me is nice, so it should be fun. And don't worry, my brothers have already given him stern warnings about how to treat me. The guy (his name is Jackson) is in my European history class and he's also on the basketball team. He's probably a little too tall for me, but I'll wear heels so dancing isn't weird.

Are you tall? It's funny to think about how little I know when it comes to what you look like. You're probably pretty athletic since you do soldiery stuff a lot. I mean, at least I assume so. And you said you're training—are you still training? What is happening with that? Are you really getting ready to deploy again soon?

I have dark hair—we all do thanks to those Delmonico Italian roots, I guess. They were no match for the English ancestry my mom brought into the mix. My eyes are brown and I'm pretty fair. Also, I'm on the short end—five foot three. I'm not a big dancer at these things unless I'm with friends, but most of mine have serious boyfriends and dates they're going to hotels with after. I'm not about to do that with Jackson, even if we are kind of a thing right now, so I'm hoping we can do a few dances and call it good.

Are you a dancer? I can't really imagine it—*the* Tristan Donnelly slaying on the dance floor. I think I'd pay good money for that, even if it did mean surrendering a few months' paychecks. What would your song be? Maybe you're the guy out front leading the "Cupid Shuffle."

Just kidding. I know you're shy, and I can't imagine you out there leading the moves, because I'm betting you never have. But did you go and *wish* you could dance? Were you shy but wanting to twirl someone around? Not that you'd twirl... anyway. All I'm saying is I'd dance with you so you could fulfill your dreams of dancing with someone a foot shorter than you.

My dress is pretty. Maybe I'll send you a picture, though we don't really do that, so probably not. I don't want to make it weird. Plus, I am going to mail you a graduation announcement, which will have a cheesy senior picture of me in it for sure, so that should be enough to haunt you for a while.

That's all from me for now. Stay safe, friend.

Winn

CHAPTER FIVE

Winnie

After a fitful sleep, I snuck into the kitchen as quietly as I could. I hadn't eaten much last night despite the food looking amazing. I'd wanted to talk through some of this madness with Tristan like I would've over email, but the quick, cordial process of getting married had caused an inward collapse.

His supportive friends who'd showed up for our sham wedding drilled home how much he was sacrificing for me —he had a real life here. He had friends who would learn about this and would have to wonder.

And then the ceremony was so cold and formal, so completely void of any romance or sentiment in the vows I could barely recall. It was simple and effective and so unlike what I would've dreamed... though I hadn't dreamed about a wedding since middle school.

A light on the coffee maker gave me a jolt of hope.

Juniper must've been in Tristan's room, and the fire in here had burned to a low flicker behind the doors of the fireplace. I may have felt completely unmoored, but the idea of having a few moments to sit in the quiet darkness of the morning and sip coffee sounded like heaven.

I just needed a few minutes to get my thoughts together in a safe place, and this fire-lit moment offered me just that. Soon, I'd need to figure out how best to work remotely here so I didn't fall too far behind. And hopefully after a moment to myself, I'd be able to actually talk to Tristan instead of being shuttled around like a zombie and then dumped into bed early. I didn't blame him for suggesting I head to bed at eight o'clock last night, and in truth, I'd needed it. It might've only been an hour later according to my body, but I felt like I'd traveled years to get here. I'd fallen asleep almost instantly... but then after four hours, I started my nighttime mental guard duty until the morning.

I'd paced around the lovely bedroom, worrying over every person in my life and whether I'd done the right thing. This was nothing new, but I'd hoped that having done the deal and signed the papers and confirmed the "I dos," I'd at least feel some measure of peace. I did to a degree, but even that had caused a spiral of guilt and worry to coil up and rest on my chest like a weighty, cold snake.

Mugs were nestled into a cabinet just above the coffee maker, so I helped myself to one and poured the dark brew into the large vessel. I preferred a smaller mug, but it made sense a large man like Tristan would want something sturdy.

A search in the fridge revealed well-stocked shelves, and my heart flipped when I saw not just milk but a small bottle of coffee creamer. At one point over the years, we'd talked about how we take our coffee, and I knew for a fact he didn't take anything in his. So this... this had to be for me.

Or anyone else he has coffee with.

Woof, I didn't like that thought. I didn't think Tristan routinely entertained women, but now that I thought about it, would he have told me? I had told him about a few disastrous dates I'd attempted before my dad's heart attack, and he knew I'd had a boyfriend in high school who disappeared after Thomas's death. My grief had been too heavy for the guy, and though it'd hurt at the time, I could understand in retrospect. Otherwise, my dating life had largely been nonexistent or anticlimactic. And Tristan's...

I honestly couldn't think of him ever mentioning anyone. And now, it felt like I had gotten comfortable with the idea that he just didn't date for... reasons... but that couldn't be right. I mean, look at the man. He was this tall, handsome, intelligent, fit, gentle person. And while I had only interacted with him in person for less than a day, you don't spend nearly fifteen years talking to someone with some regularity through the major ups and downs of life and not know him at least a little. This time next year, it would officially be half my life we'd been talking.

Enough to know any woman would be lucky to be with him.

And enough to know my heart wouldn't handle seeing him with someone else. I'd always known that and maybe he had, too. Maybe it's why he'd never mentioned being with someone—because he knew I couldn't handle it. My crush on him had glared at me right in my face, and it must've done the same to him from across the screen. But he was eight years older, and of course, that wouldn't have worked for him... at least not until more recently. The barrier of distance had made it impossible, anyway.

"You sleep okay?"

The words came low and rumbly but still sudden enough I startled and dumped coffee down my chin. I swiped at my face before the burning liquid slid all the way down my neck and turned to see him standing in plaid flannel pajama pants and a loose T-shirt. Seconds later, Juniper trotted in and bumped against my legs, happily panting, then did her little circle dance as she inched toward the door.

Tristan's eyes softened when he looked at his dog, and therefore, my heart melted. It was too sweet, the way this solitary man loved his animal, and it made me want to hug him.

While he let Juniper out, I found my words.

"Pretty well. You?"

He nodded. "Just fine. Ready for coffee, though."

He plodded into the kitchen looking charmingly sleepy and his hair revealing someone had run their fingers through it all night.

I blinked and turned away from him because *what an unhelpful thought.* Of course that hadn't happened. I'd seen him run his hands through it a few times yesterday, plus he'd slept, so there was the explanation. Not some liaison in the room next to me...

As much as Tristan felt both familiar and like a friend, the reality here hit me yet again: I didn't know everything about him. Obviously. And yet, so much of the planning for this trip had been working on my parents to make sure they weren't worried about me—not that they would've been— and that my brother would be leaving them alone.

Tristan had taken the brunt of the planning—he'd gotten the rings, made the appointment for the courthouse, arranged for the documents we'd need for our license. And as I stood here in his kitchen, watching him pull a giant mug from the cupboard and fill it just shy of the brim with coffee, I had to own up to the fact that we hadn't talked about how this would work.

"If you'll give me a few minutes, I can make us breakfast."

His eyes tipped to mine over the rim of his first sip of coffee. Then came a slow blink that did something to me—it sent a tight, achy sensation into my belly when I recognized it as pleasure.

Whoa.

That was not about you. Not for you. No heavy-lidded blinks for you!

"Uh, okay. I mean, you don't have to do that. You don't have to cook for me. I can just grab cereal or—you know? I can run to the store. I don't mind, and—"

His warm hand on my wrist halted my words. The slight pressure grounded me enough to stop the flow of babble, but his steady gaze seeing right through me jump-started it again.

"You've done so much for me already and—"

His hold tightened just slightly and relaxed again as he shook his head once. "We talked about this."

Something had happened to me overnight. Maybe some of the rampant fear had drained away and I could now more aptly appreciate how ridiculously handsome Tristan was, or maybe I felt foolish for only just now recognizing how few things we'd discussed ahead of time.

Would we share groceries or split them like roommates? Would we date other people? Would *he?* Would we go out in public together, or tell people here what was going on?

And maybe worse, the gut-level need to know everything about him and see more of those lazy, pleasure-filled blinks at his first sip of morning coffee and ideally at other times, too—but the cruel slap of reality saying I wouldn't get to. Not for long—not for long enough.

"Honestly, we haven't talked about much, Tris. I'm just..." I swallowed, trying not to internally melt when his thumb arced over my wrist before he released me. The gentle gesture tipped me over the edge, and I spoke without screening myself. "I'm scared. I don't want to disappoint you or inconvenience you. I don't want you to hate me after this. And I don't want anything bad to happen to you or me *or* my parents."

Because there would be an after, and I had to keep that in mind.

He studied me, his face unreadable for a moment before he set his mug on the nearby counter and took mine from my hands. I let him, and he set it next to his.

"I'm going to hug you now. Then we're going to eat breakfast. After, we'll get cleaned up and talk through anything you want. Everything you need so you feel like your feet are on solid ground. Okay?"

I huffed a breath because I couldn't figure out what else to do when confronted with someone who said exactly what I needed, and nodded. "Okay."

He wrapped me in his arms, and I welcomed his touch. His body was firm and warm, and he ducked his head down close so he surrounded me, and I breathed in his nearness. It was the second hug he'd given me, and I could now confirm his touch—particularly his hugs—had a deeply comforting effect on me.

I inhaled his scent—something woodsy and clean, probably his deodorant and just the natural alchemy making up Tristan Donnelly and a hint of coffee.

The unwelcome sensation of heartache needled me as I

hugged him tighter before releasing. He was doing so much for me, and I hated it. I didn't want him to have to do *any* of this, but I couldn't change it. So what I needed to do now was whatever I could to make this easier on him.

The fact that he seemed to be doing everything in his power to make this easier on *me* only made me more determined to make sure he knew just how grateful I was.

Twelve and a half years ago

To: Winniechickendinny
From: Tristan Donnelly

Winnie,

I hope prom went well, and I hope this Jackson kid behaved himself. I'm sure Thomas and Jeremy did their best, but feel free to remind Jackson you know a guy who is trained with a variety of weapons and isn't half bad in a fighting ring. Not to pull the macho friend card or anything, but if that kid does anything to disrespect you, I'll find a way to make sure he doesn't have the chance to do that to anyone else.

Winnifred Maria Delmonico, did you think I meant murder? I'm not about to roll up to your high school and disappear this guy. But I do want it noted that he best watch himself.

Nah, mostly, I hope you guys had a great time.

I was never a big dance guy, you're right. My folks

passed toward the end of my junior year and that was it for me. I took the GED after studying all summer, and since I was seventeen, I went ahead to basic training and never looked back.

So do I even know what the "Cupid Shuffle" is? No. But it sounds terrifying. You're a braver woman than I realized, Winn.

I am always training. That's pretty much all we do in the Army until we go do the thing. Then we come home and train again until it's time to leave. It can be exhausting, but I don't mind the battle rhythm. It's predictable and, at this point, familiar.

Have fun wrapping up your school year,

Tristan

CHAPTER SIX

Tristan

Winnie looked like she might cry when I set her breakfast on the table in front of her.

"This looks so good. Thank you so much.'

The gratitude in her voice was downright palpable.

"No big deal. I'm happy to cook for someone besides just myself."

Interestingly, that was true. I didn't often think about how much time I spent eating alone and cooking for one. It'd been my life since my folks passed just before I graduated high school.

Those first weeks had been so, so quiet.

And through the first years in the barracks, then later moving out into an apartment, then a house. and now here in my little sanctuary, I'd gotten used to the trajectory of my life being largely solitary. Of course, I'd come here to

Silverton to be near the men and women who'd become as close to me as anyone had, save Winnie.

This was different, though.

"Is Juniper okay outside in this cold? I can't believe she's still out there."

She peeked over at the door where Junie had definitely not yet notified me she was ready to come back in.

"She loves the snow, but her paws will get too cold soon. I promise I wouldn't leave her out there longer than she likes." I took a bite of the scrambled eggs on my plate.

"I never had any doubt."

She focused back on her food, and we sat eating and lightly chatting on and off about inconsequential things. We both knew harder conversations would come soon enough and had tacitly agreed not to rush them.

After we finished and I insisted she go get ready while I did the dishes—a battle in itself—I cleaned up the kitchen and got dressed in the spare room. I'd never minded not having an actual spare bed since anyone in the world I cared about lived here in Silverton, except for Winnie, or was on active duty and wouldn't be likely to come to visit. But after last night's sleeping adventure, I did wish I had another room for a bed.

The borrowed air mattress had deflated enough that I ended up flat on the mat underneath me. While the tatami-style mats were perfectly fine for sparring and working out, I'd never mastered sleeping on them. Maybe it was one too many high altitude jumps or the fact that as I neared forty, just turning my head quickly could catch up to me on the wrong day.

Either way, I needed a different setup or I wouldn't be much good to anyone in another few days.

Juniper settled on her bed in the corner, and I'd stoked

the fire while the eggs cooked earlier, so we sat in our usual spots and I gazed at the flames dancing in the hearth. The house already felt different, even after one night of having her here. Her scent hung outside the door to the bedroom, and though she hadn't left any physical evidence of her presence, I knew she was here.

Just behind that door was the woman I'd cared for through so many events. Through a long deployment for me when her family first adopted me and her wrapping up high school, then her brother Thomas's death. The rest of the family had rarely written—understandably so—but Winnie kept going.

She'd brought me along into their lives and sent me care packages when I deployed. I remembered her finishing high school and entering college, and my deployments, then assessing into special operations. Then even more time overseas. I couldn't tell her many details, but she'd learned enough to know what I was doing was special. She'd made it feel like a big deal, and even though I knew the truth of it well enough, it'd been good to share it with someone.

At that point, it'd already been so long since I'd shared much of myself with anyone, so having her there, even distantly... it mattered.

Some years, it was a handful of emails, but as time went on, we'd gone back and forth at least once a month. When things were hard or particularly good for one or the other of us, it was a little more.

The frequency didn't determine how much I'd cared for her since almost the very beginning, and certainly not as time had passed.

I knew with no room for doubt that she hadn't wanted to reach out to me about this mess, but she did it. It meant the world to me—for her to even have asked. And it had to have been more difficult for her than I knew—I could feel it between us, this sense that she owed me so deeply. But even if she hadn't asked me for help, if I'd found out what was happening, I couldn't have stood by. I couldn't have pretended like she was just some woman who'd written to me and didn't actually matter to me. She did.

She does.

Even Bruce and the guys knew about her—they'd always known how much her communication meant to me. Some had assumed we were together or that I wished we were. I'd genuinely only ever felt grateful for her and, yes, a bit protective of her.

I'd never wished to be with her because I'd seen a future on my own, ideally with Winnie safe and happy, living her own life and occasionally letting me in on it through a letter or email. I'd convinced myself it would be enough for me.

Until now.

Now, everything was jumbled up together. It didn't matter so much that she was easily the most beautiful woman I'd ever seen in real life. I'd known she was beautiful for years. She'd sent me a high school graduation announcement with a senior picture, and even at eighteen, she'd been gorgeous. The age difference between us meant I wouldn't think of her like that, and though I'd never felt like she was a sister, I still didn't feel attraction. Only affection.

Again, *until now.*

And now, when she was fleeing danger and needed me to be a good man, to protect her and help her, was not the time to catch the wrong kind of feelings.

I tried to focus on the book in my hands instead of the awareness shooting through me when I heard the bedroom door open. Not *romantic* awareness, though. Just trained operative awareness. Obviously.

"Hey, sorry it took a while. You have great water pressure."

She plunked down on the couch next to me, and I ran a hand through my hair and forbid myself from thinking about the shower or her in the shower because I was not a jerk.

"No problem." I shifted, turning a bit so I could face her. "You ready?"

With a giant inhale, she summoned a smile. "Yes. No. I don't know."

"At least you're honest," I said, refusing to be sidetracked by how darn charming I found her. "Tell me your biggest concerns and let's hash through those."

She tucked her hands under her thighs and glanced at me before returning her attention to the fireplace. "Um, so I know you're not being forced into this, but honestly, one of my biggest concerns is that when all is said and done and I'm back in Kansas and we're divorced and have wasted all this time, you're going to hate me and never speak to me again."

Her gaze tracked all around the room until finally, finally, it landed on me. I held her there, our eyes locked.

"I can see why you'd be worried about that. Do you trust me, Winnie?"

Her lashes fluttered, and she nodded. "Of course I do."

"Good. Then please trust me when I say you don't need to worry about me. There's nothing you can do to make me hate you. I volunteered for this and I'm not being coerced."

She swallowed, mind running a mile a minute, it seemed, then yanked at the hem of her sweater, pulling it up and over her head like she'd become unbearably hot in the space of a heartbeat and tossing it on the couch next to her and leaving her in a thin T-shirt. After tucking her hair behind her ear, she finally responded. "I do. I mean yes, I can do that. I... okay."

Then I saw it. Everything in me locked up, cementing into something cold and wrathful as I registered a bruise that had without a doubt been caused by a hand.

It took everything in me not to demand she tell me what happened, but that was part of the goal here. We'd sat down with the express purpose of getting to the truth of things, and I hoped she'd tell me everything, not just the more palatable version, which I now understood was what I'd gotten thus far.

"Good. Then please tell me..." I exhaled slowly, ratcheting down the fury I felt rising by the second at the thought of someone harming her, the thought of someone daring to put his hands on this woman, and notched my eyes toward her arm, then back to hers. "Who did this to you?"

She tucked her lips together, anxiety and fear cloaking her posture and demeanor in an instant.

I hated that, but I'd do whatever I needed to keep her safe—and I couldn't do that without the truth.

"Um. Yeah. So..." Her eyes darted away. "The guys after Jeremy... they came by the office the other day."

Her cheeks reddened, maybe from getting hot next to the fire, or maybe from shame. Her shoulders hunched in, and where she'd been buzzy with nerves moments ago, now she held a defeated posture.

"You can tell me what happened, Winn. And please know, none of this is your fault. Absolutely none of it."

She blinked hard, staring at her hands again. "They were talking about owing them, how Jeremy had said I had money and I would help him—which is complete crap because I've made clear I won't do anything else. I didn't tell him I might help him with his debt when I get the money from the trust—as far as he knows, it's all going to save the business."

I waited, but she didn't budge, so I urged her on. "And? What happened then?"

She swallowed, and her gaze flicked to mine. "Anyway, yeah, so then they said if I didn't want to help financially, maybe I could help another way. I think they meant by... you know."

A beat of silence passed as her statement hit the air between us, blood dropping into water, and I spoke as calmly as I could considering the wrath growing in me.

"They said that?"

She swallowed again. "I think it was just a threat. Trying to scare me. I'm sure it was just trying to get me to talk to Jeremy for them."

There had to be more. I could feel it, by the way she'd hollowed out and the color had drained from her face now. Eyes on hers, I nodded, begging her to finish.

"Then the ringleader guy grabbed my arm and then—" She cut off, calming herself.

I wanted to take her hand or wrap my arms around her, but that didn't fit. Not yet, anyway. Yes, we'd hugged, but both times had been purposeful and not off the cuff. In the context of her being told she'd be forced to do *anything*, I didn't want to encroach on her sense of personal space.

"It's okay to tell me. But if you don't want to, that's okay, too. You get to choose."

I didn't know if I'd managed to imbue gentleness into my voice, but I'd kept the fine edge of rage from it, at least.

"He licked me. My neck."

Fury pulsed in my veins, but I held it tight, waiting, and all the while mentally calculating how quickly I could find this person's information and set the police on him so he'd never even think about Winnie again.

"I tried to pull back and he tightened his hand, and then he tried to do it again, but I jerked away and ran to my car. I couldn't get out of his grip at first, and I was so scared." Those big eyes hit mine. "I was so scared, Tristan."

Needing to touch her if she'd let me, I held out a hand as I stood.

She set hers there and rose and met my eyes.

"I want to make a few things clear, but I need to say this first. Any anger you see on my face is not with you—it is never with you."

"I'm sorry I didn't tell you sooner, though. I should've. I'm sorry."

"Winnie, no. You get to choose who you tell and what you tell them. You were hurt and threatened after a lot of other crap the last few months. I'm sorry any of this is happening. You don't owe me anything. Do you hear me? Not apologies or gratitude or *anything*."

"Okay," she said in a small voice, so quiet, I might not've realized she'd spoken if I hadn't been watching her face.

"Good. The other thing you need to know is this." I clenched my jaw, spending a bit of that energy with the firm press of my molars against each other before continuing. "No one is ever going to touch you like that again."

"I don't want you hurt."

The pinch of her brows told me she meant it—she was less concerned for herself and more worried I'd get hurt defending her.

I shoved that aside to think about later because it'd upend me if I let it. "Do you know what I did before I retired? What kind of soldier I was?"

Her brows furrowed even more, and she clearly didn't

understand what this had to do with anything. "Um, you were special... something. Right? I mean, I know I should know this, but it's been years and years since you could tell me much about work."

I couldn't help but be charmed by this, like so much of who she was, but I wanted her to understand something before I had to get to work.

"I was special operations, in a group called the Exceptional Mission Unit. The point is, I've faced plenty of actual bad guys. Sometimes with a whole crew of operators with me. Sometimes with only me, depending on the mission. I'm also decent at hand-to-hand combat, an expert shot, and happen to know a crew of people who are the best in about every possible field having to do with protecting people."

Those same perfectly arched brows rose high now. "Fancy."

Despite the gravity of the moment, a chuckle slipped out. She'd always had this potent mix of deep feelings and humor that cut through me and made me smile. In the face of considerable challenges, she'd kept that sneaky sense of humor, and it made all of this so much more poignant and real.

"I'm not trying to brag. I just want you to understand. This is why I wanted you here. You have me, and you have everyone in my company. And as people get to know you here, you'll have the town on your side. You will have so many people at your back ready to help you, you won't need to worry."

She took a big breath, like this both overwhelmed and reassured her.

"And until you get settled in, you have me. I mean that. No one is going to touch you unless you give them permission. You are safe here, with me, and I will stop at nothing to keep it that way."

I wanted to say more—I should've. About how good she was, and how kind. About how her brother was an idiot and he should be ashamed of how he'd let this situation get out of hand and how it'd affected her. I wanted to rail against her parents for being so blind for so long, for being willing to send her away and let her marry someone they hadn't even met, nor had she. I wanted to wrap her up and hold her, assure her that whatever came, whether with my home or my body, I would protect her.

But for now, I took her whispered acceptance, and I brushed a thumb lightly along her cheek before nodding and stepping back, away from the temptation to physically shield her from the world or press my lips to hers. Away from all the mistakes I wanted to make with her, away from breaking my promise that she'd be the one to give permission even if I hadn't been talking about myself. It still applied.

And I had to get to work.

LETTER

Twelve years ago

Winnie,

I'm so sorry to hear about Thomas. Writing that, I know how short it falls. I remember how hard it was to do the most basic things after my parents died. Brushing my teeth felt like a chore and eating felt pointless. That lasted for a while, but at some point, I figured out how to do it without wearing myself out. You'll get there. I promise.

Nothing I can say will make this better for you. Please know that I am here and I'm thinking about you. You will get through this, and I can tell you all kinds of other stuff like that if it helps, but right now I wish I could just sit by you and let you know you're not alone.

Thinking of you,
Tristan

CHAPTER SEVEN

Winnie

I spent the first hour after Tristan went to work snuggling Juniper and staring into the fire rather than working. I rarely sat quietly and still because when I did this at home, anxiety over the mess swirling around me invaded and ruined it.

But after the last twenty-four hours, I needed the quiet. I couldn't form a coherent thought beyond a feeling that I was safe here. Tristan had said it, but I felt it, too—safer than I'd been in a long time.

I felt safer being away from the situation at home, and I felt safe in this beautiful, cozy little cabin with a sweet, giant dog snuggled next to me, and I felt safe with him.

The low-level rhythm to my heartbeat said something about this situation—no anxious racing. No dread tightening my chest. It was a simple, even beat giving me more hope than I'd had in a long time.

"You are safe here, with me, and I will stop at nothing to keep it that way."

So many of the things he'd said kept circling through my mind on a loop. The intensity in his face, his voice, his entire *being* had spoken so loudly and fiercely, I had no choice but to believe him. And yet with all that intensity, I hadn't been scared of him—not a bit.

I still had concerns, but the relief I felt now that he knew everything that'd happened in the last week to pile on top of the larger situation had me sighing an exhale. Juniper perked up and propped her head on my knee.

"What do you think? Should I go check out my new home?"

New home. What a strange thought. I'd lived in a small apartment about ten minutes from the farm office since I'd graduated college. It wasn't in a great neighborhood, but it'd been my space where I got to do what I wanted.

But that had been ruined, too, thanks to Jeremy's foolishness and his apparent lack of care about his creditors coming after *me.* They'd shown up at my house once before, but they hadn't threatened—or at least, I didn't realize it was a threat at the time. That'd been when I was naïve enough to think they were simply looking for Jeremy to talk to and not them proving they had found me, my house, and could've harmed me if they'd chosen to.

Not wanting to spend another minute dwelling on the past and knowing that the more people who knew me in town the better, I rushed through getting ready for the day, answered a few emails for work, and took the keys from the counter where Tristan had left them. When he'd told me he'd leave his truck for me, I'd protested, but he'd insisted he didn't always drive to work anyway, and he wanted me to be able to come and go as I pleased.

That's how I ended up pulling his big black truck into a small lot in downtown Silverton and walking until I reached Silver Street. I'd checked out the shops on my phone and already knew where I wanted to stop first. I wound my way down the street, passing several cute storefronts until I arrived at my final destination.

All Booked Up sat next to a gorgeous flower shop called Bloom and a few doors down from what looked like an ice cream shop adorably named Scoop, though it wasn't open yet today. My heart fluttered as I opened the door and the smell of books and coffee wafted in and instantly set me at ease.

Maybe I should just move into a bookstore when all of this was over and I had to leave Tristan. I wouldn't have him or Juniper, so I'd need reinforcements in order to have that feeling and this could be a decent substitute.

"Welcome in," a woman's voice greeted me. "Let me know if I can help you find anything."

She stood at a circular counter-height section where a computer sat and she tapped away on a keyboard, only looking up after a minute. She was young—probably a few years younger than my thirty, and she had medium brown hair pulled high into a bun. Her glasses perched on her nose, and she grinned at me as I entered, slowly making my way in as I appreciated the displays and endcaps featuring different books.

I hoped there'd be a romance section. A lot of indie bookstores still hadn't caught on to the fact that romance was the top-selling genre in the world. I'd resorted to requesting them through my local place because they simply didn't stock anything but the biggest names, and though they were good, a girl with a healthy bookish appetite had her needs.

I was about to ask when a bright archway of books caught my eye and I gasped.

The woman behind the desk chuckled. "It's impressive, right?"

With a glance at her, I moved closer, trying to see if I was right and... *yes*. This arch was made of stacked romance novels and led to a corner of shelves holding what looked to be exclusively romance titles.

My head snapped to the young woman. "Um, this is amazing."

She beamed and rushed over, clearly delighted by my response. "Isn't it?"

"I'm so used to local shops only having one shelf begrudgingly dedicated to romance, if that. This is dreamy."

The woman chuckled and wrapped her arms around herself, swaying side to side like she was hugging herself. "I told my dad it would be a good investment to have a solid romance section, and fortunately, he believed me."

"Your dad's the owner?"

She grinned. "He is. He moved here a few years ago and started a bookstore. Fell in love, got married, and there you have it."

The smile pulling at my lips felt so light and natural, I wanted to bottle the sensation and save it for later. "I love that. And you came with him?"

She scrunched her face a little, an adorable gesture. "Originally, just to Salt Lake to attend the U for my master's degree, but I visited him a lot and got reeled in. I just officially moved to town this summer."

"So you're kind of new, too?" I asked, a little leap in my chest.

Her brows rose a little. "Oh, are you moving here? This time of year, it's tourist city so I never know."

It tracked, being January. "I guess that makes sense for a ski town. And yes. I just moved here yesterday."

Gosh, had it really only been yesterday?

If I thought this woman was smiling before, I was fooled. She was now smiling so wide, she'd rival Julia Roberts's grin.

"Oh my gosh! Well, welcome! And hey"— she held out a hand—"I'm Josephine Malcom, but I go by Jo."

"Winnie D—" I coughed, then course-corrected. "Well, sorry. Winnie Donnelly."

Her head ticked to the side. "Why 'sorry'?"

My cheeks heated. "Oh, it's just new."

And thrilling and amazing and terrifying.

"Wait." Her brow furrowed, and she was studying me now. "Donnelly."

She looked at me like she might decipher it, and instead of making her wait, I decided to just get it out there. She might not even know Tristan, but if she did, she'd end up finding out what we'd done soon enough.

"Yes. Tristan Donnelly—do you know him?"

Her beautiful, dark eyes widened, and her mouth dropped open before she nodded. "Oh my gosh. Oh my *gosh.* How did I not know this? When did you get married? He doesn't wear a ring—not that I was checking him out or anything, I swear, I just... I've been around him on and off since he moved here. It really is a small town when you drill down past the tourists and... *wow.*"

I couldn't help smiling at her rambling, both because it was nice to see I wasn't the only one with the same habit, but also because it seemed like she might actually be... excited. She confirmed it when she continued.

"I love this. I just love this... I mean, he's so gorgeous

and kind." She widened her eyes. "I'm sorry but *wow*, girl, way to go."

I grinned at this because she was not wrong. "I can't disagree."

All this might be a little easier if he weren't so gorgeous, though in my heart I knew I was a goner long before I ever saw his too-long hair or soulful eyes or deeply, problematically kissable mouth.

She wrinkled her nose like this gave her a great deal of joy. "Okay, but how did I not know he'd gotten married? And oh my gosh, hi, nice to meet you Winnie Donnelly, welcome to Silverton, please be my friend."

A startled laugh jumped out. "Thank you. And... yes. I'd love to."

We shared what was no doubt a triple-cheese grin and then the bell at the door rang. She glanced toward the customer and made a face.

"I better run, but have a look around and stop by the desk before you leave either way—I just started a romance book club and you *have* to join."

She jogged toward her post, and I turned to the welcoming, colorful romance section to browse, my cheeks aching from so much smiling.

When Tristan had mentioned getting to know people in town and them having my back, I hadn't realized he'd meant it literally. I believed Bruce and Nikki would help us out if something came up, but now, as I took in the lovely assortment of authors and subgenres in this little nook, I accepted he'd indeed meant it literally.

A tiny spindle of hope peeked out in me amidst the snowy planes of worry and fear and bleakness.

Maybe this could be more than a plan Z. Even if just for a little while, maybe this would be something... good.

Twelve years ago

To: Tristan Donnelly
       From: Winniechickendinny

Tristan,

I should be crying more, shouldn't I? It's been two weeks and I haven't cried since the funeral. I feel numb. It's like I'm walking around in a fog and I don't know when the sun will rise and burn it off.

Thank you for your letter. I like your handwriting. Thank you for what you said.

And for the record, I'm so sorry you lost your parents. I'm sorry you know how this feels—probably more so in some ways, since I still have family left. Sorry, I'm not making sense.

I just want to say thank you. Thanks for being there. Even though you're nowhere near me, it feels like you're close.

Thank you.
Winnie

CHAPTER EIGHT

Tristan

Pacing the living room hadn't done much to get my mind off things, but it was too cold outside to go for a walk, and it was nearly time to leave.

"Almost ready!" Winnie shouted from inside her room.

My room.

Inside *my* room she was using as hers, and for some reason, this knowledge had continued to plague me in an unfortunate way. First, thinking of her in my bed made me antsy. I couldn't explain it and I wasn't going to dig around in the thought, because what good would that do?

And second, because sleeping on the perpetually deflating blow-up mattress was not doing my back any favors. I'd be aching tomorrow during our self-defense workshop. I could go buy my own mattress, but I hated wasting things. I'd patched the leak in the material this morning after waking on a fully flattened failure of a mattress, so tonight would be better.

Winnie scuttled out of her room, sliding an arm into her jacket as she did, and maybe also looking at her phone? I'd noticed she had a propensity for multitasking, and though I liked how she could end up so absorbed in whatever she did on her phone or tablet, I worried it provided potential threats too much of an opportunity.

This was one of several things we had to talk about, and soon. But for now? We needed to deal with tonight.

I would definitely focus on tonight and not on how soft her hair looked or how my hand practically ached with the need to run my fingers over it and just *finally* feel it. Had I always wanted to feel her hair? Was this something creepy I'd just now recognized in myself?

The air mattress was to blame here. And yes, she had gorgeous, long, dark hair that probably smelled like her and—

Crap. *Focus*. Tonight. Nothing else.

"We should talk a bit before we go." I glanced at my watch. I'd planned to be exactly on time, but others would be late, so if we ran a few minutes behind, it'd be fine.

Her eyes jumped up to meet mine. "Okay. What should I know?"

We'd already discussed how her coming with me tonight to the weekly Saint Security after work drinks would force us out in the open. A few of my closest friends knew what we'd done already, but it would be notable to some to have me showing up with—well, with anyone.

"This is our first time being out in public as a married couple. You've confirmed you want to maintain that this is a genuine marriage in any public-facing engagements, so I just want to... reconfirm. If it's still the case, there are certain implications."

Was I seeing things, or did a smile just flash at me before she steadied her expression and grew serious?

"Of course. Yes. You know I already told Jo from the bookstore, and I think that's best. I mean, you do, too, right? Still think it's best?" Her long lashes blinked at me.

Not the time to be mesmerized by those dark eyes, but it took work to resist. "Yes. And so, we'll need to be convincingly together."

She nodded. "Right. We'll need to be affectionate and comfortable with each other. I feel like we're pretty good on the comfort part, even if you don't talk much."

She winked.

The woman *winked* at me.

"I am not particularly loquacious, so that won't be a surprise to anyone watching."

She tilted her head to one side and eyed me. "See, I hear you saying that, but whenever we talk about the logistics of the plan, you seem pretty chatty. And in your emails over the years, you were, too. So I'm just trying to figure you out."

I didn't smile or react to this, even though some part of me knew I spoke more to Winnie, both present and past, than I did most other people combined. "I am an expert at planning operations. This, in essence, is a mission. And we're going to do it well."

She hummed, and her eyes glinted in the light as we moved toward the door. "I bet you're used to doing everything well, aren't you?"

I blinked, the words hitting me like a sideswipe. "I— suppose so. I prefer to do something once and do it well."

She had opened the door and stepped out into the night

air but turned back. Her bright white teeth bit into her bottom lip, and she had this look in her eye that told me she had something up her sleeve.

"But sometimes, if you're really good at something, you want to keep doing it, right? Seems like it'd be a shame to waste all that... expertise." She turned and continued walking toward the car.

I carded my fingers through my hair, shaking off the troublesome thoughts trying to invade. Something about that little look and the way she was talking made it feel like she was baiting me and leaning into what could be an oddly sexy double entendre.

But Winnie and I had never flirted. *Ever.* At least not to my knowledge. And though I was shy, I wasn't dead.

Granted, over email, maybe I just hadn't realized?

But no. We'd been on the same page—friends. Always and only pen-pal-style friends, until recently when we'd become... more. Not more romantically, but a real-life version of this thing we'd cultivated for so long.

Now that she'd shown up with her shiny, dark hair and glittering eyes and gorgeous... everything... I struggled to keep my thoughts about her focused on concern and care.

Changing the subject was the only chance of survival here, especially with my own brain ambushing me and her giving me little smiles and generally kidnapping my attention at every turn. Attempting to flirt back? *Well.* That way lay ruin.

After sliding into the truck, I broached the topic. "I want you to think about attending the workshop tomorrow."

I'd mentioned it yesterday when we'd done a short calendar sync. I'd asked her if she had anything I should know on her schedule, and she'd mentioned an upcoming book club. I'd noted a few obligations, including upcoming weekends away for assignments I'd volunteered for long before this all got started. I could change them, but I wondered if she might like the house to herself a bit.

"The self-defense one?" she asked, elbow on the door and denim-clad legs crossed in my direction.

"Yes. It's two hours with a break in the middle. We like to do this quarterly in addition to our regular classes."

The cab was quiet for a few minutes as I drove. It was a brutally cold January evening with a crystal-clear sky like a black diamond above us.

"Do you think I'll need it? The training I mean." Her voice emerged small and empty of the cheekiness she'd had as we'd left the house.

I weighed how to put this best. "I hope you don't. I always hope that for people. But there's value in being prepared and never needing the knowledge versus the alternative."

"Right," she said softly. "Then I'll be there. I don't want to—" She cleared her throat, and I forced my eyes to remain on the road instead of finding their way to her to check if she was crying. "I don't want to feel helpless again."

My jaw clenched, and I squeezed the steering wheel, a hit of anger at Jeremy for putting his sister in this situation writhing through me. Instead of saying anything negative about her brother despite the deep desire to call him any number of names or promising that if I ever saw him, I'd show *him* the need for self-defense, I reassured her.

"We'll start tomorrow, then."

We parked as close to Silverton's Irish pub, Craic, as we could since it was so cold. I'd thought about dropping her off at the door and then parking, but I hated to leave her there alone. My job was to keep her safe, help her adjust to a new place, and be here for her however long this lasted.

When my gut clenched at this last thought, I shoved it away. I had no business getting attached to the idea of Winnie and me together, even if it had been the far side of wonderful to walk in the door from work yesterday and today and find her snuggled on my couch with Junie.

I didn't have any specific memories of the last time I'd come home from football practice and found my parents laughing together in the kitchen, but the scene had been a staple in my life. And missing it—the way I missed just that one feeling could gut me if I lingered with the sensation and lack of it. If I allowed myself to remember the whole, full-bodied life I'd had with them and they with each other.

It'd flickered to life upon entering my home and finding Winnie and my sweet dog relaxing together, safe and at peace. A blissful, agonizing peek at a life I couldn't actually have. At least not for long.

She'd given me space since arriving, clearly not wanting to impose on my life. I needed to address that and make sure she understood I wanted her around. But until I could do so, I'd at least make sure we sold this marriage and got the entire town on our side.

If the idiots after her brother's money were stupid enough to come to Silverton, they'd have Saint Security to deal with, obviously. But I wanted to make sure they had the whole town against them.

I helped her out of the truck and took her hand in mine. We both wore gloves to ward against the chill, so it wasn't an intimate thing. It didn't make my senses light up like any other contact had done thus far, but it did feel good to have a connection to her.

"Are you nervous?" she asked, her tone a little breathy, maybe because I was walking us too fast.

I slowed a touch. "No. Are you?"

Frozen white air billowed out with her exhale as she set her eyes on the bar at the far end of the street. "Yes. But... we can do this, right?"

That little *we* burrowed in between my ribs.

I hadn't been a part of a "we" in so long—not like this. I'd been a part of the EMU team and I was a part of the Saint Security team, and Juniper and I were a team of sorts, but this... this was different.

So I told her what I not only believed but knew for a fact. "We can."

CHAPTER NINE

Winnie

Walking into Craic with Tristan leading me by the hand felt like a dream. Maybe the worst part of all this was how amazing this man was. All these years of e-mailing, I'd dreamed of meeting him, and now I was discovering he was, in reality, even better in person.

Knowing all this but having the context be me using him to satisfy the stipulations of a trust and then for safety and security in the midst of a mess of my own making?

Much less a dream and more of a nightmare.

And fine. I needed to stop blaming myself for everything happening. Had I caused Calvin and his gross dudes to grab me or him to lick me? No to infinity. But had I possibly made things worse by not letting my parents in on what was happening a long time ago? Or even forcing Jeremy to go to the police? Something?

It wasn't an easily solvable situation, and I needed to

stop the self-blame and do what I could now. Sitting on Tristan's couch, Juniper snuggled close to me, my gaze drifting into the flickering flames from the fireplace, had been conducive to a lot of thinking and really looking at my life with the perspective physical distance granted me here in Silverton. I'd been working on myself in this regard for years—trying to tease out the strands of my life from those of my family's. I wanted freedom and independence, but how could I separate myself from them when it might mean more loss?

Shouldn't I, as a woman of nearly thirty years, be able to simply live my own life?

Maybe I could've if we hadn't lost Thomas so suddenly—a hole in his heart we never knew about and a cardiac arrest while he was out for a jog on a regular Tuesday. An event like that changes not only a person but a family. And it had irrevocably stripped away all the things I'd had planned, all of my ability to think of only myself. I'd been working toward taking the reins of my life more directly in hand when Dad had his heart attack, and it felt like such a foreshadowing, triggering mess, I lost the thread. But maybe there was still hope that, even in the midst of all of this, I could still find myself. Or at least, a way to forgive myself and make new choices going forward.

"There they are!" Bruce hopped up from his seat and held his arm wide to welcome us to a cluster of tall bistro tables.

"Wow, very nice, Oak," a cheery voice said with something like awe, the man's boyish features making him seem a bit younger than Bruce and Tristan.

Hard to say for sure, but I'd put him closer to thirty than forty. His gaze ticked back and forth between me and Tristan, and the latter released my hand and slid his arm around my waist.

A thrill raced through me, though I knew it shouldn't. This was all to make it look real—or not simply legal.

Another man sent the younger one a scowl right as Bruce said, "Everyone, this is Winnie. Winnie, this is everyone." He waved a hand, all casual and fully in control, then notched his head to the younger one. "That's Kenny. He's the baby of the family."

This had Kenny sending a dirty look to Bruce and then the other man.

The names rang a bell. Tristan had mentioned a Kenny and several others in emails here and there. I hadn't fully registered I'd be meeting some of the people who'd been a part of his life for so long, but of course.

"This is Adam." Tristan nodded to the man next to Kenny, who had short light-brown hair and a neatly trimmed beard.

Couldn't tell his age, but he had a certain wizened quality to him.

"Nice to meet you, Winnie." He held out his hand with a warm smile, and I took it with a gentle shake.

"Nice to meet you, too." I smiled at Kenny as well, just to make sure he wasn't left out.

A petite woman with bright green eyes and dark hair pulled back from her face caught my eye.

"I'm Jess, and I'm going to go get a few more glasses because if you're going to spend time with this crew, you're definitely going to need a drink." She winked at me and turned toward the bar.

I took in the beautiful, polished wood of the bar itself and the bustling crowd standing in small groups all around. Why was everything in Silverton so much cooler than anywhere else I'd been? Granted, I'd been to very few places, but this bar was gorgeous.

It was cold outside but warm enough here for most people to shed their layers and hang them on various hooks on walls or drape them over backs of chairs. Even Jess wore only jeans, boots, and a simple black tank top showcasing her muscular, feminine form.

"Want to sit?" Tristan asked in a low voice so only I could hear.

I turned to see his gaze on me, so intense and inscrutable yet warm. *Oof.* These other guys were all wildly handsome, but Tristan's attention felt like something out of a romance novel. Heady and enough to make me forget anyone else was watching me and momentarily lose focus on what had brought us here. Granted, I read romance like it was a part-time job, so that's naturally where my mind went.

Thankfully, my body didn't seem quite as insistent on living in a fantasy, so it took him up on the offer and slid onto a stool.

"Oak, seriously? She's like—"

Tristan's gaze tore from mine to pin Kenny's. "Careful."

Kenny seemed delighted by this and grinned wide. "I got it, man. No talking about your woman, even if it is to remark on how fine she is and how I don't know how you—"

"Kenny, bring it down a touch." Adam's hand clasped Kenny's shoulder and gave it a shake, like he might be able to jar the loudmouth out of him.

My cheeks burned, but I took no offense. Having just encountered more than one man who came on to me in the worst kind of way before I arrived in Utah, Kenny wasn't anywhere near that. I suspected his enthusiasm came more from his excitement for Tristan than from anything about me in particular. I remembered some of Tristan's stories about him, and so far, he was living up to the reputation.

Kenny held up his hands in innocence. "I'm just trying to say congratulations, alright? Is that allowed?"

I chuckled, and Tristan's arm tightened around my waist in a comforting gesture, then released.

Sad. I wouldn't have minded him keeping a hand on me all night.

"Oh my gosh, hi!"

The voice had me turning around to find Jo Malcom beaming at me, then throwing open her arms. And because she had that warm, familiar air and we had just talked yesterday, I accepted her hug.

A fleeting joy sparkled through me, laced with a cruel dose of regret. What was I doing hugging this woman under false pretenses? I'd be here, be her friend for, what? A few months, at most?

I banished that horrid voice and promised myself to be here now and not to worry and ruin everything because of it. I could ignore it for now.

When we pulled back, Tristan's attention made me explain. "Remember I said I met Jo? At the bookstore?"

He blinked, then nodded, a little furrow in his brow revealing his confusion. I couldn't be sure about what, but I forgot all about it when he offered Jo a polite smile. "Good to see you, Jo."

"You too, Tristan. Congratulations. I'm so happy you married a romance reader." She grinned.

Tristan smiled wider, shooting me a quick look. My stomach tumbled at the sight of his smile because *wow*. It wasn't that he never smiled, but I was still figuring out what he normally did. We hadn't found all this out about each other yet, and this gorgeous little flicker of humor and pleasure made me feel like I'd won an award.

We hadn't discussed my reading habits in person yet, but I'd detailed my love of romance enough over the years that this wouldn't be a surprise to him, hence the smile, no doubt.

"I hear romance readers are the best sort of people, so it works out well for me." And then he did the wildest thing.

He stepped close, right between my legs, slid his large, warm hand to my jaw, and dropped his head. In a flash, he pressed a kiss to my cheek, then slipped back, his fingers burning a streak along my neck as he retreated. My eyes had to be huge, and my lips had parted, but there was a look in *his* eyes that made my stomach flip and drop low. Then he winked.

Quiet, sturdy Tristan *winked at me.*

I'd winked at him earlier as a joke, and now here he was, stealthy humor and all kinds of hotness staring me right in the face.

"Need a moment alone, guys?"

Kenny's voice broke through the gauzy quality of the moment and brought us back to the space bustling with people and conversation.

My eyes shot to Jo's. "So, uh, you're here! Do you come to the Saint Security thing on Fridays?"

Tristan had explained how this standing event would be good for us to show up for since it was casual and would get the big reveal over with. My question made sense, in theory, but oh, boy, I sounded as shaken up as I felt.

All from a little kiss.

But one he'd executed out of nowhere, and so quickly! I shouldn't have been surprised the man had moves, considering what he'd done for a living the last twenty years. I knew he had expertise in hand-to-hand combat and obviously moved with amazing speed, but... this all seemed so natural for him.

"No, we do a girls' night most Fridays, too. You know Nikki, right?" She glanced over her shoulder at a table where the beautiful redhead who'd also been witness to our wedding stood along with two other women.

"I do. She's lovely." I waved when Nikki saw me and lifted a hand. The two women with her smiled over, and I hoped they'd be a part of the book club.

"That's an understatement," Bruce said, his gaze on Nikki like it had no choice.

Jo caught my eye, and we smiled at each other. There was really nothing like seeing a ridiculously handsome man like Bruce be completely gone for his girlfriend, and I was all for witnessing it.

Jess returned with two pint glasses and filled them without comment, then slid them toward me and Tristan.

Jo set a hand on my wrist. "Well, I don't mean to interrupt. I just wanted to say hey and grab your number since I forgot to at the store. I'll get you the book for book club and hopefully you can join us—don't worry about reading the book if you don't have time."

"What are you guys reading this month? Something seeexy?" Kenny drew out the last word, and I caught the waggle of his brows.

Jo hid her smile. "As a matter of fact, we are. *Very* sexy."

His eyes widened. "Really? What's the story?"

I laughed right along with Jo. I couldn't tell whether Kenny just liked the idea of women reading sexy books or if he genuinely wanted to know. Either way, his earnest interest tickled me, and he appeared to hang on whatever Jo said next.

"Now, now, Barbie. We've talked about this." Adam's hand came back to Kenny's shoulder. "You'll have to do your own reading if you want to know the story."

While I internally reveled in learning Kenny's nickname was Barbie, out of the corner of my eye, Jo's posture changed. The relaxed stance shifted to something straighter, more alert, and she said, "Oh, hey, Adam."

Adam greeted her with a soft, familiar smile. "Hey, Jo."

Well, what do we have here? One more reason I couldn't wait for book club—I'd be asking about this little firework show for sure.

"Ugh, I'm out, y'all."

Jess's irritated comment came suddenly enough we all looked up in time to see a giant of a man walking toward the table and Jess shooting him a vicious glare.

If it weren't for Tristan's and Bruce's continued ease, I would've been concerned because this man looked like a—

"Beast. Didn't know you were coming." Bruce extended his hand, and the giant of a human accepted with no change of expression.

If Bruce was beautiful and charming and Kenny was almost prettily handsome and Tristan was ruggedly, heart-racingly gorgeous, this man was what I'd call brutally good-looking. He was huge and had a slightly dangerous edge to him, maybe.

The other guys chimed in, each nodding or verbally acknowledging the man whose nickname was, evidently, Beast. *Perfectly accurate.*

The only person who didn't outright greet the newcomer, Jess—also a completely beautiful person—leaned into the table. "Great to meet you for a minute, Winnie. I'm sure I'll see you again soon. Congrats again."

And then she was gone.

The mood in the group was... odd. Off, somehow. I wanted to ask about it, but I'd keep it for later when it was just me and Tristan.

Kenny slapped his hand on the table and I jumped, but when Tristan's hand settled on my arm, just a slight touch of reassurance, I relaxed fully as Kenny launched in.

"Okay, so tell us everything about you. We know you two have been writing letters and whatnot for years, but now you're married? When did you get engaged? And why the crap didn't we get to go to the wedding? I make an excellent groomsman."

Maybe I hadn't relaxed fully, because my throat wouldn't quite work to swallow and I found myself doing my best slow turn to look at Tristan, just praying he knew how to answer all of these things.

We knew it would come, and sure enough, our first test had arrived.

Ten years ago

To: Tristan Donnelly
     From: Winniechickendinny

Tristan,

I'm so happy to hear about your promotion or acceptance to this new unit. You really can't tell me what it's
called? That sounds like spy stuff. Are you actually a spy?

Wait, is someone reading this before you can even see
it? Is your mail getting screened to make sure we're not
passing government secrets?

Little do you know, I'm secretly a KGB agent sent to
undermine the entire US Army via *you*.

Okay, but seriously, if someone *is* reading this, I'm officially stating on the record and for all posterity that I have
no affiliation with any foreign governments and I am just a
nerd who likes to write Tristan letters.

Also, your nickname is Oak? Is it because you're a
nature lover? I hadn't totally picked up on that, but I guess

you've mentioned how you like to be outside. Have we talked about dream homes? I do think I'd like tall trees and open space. The Kansan in me, who's used to wide open spaces, probably couldn't live in a city, but I wouldn't mind a town a bit bigger than mine. I would take some mountains or lakes or something other than corn and soy fields too, if we're just ordering up any old thing we want.

No surprise, I've rambled. I'm not nervous when I write you, but I think I channel the same energy I get—my mouth won't shut off in those circumstances and here, with you, I think I just feel free to let it all hang out. Words-wise. Metaphorically. On the page. *Moving on...*

Stay safe, Tristan. Thanks for letting me babble. And to answer your question... it's okay. I'm mostly staying distracted. Changing my plans for college—I can't imagine leaving anymore. That's okay, though, I'll stay local for now.

Keep me posted,
Winn

CHAPTER TEN

Tristan

It was only fair I be the one to speak up and start our explanation. These were my people and Winn had just met them, but it took a moment to push through the desire to simply excuse us both and walk back to the car.

Why did we need to explain anything to them, especially Barbie? And yes, I heard the petulant child in that thought. If Winnie was any less tense about all of this, I probably would've just told them the whole deal. Bruce and Nikki knew, and none of these guys would reveal the truth if Jeremy or the loan sharks came to town.

But the logic of keeping the true nature of our relationship under wraps made sense—we'd determined this course of action for a reason, and the heat of the moment wasn't the time to change the plan.

So, I leaned into it, sliding the hand resting on her arm around, across her back, and to its new home on the far side of her body so I effectively cradled her. This served to be an affectionate gesture, and it just so happened to feel great. No surprise considering the more of Winnie I got to know, the more I liked. The more I saw, the more I wanted to see.

The more I wanted. Period.

"It's been a long time coming."

Adam nodded, as though this wasn't hard to believe. Bruce did the same, saying, "Of course" since he wouldn't do anything to let on that he had insider information. Beast kept his unaffected expression but also dipped his chin. I didn't know how Jess would've responded, but she wasn't likely to give us a hard time. But Barb?

"Okay, great. But... what else? How'd you pop the question? How the crap didn't we know it'd happened? I know you're private, Oak, but come on."

It was the genuine upset underlining his words that made me tread cautiously instead of brushing him off. Kenny had a lot of growing up to do, but one thing I knew as well as any of the other Saint Security team was that he'd found his family in us. While he was in the military, his choice to get out and come with us, especially to follow Bruce, me, and Adam, made sense.

So it must've indeed seemed like a kind of betrayal to not know before it happened.

"Everyone's been so busy, and we didn't want a long engagement." It fell short as far as explanations go and I knew it.

Winnie leaned into me, almost like she wanted to offer me comfort. It did that, but it also sent my pulse a little haywire. Kenny was right next to her, and she turned to him, gently patting his arm where he leaned on the table. It was a simple move but one that clearly ratcheted up his attention and affection for her in an instant.

"I think it's probably my fault Tristan has been so quiet about everything, and I'm really sorry for that. I see how close you all are—I've known it for years. It's just... it's a complex situation back home, and Tristan was respecting my preference for privacy."

Her voice was so sweet and almost pleading, and Kenny fell for it hook, line, and sinker.

"That makes sense. I'm sorry if I seem pushy. We just love this guy and want the best for him. But I can see how happy he is already—and now that you're here, I'm sure we'll get to see it every day. I'm really happy for you both."

"Thank you... Barbie? Should I call you Barb?"

Kenny flashed his eyebrows. "Oh, I think since you're now officially a part of the family, you can call me anything you want."

"Hey now," I said as everyone laughed, simply because Kenny sounded too silly and flirtatious not to, even though we all knew without a doubt he'd never actually flirt with Winnie now that she was mine.

Mine.

That hit me right in the solar plexus like a punch with no guard up. How many times would this keep happening? This feeling of needing to protect her and keep her safe, but also the need to... the desire to... the desperation to have this be something more.

But no. It wasn't what she needed.

Even though her explanation had been vague, it was true. She did need privacy, she did need protection, and she did need to keep the mess back in Kansas under wraps. If she had any chance of recovering from the stress and madness of the situation in Kansas, she needed all of that.

And she most assuredly did not need me pining for something more with her. What would that be? I didn't even know what that would look like at this point, and I had to keep myself straight.

"Sounds fun. Don't you think so, Tristan?"

Winnie was smiling at me, expectation on her face like I'd heard what whoever had said. I honestly had no idea because my mind had been talking too loudly at me.

"Uh, sorry. Missed it. What?"

"I was just saying we need to get you two some time away," Kenny said. "You barely took a day off this week. What about a honeymoon?"

"The schedule isn't bad right now. We can cover down on whatever you need," Adam offered.

Bruce narrowed his eyes a touch as though he were waiting for a signal, but I couldn't figure out which one to give him. Instead, I scrambled into an explanation, never having even thought about how odd it would look that we hadn't taken a honeymoon, nor did we have one planned.

"That's nice, guys. Bruce and I have actually worked it out. I have a little surprise trip planned for us, and if we keep talking about it, it won't be much of a surprise."

Beast grunted and slugged back a large swallow of his beer while Kenny practically giggled and Adam nodded in approval. Thankfully, Bruce redirected us to more detailed introductions of each of the men and a brief review of the people who weren't in attendance tonight but who regularly worked at Saint based here in Silverton. We'd cover the international folks at some point... maybe.

The evening wore on, and Winnie and I sipped our beers slowly, sides pressed together. I wondered if she'd prefer I give her space. I wondered if *I* would prefer that—no. The thought was enough to confirm I didn't want more space.

These guys had never seen me with a woman, much less

a spouse. They wouldn't know how I typically behaved, but neither did I. I hadn't had a relationship in years, and I'd never had one with someone like Winnie.

We had history. We'd been through incredible highs and lows. And yet, we'd just met a few days ago.

Oh, and now we were married.

In reality, I didn't know how I would behave in a marriage. This was my first time.

Thoughts like that grated. *First* time, as though there'd be another. I couldn't imagine it, just like I'd never imagined there'd be a first to begin with. But here we were. And as I overanalyzed everything from where my digits rested against the swell of her hip and dip of her waist to whether she preferred men who wore cologne versus my soap and deodorant basic approach, I knew *this* was how I'd be.

I'd be close. As close as possible, as much as possible.

Because I hadn't had this—had hardly dared dream of it. And while it was here, even under the guise of pragmatism for her and definitely fleeting, I would embrace it.

Even if it'd be harder when the end came And it would.

Even if Winnie wanted to choose me, and there was no saying she would want to, she wouldn't. I'd never known someone more dedicated to her family save possibly Bruce, and even then, the circumstances were different because he'd had choices, and she hadn't. Winnie had been beholden to her family, wrapped up in their drama, and now put at risk on top of doing something huge to save them all, in essence.

When things were cleared up and she could return, I hated to admit there was no chance she'd choose anything but that ending—the one where she went home to fix everything, to save her family, to save everyone but me, and one where I stayed here.

CHAPTER ELEVEN

Winnie

Staring at my husband's muscles moving under the T-shirt he wore to teach his self-defense workshop should *not* have made me feel guilty.

And logically, on one hand, it didn't.

But on the other, more circumspect hand, it really did.

Because Tristan was not mine to ogle, and yet that's what I was doing. Sure, on the outside, it might've appeared like I was studying his position as he walked through attacking Bruce, who then walked us through the steps of how to stomp a foot, give an elbow to the gut, and so on and so on, and I couldn't rehash the details because Tristan was also wearing joggers.

Yes. Gray sweatpants-style joggers.

And let me just state for the record, these mock assaults had nothing on those sweatpants. They were an outright attack on my good sense, ability to listen, and desire to be respectful of a man who was giving me so much.

"Anyone have questions?" Bruce asked, his hands on his hips and brows raised in a friendly, welcoming mien.

He was also just... startlingly handsome. What was in the water here? Or, back in North Carolina where so many of them had worked before this—something?

"I'd like to see you two really go at it," someone said from the back.

The class of about twelve people turned to see Kenny leaning against the wall, arms folded across his chest and a sly smirk firmly in place. This one, too, was ridiculously good-looking, even if a bit immature for my taste. Tristan sent him a look that had me smothering a smile—if Tristan had ever had a younger brother, that's exactly how he'd look at him.

"No questions from the peanut gallery. How about any class attendees?" Bruce smiled at everyone, truly a friendly expression.

Tristan didn't have that. He didn't exactly repel people —he didn't brood like that guy Beast or anything—he just had a quieter presence. Bruce had this movie star quality, like flashbulbs would go off the second he tossed out the right smile. Tristan was... sneaky hot. Physically, he drew the eye, and by *the* I meant *my*, but I also meant *many* eyes. People noticed him, but not because they wanted a picture. More and more, I was realizing it was because he was formidable. Not gigantic or threatening, but just... impossible to ignore.

And if his gray sweatpants stretched *just right* over his thick thighs and *chef's kiss* muscular butt, well... there were many things in life to be thankful for.

"You good? Have any questions?"

Tristan's quiet words burst my reverie wide open with a shock, and I coughed on air. "Um, yes. Well. Yeah. I'm good."

Before he could say whatever was coming to match his skeptical expression, Kenny spoke up again.

"No questions, which means you two can give them a demo."

Half the class murmured in agreement, and more than one person clapped to encourage them. Bruce raised a brow at Tristan, who nodded.

How was his nod endearing? Something about the brief incline of his head and the way those serious eyes didn't waver from his target made my stomach flip. The concentration. The pure capability in a body coiled with strength and poised to strike. The confidence.

Whew.

Honestly, what was wrong with me? It had to be the leftovers from last night. All that touching—the hand around my waist and the kiss to my cheek. The bonding with his coworkers and even just being a part of the weekend crowd as a couple in this adorable town.

It'd gone straight to my head, like I'd come up from the depths too fast and now had a case of the bends. The *I already like Tristan too much* bends, and I was just asking for trouble.

Kenny was beaming from the back of the room, and everyone spread out to leave the main space at the center on the mats free for the two retired soldiers. Bruce held up his hands theatrically, and the hubbub in the room ceased.

"Now you know we're all experts at hand-to-hand combat. Saint Security isn't in the business of selling people on things we can't do better than most everyone else."

"No shortage of humility either there, huh, Bruce?" Quinn Darling-Grenier, a woman I'd met when the workshop started and who was apparently a veteran of these classes, grinned over at Bruce.

"Why are you here again, Quinn? Did you forget the advanced group isn't starting until February?" he asked.

She shrugged a shoulder. "Nah, just couldn't stay away from you pretty boys."

Everyone chuckled, and he waved her off.

"There's no value in false modesty. It doesn't do you good, nor does it do us any good either. And that's not unlike self-defense. You get rid of the pretense. Get rid of your manners and your politeness."

He gave a strong look around the room, particularly making eye contact with each woman. He'd given us all a small lecture on how being polite often got women into trouble and we had to check it all at the door.

That felt like sand under a fingernail, but after he'd listed a few examples of how dangerous the tendency to be accommodating could be, I felt more than convicted of the truth. I'd witnessed it in my own life—had I just kept walking and slammed the door on the guys after me to get to Jeremy, maybe they wouldn't have grabbed me.

"So now we'll show you what it looks like when you stop being polite. You don't worry about the optics. This is what it looks like to defend yourself when it matters."

He made eye contact with Tristan for a half second, then he attacked.

It was a flurry of rapid strikes, the impact a tangible thing, and in a few seconds, both men had used each limb to deflect and attack. This went on for maybe two more minutes, though it seemed interminable, before Kenny yelled, "Break!"

Bruce and Tristan pushed away from each other, and Tristan was smiling—*wait*. Smiling? I mean, tiny little curls of his lips at either side of his mouth, but yes. I knew this was his thing, but it was written all over his handsome face how much he liked it, and witnessing it gave me a jolt of pure joy. As though his satisfaction was a shot of espresso after a long night, watching him made every piece of me sit up and take note.

"Now show 'em how it'd really go, Oak."

"You're not going to have a go at him?" Bruce asked, clearly referencing Tristan.

Kenny's eyes went wide and he refused. "Heck no. I want to keep all the fingers I still have left. He's all yours, old man."

Kenny waved his left hand, which I'd noticed was missing his ring and pinky fingers.

Bruce cut him a look, then turned to Tristan, who waited patiently in a relaxed stance as if saying he had nowhere else to be. He could be so completely still and steady, it was almost baffling to think of how quickly and aggressively he'd just been moving.

"Go easy on me, okay? I'm still recovering from—" Bruce's eyes widened, and Tristan's chin dropped in quick agreement.

Huh. Wonder what that was. And also, what was happening right now?

Bruce shot a humor-filled glance my way. "Prepare to be amazed by your man."

And before my stomach had the chance to flip, Bruce attacked. I cringed, bracing against whatever part of Tristan he would hit, but Tristan blocked each strike. One, two, three, each lightning fast. A kick, a knee to the groin, and then—

Holy crap. *Holy crap.* Bruce was on the floor lying face up. Fortunately, he was laughing, even though Tristan held him in an arm bar that looked like it put pressure on his shoulder and elbow.

Everyone clapped, and Kenny chuckled to himself with what sounded like glee. Tristan shifted and hauled Bruce to his feet as I worked to understand what I'd seen. And maybe more so, why I found it so wildly attractive, it'd sent a fizzy sensation all throughout my arms and fingers.

I must've spaced out, staring at the spot on the mat where Bruce had just been, because when Tristan lightly touched my arm, I jumped.

"Whoa, you okay? Is this upsetting you? You don't have to come if it's a problem. We'll do our own lessons at home. And Winnie, you know I would never *ever* hurt you, right?"

The concern in his voice and the borderline panicked expression shot little arrows into my heart. Oh my goodness, how was this man both lethal and so darn sensitive to me? How was he so completely badass one second and then capable of this gentleness?

"Of course, of course I know that. And no, it's no problem," I rushed out, not wanting him to misunderstand my... whatever this was. Confusion? Attraction? Longing to be good at something I loved as much as Tristan did this? I really didn't know.

"We'll skip next week. I don't want you to be triggered by this or anything else." His fingers carded through his hair, and he looked almost angry. "I should've realized this wouldn't—"

My fingers touched his lips in a desperate move to stop his worry and overreaction.

"Hey, no. I'm fine. I was just... processing. And, uh..." I scrambled for some way to explain my feelings and the jumble of thoughts. "I know I'm a beginner, but I was wondering if you could teach me to do that."

CHAPTER TWELVE

Tristan

Standing across from Winnie in the now-empty Saint Security training room was potentially not my best idea.

That said, refusing her request to teach her anything would've been patently impossible. I made no attempt to fight it because there was no point. I would do whatever she asked, and I'd long since resigned myself to it.

But teaching her how to throw me? Well, that took a lot of close contact I hadn't planned on. Her outfit consisted of skin-tight exercise pants and a purple shirt fitting her very well. She'd pulled her hair back in a braid, and a few strands had come loose around her face. She was red-faced from exertion, having tried several times to muscle me over her shoulder.

I outweighed her by more than fifty pounds, easily.

She'd need momentum and I wasn't giving it to her, but this was all with an eye to teach her.

"Okay, I give. I cannot do it, even if I start bench-pressing Juniper tomorrow."

The image made me smile, but I shoved it away. "Correct. What you need is momentum. Now come at me slowly and I'll show you how I'd do it to you. Then we'll run it through in regular time. Then we'll work on you throwing me."

She made a slow-motion punch, and I set a hand on her wrist. I blocked out the sensory receptors telling me I liked the way her skin felt under the pads of my fingers. I flatly denied the impulse that told me to press my lips to the slope of her neck when I pulled her off-balance, and I rejected the desire to wrap her in my arms and cage her in.

I did not let my focus drift to her lips or the way her chest rose and fell in measured breaths. I avoided the knowledge that she would be coming home with me, that she was my wife, and that she trusted me, because none of those things would help my self-control.

Instead, I finished the move, indicating where I'd actually flip her, then backed away, hands up as though I'd gotten caught doing something I shouldn't.

This wasn't it, though. This scenario wasn't a forbidden one. She'd asked. She had to have known we'd be touching. And that hadn't been a problem.

It *wasn't* a problem. It was a pleasure—*no*.

Not a pleasure. A duty.

I was doing something for her so she could defend herself. So that if anyone dared get close to her and somehow got through me, she'd have options.

"Alright, ready for the real thing?"

She hesitated for a second, but because we'd done a few

role reversals with partners attacking each other during our class, she followed through, a jab toward my midsection. In a few moves, I pulled her arm to disturb her balance and moved my leg to sweep her feet as I dropped to a knee, edged a shoulder into her torso, and then tried to lower her gently to the mat.

A breath gusted out and she blinked. "Okay. Effective."

Her voice came out a strained whisper. She saved me from asking if she was hurt or needed another minute by jumping up and readying her stance.

"My turn."

Her refusal to quit or give in? I loved that. I'd loved Winnie as a friend for a long time, and her determination, even when I didn't agree with her, had always been admirable. But now, seeing it in person both in big things like her mission to protect her parents and this small moment learning a self-defense move she was by no means ready for, I felt it again.

And the only thing I could do about it was give her exactly what she wanted. "Okay. Your turn."

Winnie emerged after what felt like an eternity, her hair high on her head, in sweats and, in an effort to murder me, a T-shirt that left about two inches of her firm belly and a glimpse of her hip bones bare.

"You okay? You're not hurt, are you?"

I may have jumped up and caused Juniper to swirl around and get excited, but when Juniper reached her,

Winnie dropped to one knee and pet her with as much enthusiasm as Junie had given to Winnie.

"You're so sweet, you know that?" she asked my dog. "You're such a good girl, you know?"

And I was not jealous of my dog or the attention she was giving her. I loved the beast and wanted her to love her, too. But it did do something to me... seeing her lavish Juniper with affection and yet feeling oddly deprived of it myself.

"I soaked in your giant tub and read a book. I'm going to be sore tomorrow." She shot me a little grin that flipped the table in my head.

Before this moment, my resolve, concern, muddy feelings, and everything else I'd been actively ignoring all day had been set in neat piles on the table, all right angles and order.

Now?

With a single small smile, she'd mixed everything up, all contents of that level plane now dumped in a messy heap on the ground. This meant I was mentally scrambling, less able to shove away thoughts of Winnie in the bath reading a book and less equipped to hold in my worry for her. Had she gotten hurt—had I hurt her? Was she okay? Was she *really* okay?

"Is that all right? I'm sorry if I took too long. I know you were hungry and I hope you ate. I don't want you to feel like you need to wait for me when you'd rather just go ahead and do what you need to. I—"

"No, Winn, no." My sluggish brain finally jump-started, straightening the mess and finding its path into the right way to respond so it didn't confuse things between us. "I don't mind waiting, and you don't need to apologize."

Something flickered across her face as she stood and paced toward me, and it looked a lot like another apology.

We'd touched fairly intimately while sparring, bodies pressed tightly together, sliding against each other, but that's what happened when sparring at times. I didn't want to assume she'd allow me to touch her now like I had then, but I chanced settling a hand gently on her shoulder.

"Don't apologize to me."

Her shoulders rose with a breath and she held my gaze, her lovely face solemn. I pressed on since she didn't seem inclined to respond.

"Seriously. I don't want to hear it. I know you're used to having to placate your family, but you don't do that with me, okay? Not here."

Her eyes widened even as her brow furrowed and a bit of heat entered her eyes. Not the kind I'd like to see, either. The kind that told me maybe she wasn't ready for me to address what we both knew.

"Okay."

I would've liked to blame the mess in my mind for why I pressed her now, but maybe I was just a fool I'd wanted to say this a thousand times by email, and I'd hinted at it while internally screaming at her to just stop catering to her family. Stop bending to their needs as though hers didn't matter.

"I want you to feel at home here. You don't have to explain yourself or meet *my* needs. It's not about me. You can do what you want without apology."

It took seconds for her face to clear and her energy to shift from that concerned, almost caught expression to something completely... vacant. Her brow smoothed out, and she blinked as though she'd set a new lens into place.

"Okay."

My turn to blink. "What just happened?"

She shrugged a shoulder and offered a placid smile. "Nothing. I'm just tired. I'll see you in the morning."

And instead of joining me for dinner or sitting on the couch to read or talk, she turned and disappeared back into her room.

I sank into the cushions and let my head fall back so I stared at the ceiling. I'd pushed too far and she'd shut down completely—no hope of conversation. She'd given me the version I would bet money she showed her family in times of strife. She wouldn't respond and pick a fight. She wouldn't challenge me, even though she clearly didn't like what I'd said. She couldn't find a way to make the situation better, so she was withdrawing.

I hated it.

And I'd also overestimated how much I could say to her. I didn't want to push her away, but I needed her not to cater to me. Her life was upside-down right now, and I wouldn't allow myself to be one more person she bent to.

A person can only bend so many times for others before she breaks.

CHAPTER THIRTEEN

Winnie

There was nothing like having the person who'd become your best friend call you on your worst habit. I could easily say it ranked up there with my least favorite things, especially when my retreat resulted in such a crestfallen, worried expression.

And maybe even more so when I felt an apology rising to my lips even as I retreated to the safety of my room. *His room.*

I'd planned to relax on the couch and hang out with him until book club, but my pride wouldn't let me stay there. At the same time, the letdown of finding out I'd defaulted to the same way of functioning with him as I did with my family gave me heartburn in the worst way.

Instead, I hid away in my room, devouring the latest Josie Wade novel after failing to focus on work and wishing I could escape the reality that I'd have to go back out there.

Maybe he would leave, but I doubted it. Tristan had proved to be quiet and tended to give me space, but he wouldn't shrink away from me, even if I'd retreated.

So when the time came to leave, I cautiously exited my room. Tristan sat on the couch, with Juniper nestled into her bed, the fire flickering between them. He didn't look up, though I knew he'd heard me. The space was small enough, and my boots made a *tack, tack* sound on the hardwood floors that would've alerted him if the sound of my door hadn't.

"I'm ready to head out," I said, as though I hadn't run away from him hours earlier.

And then he turned and I saw them.

The glasses.

Ugh.

Of course this gorgeous human had an imperfection. It wasn't his shyness or his ability to see through my apologies. It wasn't something truly off-putting. It was completely benign and yet totally damaging to the promise I'd made myself to remain emotionally aloof and ignore the attraction snapping between us whenever we shared the same space.

Reading glasses.

I couldn't explain why, but in this moment, with his head ducked into a book and his glasses on, his stunning face etched into something solemn and familiar even though it'd only been days I'd had the privilege to learn it well, I wanted to cry.

"I'll drive you, if that's okay." He didn't rise from the couch, didn't budge beyond regrettably removing those wire-framed lenses and waiting for my reply.

"That'd be good. Thank you." The words emerged stilted and awkward. Everything felt a little wrong, and my heart hadn't stopped fluttering in my chest.

He closed his book and set it aside, but I saw the cover and a bolt of lightning hit me when I did. "You're reading a Josie Wade book?"

A smile flashed and disappeared. "I've picked up the ones you mentioned with the most enthusiasm over the years."

He stood and left his glasses on the book, his large hands making the spectacles even more alluring for some reason.

"You—you've read books?"

He laughed lightly. "I do read. Yes."

Shaking my head, I rushed to clarify. "No, I mean, you read books I read? Like, you're reading romance because I do? Or because you just like them?"

His eyes narrowed on me as he approached. "Am I not allowed to read them?"

"No, of course not. I just... you never said anything. I never imagined you reading romance."

Probably for the best because had I read any romance with Tristan in mind, it would've been dangerous. I'd already felt more emotionally invested in him than I did anyone I'd ever met or dated, and imagining him as the hero of every book? Or even to think of him reading them—the steamy kisses and heroic moments, and knowing I'd read them, too?

I could've died. Or passed out. Or melted into a puddle on the floor in front of the fire. But when I studied his face, there might've been a slight blush to his cheeks.

"Guess I should've told you."

It came out quiet... maybe even shy.

My stomach flipped, but I crushed the feeling down. I was far too flustered by his too-accurate assessment of me earlier paired with the glasses and the reality he was not only a reader but a sometimes *romance* reader to segue gracefully, so I simply asked, "Um, so, are you ready to go?"

He grabbed his keys and jacket and walked to the door. "I'll be back in a few minutes, Junie."

Juniper's head perked up, then settled back down where it lay on her bed.

I slipped into my coat, and we exited the back door. As we loaded into the truck and he cautiously backed out of the garage, proceeded down the long driveway, and began the drive to the bookstore, my nerves spiked.

It didn't take much lately, to be honest. Things were going as well as they could here, or so I hoped. I hadn't handled the conversation this afternoon well, but that didn't come as a huge surprise. Tristan and I usually corresponded with time and space between responses—we had a moment to consider our words rather than being face-to-face, where we had none. I wasn't used to him being the one to push me, and I certainly wasn't used to anyone suggesting I should do what I wanted rather than what *they* wanted.

My parents loved me. I knew Jeremy did, too, in his own messed up way. But I'd long wondered if maybe their love wasn't quite... whole. Or maybe it made more sense to say it was conditional.

I could admit one of the biggest reasons I loved romance was the frequent thread in my favorites that spoke to an *unconditional* love. A love that persisted and lasted and didn't shatter when something went wrong or someone made a wrong choice. To me, this was unequivocally the most romantic notion I could fathom.

We drove the ten minutes into town with only the low melodies of a country station playing quietly enough I couldn't quite make out the tune. The landscape was blanketed with snow, and fat flakes made splotchy, wet sounds against the windshield. Time was running out, and I couldn't stand the thought of going to this event and ending up thinking about how off everything had been in the last few hours, so I finally spoke as he pulled up to the curb outside All Booked Up.

"Listen, about earlier..."

He left the engine running but shifted into park and faced me, his eyes glittering in the darkness. I could just make out his features thanks to the streetlight not far from the truck.

"Me reading romance?" he asked, as though that was the cause of my quiet.

"No. I mean, I do want to discuss that further and in great detail as soon as possible, but no... before that."

"I shouldn't have said anything. It wasn't my place." His gaze shifted to look out the front windshield.

The other storefronts on this side of the street were closed. The restaurants and bars around town would be open, I guessed, but by eight on a Saturday, most everything else had shut down. We had privacy and were five minutes early, and I needed to stay here and face him on this. I needed to be honest.

I was terrible at this. Not that I thought of myself as a liar, but I was absolutely used to appeasing people. He'd seen it, clear as day, and I didn't want him censoring himself. I didn't want him not to tell me the truth when he saw it.

I reached for him, setting my hand on his where it rested on the fabric of his seat, which drew his attention back to me.

My heart rate surged, and I huffed an exhale to try to find some calm.

"I'm sorry I reacted poorly. It hit pretty close to some

truths I'm wrestling with." Gaze connected to his, every bit of me that tended to want to run away from this discomfort balked, but I gripped his hand tighter. "I'm not used to someone talking to me like that, and I didn't handle it well."

"Winn, I'm so sorry. I never meant to hurt you. It came out like a criticism, but I never—"

"No, Tristan, it didn't. I took it that way, but I know you were just trying to get me to... be normal. And I know I'm not. I know it's been too many years of placating my parents and tiptoeing around everyone's feelings. And right when I thought I was doing better, that I was making plans, I—then Dad had his heart attack and it was like something in me reset. I lost the ability to see my way forward without doing everything I could to make sure they were happy, even when I could feel it made me unhappy."

A raw, vulnerable feeling made me squirm in my seat as I realized what I'd said and just how true it was. Resoundingly true and unimaginably painful to admit, but there it was.

I'd acknowledged I had growth to do, especially when it came to my parents and Jeremy, but I hadn't ever confronted how it'd made me feel... sometimes just tired, but sometimes deeply sad. A little used. And then maybe self-pitying and annoyed at myself for that, because wasn't it my choice anyway?

It wasn't that simple, but clearly, his words had set off a long train of thoughts.

Tristan's hand turned and grasped mine, effectively claiming my hand with his warmth and gentleness. He searched my eyes, then his free hand slipped through the strands of his hair, a gesture I'd already come to adore. It was his default move, something a little messy for a man so steady and sure.

"I'm sorry it hurt you. And Winn"—his eyes held mine as he shook his head slowly—"you'll never be normal."

My brows rose in a pop of surprise, and when I saw the sliver of a smile on his face, I burst out with a loud laugh. "Well, okay then, so much for you being all kindly and gentle."

His head ticked to the side like a question, but then he grinned before stuffing that expression away for a more serious one.

"But really, I need you to know I'm not over here judging your life or your choices. I think you're—" He focused on me so intently, I could almost feel the heat of him zeroing in on me. "I think you're incredibly loyal and generous. You're thoughtful and loving to your family, even when they don't deserve it. And I appreciate your patience with me while I figure out how to support you."

His large, warm hand squeezed mine, then released. While I worked to keep the threatening tears at bay, he slid out of his seat and walked around to my door, opened it, and held out that same hand.

There was no reason for him to escort me like this. He'd parked directly in front of the shop's adorable blue door, and there probably weren't even twenty feet between my side of the truck and the inside of the bookstore, but here he was.

After saying... what he'd said.

So instead of insisting he didn't need to help me out of the truck, I took his hand. He walked with me, his gaze taking in both sides of the street, and stopped just before the door.

"Have fun. Text me when you're done, and I'll be right here to pick you up."

And then, in what must've been slow motion, he leaned

toward me, his hand dropping mine and slipping in to rest at my jaw, and pressed a kiss to my cheek. He pulled back before I could do anything other than inhale the freezing air into my lungs and nod, and I could've sworn there was fire in his eyes.

But he didn't walk away. He waited there until I fumbled out, "Oh, right, inside," and then scrambled into the store, shut the door behind me, and turned to watch him stride away down the sidewalk.

"Holy crap," I said under my breath. The man was molten hot on so many levels. The words. The earnestness. The whole protective thing. And that little kiss...

"Holy crap is right. You guys have some serious chemistry."

Nikki stood by the checkout desk grinning at me, and Jo's expression next to her featured the same pleased smile.

Jo fanned herself, the little strands sprouting from her bun swaying with the movement. "I don't think I've ever imagined a kiss on the cheek being hot, but that one was. *Mental note.*"

Nikki winked at me. "No surprise someone as private as Tristan wouldn't want any public displays to be too out there. But I'm also not shocked that he didn't just drop you at the curb. That wouldn't be a Saint man."

Jo raised a brow as I wiped my feet on the welcome mat as best I could, hoping I wouldn't track any globs of snow into the lovely store, and then joined them by the desk.

"Hmm. I guess I can agree with that. They all have that protective hero thing going on." Jo hummed with satisfaction. "I do love a protective hero." She turned and grabbed a large stack of books and took off toward what I'd assumed was the back room. "Come on, ladies, we'll be meeting back here."

Nikki and I followed, and I mentally thanked her for not trying to discuss or insinuate anything more about the front door moment. Clearly, Tristan had known we had a small audience and he'd acted accordingly. I shouldn't have been disappointed by that, and I wasn't.

Obviously, I wasn't, because why would I be?

Tristan was doing me a favor, making our relationship look real so I had the whole town behind me. That'd been his plan, after all, and I saw the logic in it.

I just hadn't imagined he'd be so thorough in seeing it through or so thoughtful in his care of me. I knew the kind of man he was in some ways, but in person, in real life, he was... so much better.

We entered a beautiful little room complete with a fire-place, cozy-looking furniture, and shelves of books built into the walls like a library. Three women were already sitting—one I knew and two I didn't.

A dark-haired woman looked at me from overtop her book. "Come in, sit down, and tell us everything we need to know about being married to Tristan Donnelly."

EMAIL

Nine and a Half Years Ago

To: Winniechickendinny
From: Tristan Donnelly

Winnie,

I'm sorry your college plans changed—maybe you can transfer in a few years? I hate the thought of you missing out on seeing other places, but trust me when I say I understand wanting to stay near family and support them. You're amazing.

I don't have much time—we're heading out on a quick mission, and I'm not sure how long I'll be gone but shouldn't be more than a few weeks if everything goes well. I'm going with Bruce and a guy named West. You'd like them. Both nice guys. And our team leader, Colby, is a good dude too. He's older and should be retiring soon, so this might be his last go-round.

I just wanted to make sure and say that if you ever need anything—I mean *anything*—promise me you'll ask. I don't know what might come up for you, but I'm there. I need you to promise me you'll do that. Don't ever hesitate to ask. And I'll promise you right back that if I really can't do it, I'll say no.

Watch some *Mission: Impossible* and pretend it's me running like Ethan, even if I am like ten inches taller than Tom Cruise...

Tristan

CHAPTER FOURTEEN

Winnie

Elise Cordero had no qualms asking questions others might consider too personal. Fortunately, aside from the one big secret in my life, I didn't have a problem telling them whatever they wanted to know.

Problem was, I wasn't sure what she was actually after. She didn't know me, but she evidently knew Tristan.

Thankfully, Nikki jumped in to save me yet again.

"I highly doubt Winnie's going to share the details of her marriage before she's even sat down and met everyone."

Jo hopped up. "Right, so continuing from Elise, that's Dove."

She gestured to a prim blond woman sitting nearest the fire and who wore a pretty, feminine dress in a blue and white bird pattern that fell to her knees. Her calves were covered in coordinating tights disappearing into heeled Mary Jane style shoes.

"Nice to meet you, Winnie. I'm so glad you're here and so happy to meet another romance lover!" Dove gushed. "Oh, and I just love your hair."

I'd braided my hair in a messy six-strand braid that looked complex but wasn't all that tricky. "Thank you."

"And I think maybe you met Jess the other night?" Jo asked, nodding to the petite dark-haired woman, whom I'd met at Craic just last night.

"Good to see you again, Winnie. And please, do *not* give us any details. Tristan is as close to a brother as I'll ever have." She shuddered, and we all laughed.

Elise cut her a glare. "You're no fun."

"You're nosy," Jess shot back, a hint of a smile on her lips.

"Come on, ladies. Let's skip talking about actual human men and talk about some men written by women—the real stuff." Dove clapped her hands together.

We laughed, and I found a spot next to Nikki on a loveseat. Jo went around distributing champagne flutes filled with pink champagne, then settled into an overstuffed chair and held up her glass.

"To the first of many meetings of the Silver Ridge Romance Readers Club."

I sipped my drink and reveled in the moment and absolutely refused to think of how many of these meetings I'd get to attend and when I'd start missing them when I left.

"I just don't get people who *don't* read romance," Dove said, her sweet voice melodic as ever.

"They're missing out. I read a variety, but it feels like coming home when I read a great romance." Jess slumped into the couch with a sigh and finished off her glass of red wine.

"I honestly never would've guessed you'd want to be a part of a romance book club, but I love that you're here." Jo smiled at Jess.

Jess chuckled. "Never would've guessed until I became a weekly customer?"

Jo shrugged a slim shoulder. "Well, yeah.'

"I may be a badass retired soldier but I..." Something sad flitted across her face before she gave us a small smile. "I've got a soft heart. It needs feeding and nurturing so it doesn't lose all hope in men and the world."

We all raised a glass to that, and Nikki spoke up.

"Romance was never my thing until I came in here at Christmas and Mr. Malcom recommended a Josie Wade book."

"That was your first romance?" Elise asked, stunned.

Nikki nodded. "I was never a big fiction reader. But I've wondered whether I might've been more..." Her intelligent eyes flickered around the room as though searching for the right words. "If I might've been more open—to love and a lot of other things."

Dove's smile stretched wide. "Happily, you had your own personal romance hero to break in and shake things up for you. And you've found your way to the light side, so that's all that matters."

Nikki grinned and a light blush dusted her pale cheeks. I hadn't seen a lot of her and Bruce together, but the little I had spoke volumes. There was no mistaking the bond between them, and I hoped I'd get to see it unfold even more.

We relaxed in the glow of the firelight and fairy lights strung up around us. We'd discussed the book of the month and had circled around a bunch of other selections for the next few months. As much doubt about the circumstances of being here had swirled around me, this night had made it feel like fate. Getting to attend this first meeting, getting to know these women so soon after I'd moved here... it felt like a gift.

"You know who else reads romance?" Jess asked, and something in her voice tipped me off.

"Ooo, who? Someone we wouldn't guess?" Elise asked, clearly interested in the gossip.

Jess's dark gaze hit mine. "You want to tell them?"

A little thrill shot through me, and a grin tugged at my lips, even as a sense of relief that I did know the truth settled. "I suppose I can."

Everyone sat up or shifted forward, eyes wide. I'd never been more glad I knew this truth because wouldn't it seem weird if Jess did and I didn't? Or would they even care?

"Tristan was reading the newest Josie Wade this afternoon." My heart fluttered at the thought of him with his glasses and a book in the quiet, lovely living room.

Jo dropped back into her chair with a sigh. Elise made a sort of groaning sound while Dove looked like she might float away and Nikki grinned.

Jess beamed. "Yep. I've caught him a few other times, too... though I shouldn't say *caught*. He never acts like it's something to be embarrassed about, which just makes me love him more."

An alarm beeped in the back of my brain. *Love him more.* Oh, dear. Did she have a thing for Tristan? Had I blown into town and sabotaged something that could've been real between them?

Wait, no. She just said she sees him like a brother. Phew. That was a wild ride of jealousy and horror, and I embraced the relief that came at remembering Jess's earlier comment.

"It's just so adorable. And oh my gosh, aren't those romantic suspense? Aren't all her heroes soldiers, just like Tristan? Gah!" Dove pressed her hands to her cheeks in delight and looked as much like an angel as I could imagine a human looking.

"It is. I can't believe he never told me."

I could probably fill multiple volumes with the things Tristan had never told me simply because we only covered so much ground in our emails. They were at once intimate and singular, all-encompassing and limited. It made no sense, but it also proved to me just how much more there was to the man, and how much more there was to me.

Frankly, I was glad I hadn't realized this sooner or I never would've thought this arrangement could work. And even though he'd never once wavered, never seemed remotely unsure we could do this and he wanted to do this, what if all this was simply because he was so loyal? So honorable, almost to a fault?

What if I'd done to him what I was slowly admitting to myself my parents had done to me—played on my loyalty to them and ended up sabotaging any sense of loyalty to myself?

Tristan was nothing if not honorable, faithful, and loyal, and I'd activated that in him when I asked him to remember the promise he'd made me after Thomas died. How could he do anything *but* what I asked him?

"Looks like Bruce is here, ladies." Nikki popped up and grabbed her bag.

"Oh, and what are we? Kicking us to the rearview that fast, huh?" Elise heckled, and we all laughed.

Nikki pressed her lips together for a moment and squinted like she was thinking. "I will never not be grateful for you all—and I'm happy to include you in there, Winnie. But like you said, I have a real, live romance hero waiting on me."

My heart glowed at her inclusion of me so soon, even as I laughed at the peace sign she threw at us before disappearing out of the cozy reading room.

Dove sighed. "Can't blame her."

"Nope," Elise agreed.

Jo shook her head. "Not at all. Oh my gosh, I had the *biggest* crush on Bruce when he first moved here."

My eyes snapped up, and Dove and Elise gave each other a knowing look. Jess was the bold one to ask the question I'd instantly wondered.

"But you don't anymore?"

Jo's cheeks reddened. "Uh, no. I mean... I can't blame myself. He's a wonderful man. But no." Her gaze softened, and the rest of us exchanged glances.

"Okay, so who's the lucky man?" Elise prodded.

Jo suddenly found the book in her hand imminently interesting, then held it up. "Oh, for now, I'm sticking with fictional men."

Elise raised her own book. "Amen, sister."

"I can get on board with that," Jess agreed.

Dove raised hers, too. "I would very much like an actual man, but for the time being, I will happily crush on the heroes in these books."

I couldn't help but smile at the ridiculous and yet very relatable sentiment. I raised my own. Since I couldn't very well complain about having Tristan—who I didn't officially have but did legally have and, for all they knew, definitely got to claim—I focused on the larger theme. "Here's to the fictional heroes."

They all toasted their books with, "To the heroes!"

Then Jess raised hers again. "And to the women who make them come to life."

Everyone liked that, so we toasted again, to the women who'd written those heroes, and to the women in the room who'd read them and made them come to life. I liked this idea, that as readers we had a part in the heroes—even the stories themselves—coming to life.

Not long after, we all tidied up the area, disposed of the empty bottles and trash and stuck our plates and glasses inside the mini dishwasher Jo showed us in the back room. We wandered out, each a little reluctant to leave the good company and the cozy store.

"Until next month, ladies. But also, Friday night?" Jo asked.

Everyone agreed, and Dove, Jess, and Elise all ventured out into the cold to find their cars. Jo turned out the lights, and we stood just inside the store while I texted Tristan. His truck was still right where he'd left it, so he must've found something to occupy him for the two hours I'd been here.

Tonight had been so lovely, I felt a little heartsick to see the evening end, even while being excited to see Tristan again. The inescapable feeling of being an imposter settled in my gut more heavily now that the warm fire's glow and cozy room was out of reach.

I'd be leaving here and leaving all of this behind. Shouldn't I just tell them the truth? Tell them I was only here for a while and not settling into a new life with a man I loved and investing in a place I'd call home, too. Building friendships that would have time to bloom and grow?

"Everything going okay for you two?" Jo asked.

I swallowed, desperately wanting to tell her the truth even though I knew I couldn't. I already trusted her, but I tended to be like that. Trusting, and maybe a little naïve.

"It's good. Just... adjusting to being together in person. That's pretty new."

"I bet it is. I know he cares about you so much, and I can tell you care for him, too. That's a good place to start."

Her words were so carefully chosen, or maybe it struck me she'd used *care* instead of *love*. A normal married couple would probably merit the use of love, but... did she see we weren't like that?

Jo had this vibe or aura or *something* about her that said she wasn't just observing, but she was *seeing*. It should've unnerved me, but in this moment, it felt strangely like a relief. I wanted to tell her everything, and maybe someday, I would. I'd have to if I wanted to survive the guilt and imposter syndrome that snuck into every good moment I had lately.

But for now, I needed to tell her something true, at least. I didn't brush away the comment, nor did I want to pretend everything was perfect.

Tristan approached with a wave of his hand as he crossed the street, and my eyes didn't waver from him as I responded through a beating heart. "You're right. It is a good place to start."

CHAPTER FIFTEEN

Tristan

My attempts at stretching and icing my back had failed to lull it into submission and force it to forget I hadn't slept on a real bed in weeks.

Still, I did what I could, and today, I finally relented and took some ibuprofen. Doc had hounded me about it, insisting it would help. I'd claimed I'd tweaked a muscle at the workshop last weekend since I couldn't very well admit I'd been sleeping on a terrible blow-up mattress in my spare room.

I could trust Adam with this information, of course. He hadn't earned his nickname Doc just because he had medical knowledge and training, though he had those in spades. He was also particularly sensitive and astoundingly in touch with his emotions. I didn't think I was too much of a caveman in that regard, but Adam made us all look old-fashioned, and not in a good way.

I'd slept in a little this morning since I had to work the weekend starting this evening. We had some personal security work to do, and our go-tos for that were still overseas save the team already escorting one or two of the celebrities attending this weekend's event.

I stirred the oatmeal, spacing out as I gazed at the snow-covered landscape of my backyard. Juniper was chowing down on her breakfast, but her ears perked up and she whined at the door. She hadn't gone out yet, so I let her.

Then she was off like a shot. Not her usual, but before I ran to see what she was up to, I saw her.

Winnie was tromping across the snowy field with a vengeance. She was too far to see her expression clearly, but her gait spoke of frustration or determination. Juniper bounded toward her, gleeful to be finding her outside no doubt, and I watched with no chance of looking away.

Winnie paused and let Junie leap and twirl around her, the Tasmanian Devil in yellow lab form. She kept walking for a few more steps as Juniper tornado-ed around her, her energy deliriously happy as she bounded around Winnie, kicking up clods of snow.

Now I could tell she was smiling, joy spilling out of her as she watched my ridiculous dog delight in her. She said something I wished I could hear, and then she kept on, still talking to Juniper as she trotted along next to her and they began to jog.

It shouldn't have, but the sight of her running alongside Juniper made my heart kick. Clearly, it didn't take much to find my weakness and exploit it. Love my dog and I'd be putty in your hands.

Her hands, anyway.

I forced my gaze away from the scene and turned off the burner. I'd known she was out there since I'd heard her leave earlier, but I'd promised myself I wouldn't ask questions. She hadn't gone on an early morning walk like this before, and she must've left before it was fully light outside. I had no concerns the idiots hounding Jeremy would find her tucked away here in Silverton, because we were monitoring them. So far, they'd been busy back in Wichita and hadn't stepped foot outside of Kansas.

Still, I wanted details. And I wanted to know what had injected such steel into her spine today. What made her look like an avenging angel heading toward this house before Junie interrupted and brought that smile to her face?

The door opened and Juniper galloped in, shook her coat, and then kept coming to me immediately and nudged at my knee before she looped through the house, making her rounds before dropping into her bed.

Winnie followed, but I made certain I wasn't looking up. My heart kicked again—recognition. *There you are.*

She'd see the look on my face, and though she never seemed to interrogate me, I hated being too obvious. I didn't want to make her uncomfortable or hint at the feeling I'd had every single time I'd seen her since the very first day.

It happened again now. *There you are.*

There you are.

"Nice walk?" I asked, dishing up my oatmeal and adding blueberries, chopped toasted almonds, and a splash of cream.

When she didn't respond, I gave myself permission to look at her. She stood frozen in place, eyes on the flames in the fireplace, one hand braced on the back of the couch. She'd taken one glove off but nothing else aside from her snow boots, which she'd left just inside the back door.

She appeared to be deep in thought, so I took a seat at the table and began eating, waiting for her to come back to the moment and guessing at what had her so wrapped up mentally. I'd heard her talking in her room last night, so it had to be related to whatever that was.

Instead of asking her if she was okay, I took another large bite of my breakfast and waited. As though she could sense her unusual mood, Juniper lumbered over to her and brushed her head under the hand hanging by her side, and the contact jolted her out of her daze.

Her eyes shot down to Junie, then instantly across to me. "Sorry."

I didn't say a word, and to ensure it, I took another bite. She was ridiculously beautiful standing there in my living room, cheeks flushed from the cold and exertion of her walk, wisps of hair that'd escaped from her hat blown back from her face, gaze fierce.

"I mean... *not* sorry. Just... *ugh*." She shook her head and inhaled, eyes closing as though to summon calm.

My efforts to give her space failed and I moved. "What is it?"

She watched my approach, gaze slipping down over my torso, then back to meet my eyes. "Is murder really illegal?"

I would've laughed, but she didn't look like she was joking. "Unfortunately, in most cases, it really is illegal."

Her eyes were full of so much emotion, I couldn't pull away from her. My default desire with her had become wanting closeness and touch, maybe because we'd lived so many years so far apart without that option, or maybe because she drew me in. Either way, in this moment, I reached for her, taking her hand in mine.

"What is it?"

She exhaled again. "Jeremy called last night. Calvin is pushing him, trying to say that if I come back and agree to be with him, he'll forgive all of Jer's debts."

Fury ignited in me like a match set to a too-short fuse. "Your brother wants you to come back there? To be with the man who is hounding him?"

Her eyes widened. "No. No, he was just freaking out. He apologized for calling."

She stepped closer, like she wanted to lean into me and take comfort but wouldn't quite let herself. I was prepared to let her, but not just yet.

"What did he want, then?"

Jeremy had always been a little lost, especially after their brother passed, but he was spiraling now. He needed rehab for whatever addictions had put him into this much debt, and probably a fair amount of therapy, too.

That said, I'd never detected any sense Jeremy *wanted* Winnie to clean up his mess for him. It was more like he'd gotten used to her bending over backward for him and was waiting for her to have an answer to this problem of his own making.

Still not an excuse to behave like an idiot or to stress his sister, who'd already given up too much for their family.

"He was checking to see if the lawyers had released the money yet. I told him it would take a few more weeks—at least that's what they told me. I—" Her gaze cut to the fire, then worked its way back to me. "He knows I want to help if I can."

This shouldn't have made me angrier, but it did. I couldn't deny the way my teeth ground together and my jaw flexed in an effort to bite back the frustration. Why should she be the one to solve this problem for her older brother?

But this was Winnie, and this was who she was. There was no escaping it, and I didn't necessarily want to. I admired so much about her, but seeing her tie herself into knots for Jeremy and her willfully ignorant parents ticked me right off.

"You're too good, Winn."

Her eyes dropped and her full lips pressed together. She didn't like my comment, but I wouldn't take it back.

"It's not that I'm too good. It's that I'm terrified."

It came out in a ragged, broken way.

I inched closer, taking her shoulders in my hands. "Tell me."

After a few seconds, she did.

"I'm scared he'll get hurt. I'm scared my parents will find out just how bad it is and my dad will have another heart attack or worse. I'm scared my mom will be disappointed in me for marrying you just to satisfy the trust, even though I don't see how she could think it was for any other reason given the circumstances, and I'm scared that I've ruined everything for everyone."

I wrapped her in my arms and she came willingly, arms clutching at my back and her face pressed into my neck as she cried. I scanned my mind for what to say that wouldn't be hurtful. I wanted to yell—to tell her Jeremy and her parents didn't deserve her help. That she'd done more than enough, and she shouldn't feel like she had to limp along a family business she didn't love and even her parents were done with.

But it would only drive a wedge between us, and now wasn't the time to broach the topic of her standing up to her family or making choices for herself.

All I could do was try to reassure her. The depth of my inexperience with this gaped at me, but I stroked my hands up and down her back in what I hoped was a soothing gesture, and tried.

"You're doing so much, Winn. You are turning yourself inside out trying to work the job of farm manager remotely, keep tabs on your parents, and deal with your brother, and as far as I can tell, you're doing a great job of it."

I pulled back and waited for her to look up at me.

My heart kicked when she did, those eyes reddened from tears and lack of sleep, but so trusting it felt like a roundhouse kick.

"I'm really not," she said, her words watery. "I forgot about a video meeting I had yesterday, and I don't even care. That's the worst part."

Another tear slipped down her cheek.

I reached up and cupped her face, wiping my thumbs over the crests of her cheeks and banishing the most recent tears.

"Don't listen to the voice telling you you're not doing enough. You've gone above and beyond, and I won't tolerate you thinking like that."

Her head pulled back a touch and her brow furrowed. "You won't *tolerate* it?"

The disbelief in her voice was exactly what I wanted to hear.

I nodded. "Correct. I will not tolerate you, an amazing sister, daughter, and woman, speaking about yourself in any way other than how you deserve."

She swallowed, eyes glued to mine. We were still in an embrace, my hands now resting where her neck curved into her shoulders and her hands linked around my lower back.

"And how's that?"

My pulse had been accelerating by degrees, but as she waited, her eyes dipped to my lips and it shot adrenaline straight to my heart.

"You should be told you are amazing. You're kind and

loving and thoughtful and generous and, Winnie, you're so damn beautiful it hurts."

Her mouth dropped open, and I indulged in a glance, wishing I could feel her plush pink lips on mine. But that wasn't why we were here—why *I* was here. It didn't matter what I wanted, and even if it seemed like she might want the same thing, it couldn't happen. She'd just been crying over her family in an extremely stressful situation and this. Was. Not. The. Time.

So. Time to redirect.

"You deserve to be respected. You deserve for your parents and your brother to acknowledge what you've done for them and to recognize how hard you've worked to support them in everything. You deserve that same kind of support—endless and sacrificial."

You deserve to be loved by someone who can love you with every bit of his heart, with no ulterior motive, without condition.

But I didn't say that.

I couldn't say that.

Because it was exactly what I wanted most to say.

CHAPTER SIXTEEN

Winnie

On my lunch break from the remote work for the farm that'd become more tedious by the day, I headed into town. At some point, I'd need to convince Tristan I didn't need him to leave his truck for me every day, but today, I was glad for it. He'd worked through the last two weekends on assignments out of town, and though he'd slept in the day before he left and day after he got back, he hadn't stayed home at all. He'd gone into the office with only spare interactions between us before departing and leaving me to the house and Juniper alone.

He'd mentioned it was a busy time for Saint Security, and at the weekly self-defense classes, Bruce had corroborated this. Adam had stepped in to teach and was a lovely person from what I could tell, but I enjoyed when Tristan was there a lot more.

Shocker. Of course I did.

In the past, we'd gone through phases where we didn't exchange emails more than once a month. Then sometimes, we sent them back and forth a few times a day, then a week, and then, slowly, they'd spread out again. It hinged on whatever we had going on and where in the world he was, just like any other relationship. And yet, ever since our conversation about Jeremy, it felt like he was holding back.

Considering he tended to be quiet and keep to himself even when surrounded by his friends, this shouldn't have been news. Even so, the dynamic between us felt different.

Maybe because you were lusting after his lips while he was trying to console you?

Unhelpful thoughts had permanently taken up residence, and while I still considered it a part-time job to worry about my brother and parents, I'd also started moonlighting as a person who couldn't stop fantasizing about Tristan.

Not even anything too racy. Just... him holding me again. Instead of him continuing to say those beautiful things he'd say to me, maybe he'd lean down and kiss me. Not that I regretted what he'd said, but they hadn't helped the matter.

As I approached All Booked Up, I found Adam standing just outside and grinning down at his phone.

"Hey. Are you going in?" I asked, nodding to the door.

His head popped up, and his face shifted from that pleased grin to a kind smile. "Hey, Winnie. I'm on my way out, actually. You meeting up with Jo?"

He had the softest touch of a Southern accent, which was more than a little adorable.

"Yes, I am. Will I see you at Craic in a bit?"

I had gone to the weekly girls' cocktail night the last two weeks since Tristan had been gone. Handily enough, it coincided with the Saint Security meet up, so I got to see all of the people from Tristan's work who were still in town, even if I didn't get to spend that time with him.

The fact that I was downright craving time with the man didn't require further thought. He was my closest friend—in life, and certainly here, though I felt a genuine care and friendship blooming with the ladies from the Silver Ridge Romance Readers Club.

"I'll be there. Oak should be back, right?" He said it casually, kindly enough, like it was something I'd know.

A familiar ache settled in and I shrugged. "I'm not sure. He hasn't really given me his schedule."

I shouldn't be bothered by that, though. Should I? I mean, he didn't owe me anything. He'd been working nonstop thanks to events in some of the fancier ski towns in the state that drew celebrities needing security. Why would he need to report to me?

Adam must've read at least part of those thoughts on my face, though, because he gave me a regretful grin. "I know he's been working a lot. That's hard when you're new in town and still figuring out married life. He committed to these jobs months ago, and I don't think your elopement had been nailed down yet. You know Tristan—when he gives his word, it's given fully. We tried to get him to find a sub, but he refused."

I huffed out a small laugh. "I do know that. He's honorable and stubborn."

"As all get out," he agreed.

"Well, thanks. Hopefully, I'll see you *and* Tristan soon."

He sent me a little wave, and I slipped inside the store, hoping to shake off the frustration that'd crept in while talking to Adam. It wasn't fair to feel like Tristan owed me anything when I owed him *everything*. He'd agreed to this so I could get the ball rolling on my trust and save the business even before Calvin and his loan shark buddies started messing with me.

"Aren't you adorable!" Dove clapped from where she leaned against the checkout counter, and Jo popped up and adjusted her glasses.

"Aw, you do look cute. You're so bundled up, I love it." Jo grinned, and she and Dove shared a little *aww* before settling their sights on me.

"Um, thank you."

They both giggled, but Jo spoke first. "Sorry, you've just got your furry hood up and your cheeks are all rosy. You look stylish and weather appropriate at the same time. It's a hard look to pull off, so just embrace it."

I took a turn to chuckle, then spread my arms wide. "Feast your eyes on my wintry fashions."

"Own it, girl," Dove said, slipping on her own coat and knotting the cerulean blue wool belt around her. The jacket was so bright and fit her perfectly, especially on top of the beautiful sweaterdress she wore underneath.

"I love your coat, too," I said, feeling a touch shabby for my more athletic wear. At least I'd pulled on a skirt and thick leggings underneath instead of jeans.

"Don't be alarmed. As you know, no one else will be dressed up. Dove is just extra." Jo winked at her.

Instead of rejecting it, Dove preened. "I fully embrace I am extra when it comes to clothes. I wear scrubs all day every day and therefore use any nonwork activity as an opportunity to wear a dress and feel my best." She beamed, a shiny white blast of straight teeth and happiness.

"You wear it all very well. Though I guess I haven't seen you in scrubs yet."

She waved me off. "Eh, nothing special. But enough about me. Is your man back?"

My stomach flipped, the thought of Tristan being *my man* far too appealing considering the arrangement we'd made.

My man legally. Not my man physically. Or emotionally. Or for very long, either.

I didn't like thinking about how it'd already been over a month since we'd gotten married. Any day now, the money would come through. I'd stay in Utah until I could get things worked out with Jeremy's creditors, but once that was all resolved, I'd have no reason to stay here...

At least in theory, I'd have no reason.

They should know that, and yet I hadn't even hinted I might not be here long-term. I didn't want to think about it now—I couldn't actually imagine when I would want to.

Instead of saying any of those things or admitting I had no idea when Tristan would be back, if at all. I simply said, "Hoping he'll be meeting me there. Let's go!"

An hour later, Dove, Jo, Elise, Nikki, and Catherine, another local who apparently usually came to these things and planned to join the romance reading club, had begun toasting each other.

They'd started this tradition in the new year. They wanted to celebrate small things every week instead of waiting for big events for the excuse.

"I'm celebrating the fact that my ex is finally getting the message." Elise widened her eyes.

We all applauded and Dove exclaimed, "Finally!" with so much relief, I believed she felt it to her toes.

Nikki leaned over and filled in the gaps. "They've been on-again, off-again and every time she breaks up with him, he ends up crawling back and talking her into trying again."

This surprised me since Elise didn't seem like a pushover in any kind of way, but I also knew that sometimes, there were facets to us different people saw.

We toasted and all took a drink, then Nikki raised her glass. "I think I finished the outline for my game, and I'm looking for app developers now."

She'd mentioned she'd been creating a math-based game to help high school students with more complex math. I had no idea what it all meant other than I'd probably be terrible at it once it wasn't formulas in a spreadsheet, but it certainly deserved a toast.

"That's amazing! I'm so proud of you," Dove said, beaming at Nikki.

Nikki grinned back at her, and we toasted this.

"Oh my gosh, that man," Catherine said, glancing away from the Saint Security table across the room.

But of course when she looked away, the rest of us turned and saw what she had—Bruce Camden looking entranced by a smiling Nikki.

Nikki whipped her head around, her cheeks flushed. "I can't look, or I'll end up over there or he'll end up over here and as much as I love him, I want to hear what else we're toasting."

Jo had hearts in her eyes and Dove sighed. My own little romance-loving heart fluttered on behalf of my new friend. To have a man like Bruce Camden look at you like he was besotted? *Hello.*

"Well, mine's tiny, but you may have heard I switched

to home health recently. So far, it's working out really well. I'm loving it." Dove touched a napkin to the corner of her mouth in a dainty little gesture.

"So you do your same job, just going into people's houses?" Catherine asked.

Dove nodded. "Yes. They needed people for the job, and I figured I'm pretty flexible since I don't have... well, anyone who needs me at home overnight or anything. I'm not sure how long I'll do it, but I've had a great first week."

Elise shook her head. "You're the best person I've ever met, and that's not because I only know terrible people."

She shot us all a look and we chuckled, but Dove ducked her head.

"I love what I do. It's easy when you love something."

We toasted her change, but her words rang in my ears. I'd known for a long time I didn't love what I did. I'd fallen into accepting staying at the family business and taking on more and more responsibility after my dad's heart attack. When they liquidated part of the farm to help Jeremy, I thought that'd be the main part of their downsizing. When they told me Dad was retiring and my mom was stepping back from her part-time role as well, the responsibility defaulted to me.

Had I dreamed of managing a farm? No. Not when I was ten or sixteen or twenty or twenty-five. Certainly not now. But somewhere in there, I'd accepted I'd have to do it. Problem was, I had no passion for it. The admin side of things had long been my home, and it'd worked while my parents were involved. There were several other employees, and God bless them, because I couldn't go do the actual farming work. Dad always said he'd sooner die on a tractor than retire—until that nearly happened. They'd hoped Jeremy would find a belated interest and take over, but after college, he found excuses to stay away, to take a different job, to delay "coming back" to the farm and settling in.

Part of what they'd grieved with Thomas's death was the loss of the legacy—at twenty, he'd been in school for agriculture and would've taken over eventually.

But not Jeremy—not after so much changed for us with Thomas's death. And not me, both because I'd never had the desire to learn all that much about farming and because I'd stuck with the office work.

What would it be like to have a job you loved so much you gushed about it at a girls' night?

I'd had plans before Dad's heart attack. I'd enrolled in a master's program online—an MBA program that would've let me develop skills for any number of industries beyond agriculture. I'd gotten halfway through with great grades. I would've slowly separated myself from the farm business and stepped closer to what I'd wanted... until stepping away would've been a betrayal.

Sitting at this table of women who all seemed so strong and self-assured, I wondered what was missing in me that I couldn't even be honest with my own parents. I'd never told them about those plans, so even if they would've supported me, they couldn't have.

And now? There was too much risk in telling them. Plus, I'd married Tristan to get the trust specifically in order to give the farm a cash infusion and help it along until we found a better manager. Who knew how long that would take, but we had to start somewhere, and I'd done it.

And they'd... they'd let me.

I swallowed against the raw sensation in my throat, then took a drink of my beer and worked to tune back into the conversation.

"I just finished a personal project. Nothing major, but I

feel like marking the day." Jo raised her glass and we joined her, toasting her accomplishment.

And then, all eyes turned to me.

"I'm making friends. Settling into my new town."

I held up my drink, hoping this would suffice. Hoping they couldn't hear the slight edge of regret I'd worked to hide since, eventually, it wouldn't be my town anymore. Once the money came through and enough time had passed, I'd go back.

I mean, I had to.

Didn't I?

Could they see the lies in my eyes? Did they show up as little angry or sad emojis instead of heart eyes?

Clearly not, because no one so much as blinked. Instead, they all beamed at me, welcoming and already so loving, it threatened to break my heart.

"To new friends and to Silverton!" Elise said, and all of us followed.

Last but not least, Catherine started, but something caught her eye over my shoulder. Her eyes widened almost comically, and everyone else's gazes shifted to what she was seeing. I turned and *oh.*

Tristan.

I'd been waiting to see him—wanting desperately to spend time with him. How had he been? What had he been doing?

Tristan walked toward me like I was the only woman in the room.

His gaze locked on mine, and it didn't just *feel* like I was the only one—in his eyes, I was. He stopped inches from me and held out a hand between us.

"Come with me."

Seven years ago

To: Winniechickendinny
    From: Tristan Donnelly

Winnie,

I don't like to think about how few people on earth I care about, but I'm having one of those moments. Probably shouldn't be writing this after I've had as much whiskey as I have, but it's happening. I probably won't send this, so it's fine.

Every year on this day, we drink to the men we've lost. It's a weird thing to be a guy in your early thirties and not only be an orphan but to have lost friends at actual war. Sometimes, that presses in on me until I can't breathe, and that's when I wish I could wake up. Other times, it feels like an honor to have known those people, and I can't escape feeling guilty about the version of me who is ever anything less than completely courageous and ready to fight, because I'm still alive to do so.

Sounds messed up, but it makes me so angry with people who haven't had this loss. What is a life like that even like? Are there hard days? Is it all just sunshine and ease?

I know it's not, but I'm feeling sorry for myself, I guess. And I'm grateful you understand what loss is, even though I hate that you've experienced it. I hate myself for being grateful you get it, and yet I am. I really probably won't send this.

I'll have a headache in the morning, but it's good to cry and rage a bit. There's nothing noble in locking it all away, no point in not feeling things. Some of us around here are better at that than others, though.

I've gone on too long now, so I'll just go. Hope your finals went well and you get to take some time off before you start working. I'm still a few credits from my degree so you beat me—point to Delmonico.

See ya, Winn,

Tristan

CHAPTER SEVENTEEN

Tristan

Fingers laced with Winnie's, I walked back out the doors of Craic, down the sidewalk, and around the corner.

"Tristan?" she asked, a little breathless.

The white cloud of air that escaped her mouth slapped me across the face, and I registered that she must be cold. I'd been numb, maybe since I'd left for the most recent job and had been separated from her but for where my fingers had knitted with hers moments ago.

I stepped close, wrapping my jacket around her shoulders and holding the edges closed in front of her. No chance I'd feel the cold seeping in through the cotton of my shirt with her so close after so long. We were standing under a streetlight and out of view of any patrons from the bar.

"Didn't want anyone wondering why I didn't kiss you the second I saw you," I explained, hoping it'd be enough.

She huffed, more frozen breath slipping out between her perfect lips. "That's not necessarily a requirement."

I'd lost my sense of humor while I was gone—or maybe I'd never had one. She had no idea what was going through my mind, and it was for the best.

"It would be, if you were mine."

She blinked twice, and her mouth dropped open before she bit her bottom lip and studied me.

Wanting twisted through me, vicious and unrelenting. It'd been worse and better to be away from her. It'd been worse and better to return to her and find her laughing with her friends—my friends—on a Friday night.

Now this... I couldn't tell what this was or where it fell on the scale of misery to ecstasy.

The gut punch of seeing her, of being close enough to touch her, of taking her hand in mine, and yet the agony of knowing I wanted so much more than quick touches and fleeting moments together. It hollowed me out sometimes, the need for her, and yet I couldn't let myself feel it— wouldn't.

But here we stood, and that hollow feeling had filled in just standing here next to her.

"You could," she said, her words just above a whisper from where she leaned against the brick of the building.

Her dark gaze on mine, her chin tilted up and head resting against the cold wall, the need to test these words, to push her into clarifying, made my gut tighten. I couldn't remember wanting anything more than I wanted her right now—her closeness, her taste. I'd thought too much about a moment like this, and I'd forbidden myself to think about it.

"Are you okay?" I asked instead, my default clicking into place.

"Yes. Fine. No news."

The slight wrinkle in her brow and the downward turn of her mouth told me she didn't appreciate the silence between us. I knew this before I saw her, and I hadn't known how to break it.

Barging into Craic had been the only way I could figure out how to cut through the odd distance I'd put between us, both physically and mentally, since the last time we'd been truly alone together.

"Good." I inhaled, willing my stubborn, riled pulse to slow. "Good."

I released the jacket, but before I could step away, she grabbed my shirt. I'd worn a soft waffle-knit shirt and her hands brushed my stomach where she gripped it.

"Wait... don't you think we should, um, you know... figure out how to handle this kind of thing? It won't be the last time you're gone and I'm out and I see you and so maybe we should—"

I stepped into her space and rested a hand by her head against the frozen brick, the other snaking around her waist under the now-open jacket. She'd inhaled sharply at my movement, almost like I'd scared her, but her fist was still wrapped in my shirt and she wasn't pushing me away.

No. Not scared.

Anticipating. Ready. *Wanting.*

She couldn't want what I did, could she?

Our faces inches apart and testing every single boundary I'd ever drawn for myself, I said, 'What should we do, Winn?"

She swallowed and licked her lips, and only because we were so close did I avoid watching the movement and falling further under her spell.

"Maybe we should practice. Just so... it's not our first time. In front of people. For the... you know, so it looks real."

Opposing points of logic warred in my mind in response to her suggestion. On one hand, no one would actually heckle us into kissing—well, maybe other than Kenny. However, being prepared was a core tenet of my approach to life.

And then there was the reality that kissing Winnie felt like both an inevitability and an impossibility.

"Practice."

Buying time, but not stepping away, I searched her eyes. Did she really want this?

"Yeah, just... practice."

"You want that?"

She nodded.

I waited. She couldn't possibly think I'd take a gesture, even a definitive one like this, as permission to change the physical dynamics of our relationship.

Snowflakes floated down in soft spirals, one landing on her cheek and melting into her heat.

"Tell me with your words, Winn."

She wasn't taking this lightly either. She inhaled slowly, taking her time as though she knew by not rushing, it'd show me just how clearly she was thinking.

"Kiss me, Tristan."

That was enough for me—more than enough. More than a fantasy, in truth, because hearing her say those words sent electricity through me and I moved.

The hand at her back pulled her close and the one resting against the wall slipped down to the nape of her neck. When she shivered, I slid it into her hair, realizing how cold my skin must've felt after pressing into the icy brick and not wanting anything about this to be uncomfortable. She rose on her toes as I leaned down and pressed my lips to hers, miraculously softly this first time.

It had to be a first.

Practice, maybe, but not *only*.

A first.

I pulled back and checked in with her, but she wrapped an arm around my neck and urged me back to her, taking my mouth and requesting a bit more. Not much, but just a little demand, enough to jar my resistance to sinking into the sensation of kissing this woman—*this* woman—and so I gave her more.

In seconds, the contact between us grew from lips and hands to bodies pressed close, to deeper kisses and so much heat we had to have created a blast zone of warmth around us that melted any snow attempting to touch us.

It was only a clearing throat that shook me out of the mesmerizing question and answer our kisses had started, and even then, it took more than a moment before I froze, registered we had company, and looked to my left to find Adam.

He flared his eyes at me. A warning? Apology? Maybe both.

"Winnie's friends are heading out, and Bruce wanted a minute before he leaves. Thought you'd appreciate the heads-up." Then he mouthed, "Sorry" and turned to walk back toward the entrance to the pub.

Winnie had her head tucked into my chest, maybe hiding from embarrassment. Regret sluiced through me, coating all the delicious sensations from moments ago in a pallid hue.

"He's gone. I'm sorry."

I stepped all the way back, and she was shaking her head, but I forged back in before she could brush off my apology. I didn't want her excuses or placating to make me feel better. I wanted...

I guessed I wanted her to be as consumed with me as I was with her, and that asked too much of her. It wasn't fair. Her world had been turned upside down, and I'd just added another layer of change, another crashing wave at high tide.

"I—we shouldn't have done that. I don't want you to miss your friends, so let's go."

I held out a hand to gesture her ahead, and after a beat of those glittering eyes studying me, she pushed off the wall and walked toward Craic's entrance.

Snow had accumulated in the last few minutes—how long had it been since we'd stepped outside? I'd been late arriving tonight, but not so late people would've been leaving already. Had they thought we'd left?

And the far worse concern, had I upset her? Yes, she'd wanted the kiss, and she'd been right there with me, but I couldn't pretend I hadn't ignored a dozen warnings blaring in my head that taking what I'd wanted—kissing her like I wanted and *did*—wasn't what was best for her.

I gritted my teeth against the onslaught of doubt and disappointment in myself. I'd always thought of myself as better than this—not someone who succumbed to physical desire when I cared about someone. But here I was. No better than any other man led around by his... hormones.

"Hey, you good?" Winnie asked just before we reached the door.

I avoided her gaze, coward that I was. "Yep. I'm good. I'll talk to Bruce out here. Just come back out when you're ready for a ride home."

If she could see through me, so be it. She didn't say anything else, only nodded and handed me my jacket. When I started to object, she said, "Mine's inside. I'll be out in a sec," and then she was gone.

Bruce must've seen her enter, because he slipped

outside and hit me with a look I would've pegged as smug if I didn't know him to be better than that.

Or so I'd thought, until he folded his arms and leaned against the wall all kinds of casually, and said, "So. That went well."

CHAPTER EIGHTEEN

Tristan

I didn't immediately respond to Bruce's taunt—and it absolutely was one. Provoking me into speaking had worked in the past, especially regarding Winnie, and since we weren't at work where we could spar, I'd have to resort to words.

But not while small groups were filtering out, giggling and chatting about what ski runs they'd start their day with or how much they loved Silverton. Good for them, these travelers enjoying their ski weekends. They were escaping reality in favor of vacation in this gorgeous place. They weren't bogged down in feelings and confusion.

I rarely envied the tourists, but tonight, I did.

"Jo's going to run me home so you don't have to. I'll see you later, okay?" Winnie was talking before she'd fully exited Craic and had moved past me before she was done.

Jo cast me a regretful smile, as though she could tell this

wasn't great news for me.

Bruce notched his head to the left, and I took the suggestion. We moved back inside to find Adam sitting at the table now abandoned by everyone else and staring down at his phone. When Bruce and I walked up and took seats, his attention moved to greet us.

"Another round?" he asked.

Bruce and I both nodded yes, and Adam poured out the last remaining beer from a pitcher. He held his own half-empty pint glass aloft without a word.

I raised mine to touch his and Bruce did the same. We drank, each of us quiet, and I rallied clarity and words to the front of my mind so I'd be ready for the inevitable onslaught.

"All in here?" Bruce asked me, and I understood the question.

"Sure," I said, because Adam could be trusted. Any of the Saint personnel could, in truth, but it made sense to go slowly with letting out our secret.

Adam waited patiently as Bruce inspected me, likely double-checking with his own senses whether I meant it or not.

"Oak's marriage isn't a love match. Winnie inherits a trust if she marries now or she'd have to wait another few years. Odd terms, but she called in a favor with Oak and that's how it came about."

Adam's expression shifted only slightly, his thick brown brows raising a touch. "Okay."

I wouldn't have expected anything different from the man, but I had to appreciate Doc's roll-with-it tendency. That said, I wanted him to have the full picture if we were going to hash this out.

"She would've just come here to get married and then

headed back to Kansas, but her brother's gotten mixed up with some bad actors and now owes more money than he can get his hands on. Long story short, they threatened Winnie and we decided she should come out here to get away from the mess."

Adam nodded. "I'm glad she did."

"Me, too." A truth so enormous, I couldn't hold it for too long at a time before dropping it. *Glad* was too frail a word to express how I felt about Winnie's being here.

Relieved. Amazed. Blessed. Burdened. Terrified. Desperate. Elated. Cautious... None of them rolled into the right way to say how essential it was for her to be here.

Bruce fiddled with the edges of a Craic coaster before directing his next comment to Adam. "As you can see, though, it may be getting a little muddy."

I had no choice but to glare silently. I was drowning in guilt and regret and a sense of failure I did not appreciate on top of it all, but Bruce had it correct. He'd seen it on my face minutes ago outside, and he'd probably seen it long before I even knew what was happening.

I'd never imagined this for myself. I'd never thought I'd want anything like this.

Adam watched me for a few seconds before saying, "Feelings are involved now?"

I raised one brow slightly as though that would properly envelop the understatement he'd shared.

"We've been talking for fourteen years. I'm not sure they weren't already, but now..." I shook my head and ran a hand through my hair, wishing tugging at the ends could distract from the truth. Of course I'd always cared for her, but having her here had forced me into acknowledging maybe *care* fell short before, and it sure did now. "She's too much."

Adam's eyes narrowed on me. "Too much?"

I wasn't usually the one on this end of the heart-to-hearts. The words stuck in my throat, but I forced them out. "Too much like a dream. But she's real. And instead of just being beautiful and kind, she's also everything she's always been for the whole time I've known her."

I took an angry gulp of my lukewarm beer.

"And that's bad?" Adam asked.

With an exhale, I explained. "It is bad because it's not right. It's not fair to her for me to feel these things and be in a position where I am honor bound to protect her and care for her, and yet want... more. Too much more."

More than I ever thought I'd want from anyone and certainly more than I ever planned on needing. It happening with Winnie, the one person I'd always relied on to be there and be a safe place for me, felt like a mutiny. My feeble little heart had always loved her in one way or another, first as a friend and more recently as something more intense as she'd grown into an adult and come to know her own mind and heart even as she bent herself into the shape her family needed. And now that she was here, it had no chance of resisting falling hard. But that just wasn't right.

Bruce leaned his elbows on the table while Adam continued studying me.

"Remember when I was being stubborn about not dating Nikki because I felt like I couldn't take care of Kiley *and* date Nik?"

I blinked at him because of course I did. It'd been a matter of months since that conversation at his house. "Yes."

"We're in different circumstances, clearly. But I think there's a lesson from my experience that just might apply to your situation."

I waited, and he let the moment hang before continuing.

"It's okay for it to be *both and* instead of either or. We come from a world where things can seem black and white from the outside, but we know how much gray there is—on a mission, in decision-making, in the moment of execution when all we can do is make the best choice based on the information we have at the time. It can be messy, and so many of us want it to be cut and dry."

Adam and I both nodded along with him. Some of us had a harder time with the gray than others, but our training equipped us for those instances. I'd never been prepared to handle a situation like the one I was in with Winnie, though.

"So the point is, just like in so many other parts of life, I'm suggesting it's okay for you to have the *both and* reality rather than the either or."

"Explain that thought, please," I said, my brain sluggish from the day's events and the glut of feelings drowning out my good sense.

He nudged his beer with two fingers, making space on the table in front of him. "You can protect her and care about her *and* be attracted to her."

I huffed. "Well, yeah. I know that." *Happening now, thanks, man.*

Bruce chuckled, and I didn't miss the look he shot Adam, who returned it.

"Right, but I'm suggesting you don't need to feel guilty about it. I'm saying maybe the attraction, and dare I say *love*, you have for Winnie will only make your ability to care for her more robust."

"It's possible," Adam encouraged. "You want to respect her and give her space to deal with the things going on in her life. I'm sure I don't have the full picture of what all that is. But she's here because she trusts you, Oak. She knows you're a good man."

I grumbled, resisting. "If I'm so good, why can't I think about anything but her? I'm on assignment and it took every bit of my energy to keep my mind on the job. I get home and all I want is to be near her, touch her..." And other things I wouldn't delineate aloud for these two. They were smart men, so they'd figure it out, no doubt. "She's not in a place to say no."

Bruce ducked his head to catch my eye. "Are you pressuring her?"

"No. Never. Kissing tonight was her idea and it—" I cleared my throat, frustration spiraling up, up, up my spine, so I stretched my neck in a feeble attempt to banish it. "She confirmed more than once she wanted it. But... I took too much."

Adam's eyes narrowed. "How do you know?"

I gritted my teeth.

Bruce's hand landed on my shoulder and shook me before releasing. "I've known you a long time, and there's no doubt in my mind you're being harder on yourself than you need to be. But let's say, just for the sake of your argument, that you *did* push her in some way. That she said yes but, as you're suggesting, she wasn't able to say no or see that wasn't what she really wanted because of how much is going on in her life."

I waited, a sick, awful feeling settling in my gut like sewage leaking into a freshwater lake.

"If that's your concern, you need to address it *with her*. Because you are making choices *for* her. And I realize I don't know everything that's going on here, but you've insinuated that was precisely what you do *not* want to do, right?"

Throat tight, I nodded. That was exactly what I didn't want to do and if he was right—and he usually was—then I'd been an even bigger jackass than I already knew.

Bruce leaned back, totally at ease. "Then don't do it."

Adam shrugged a shoulder. "Exactly. Don't do it."

A frustrated sound escaped me. "Right. That easy."

Bruce grinned. "Of course it's not. If you love this woman and she's in danger, that's not easy. You're doing something you've never done before—you married her *and* you're living with her *and* you're together in the same place for the first time in the history of your relationship."

I continued for him. "Right. And we're trying to figure out how to even talk to each other while we're in the same room, let alone navigate the attraction. I had no idea she'd be so... so... so damn irresistible. And I'm not proud of that. I've never felt so out of control or unprepared or desperate to be near someone."

Bruce and Adam were beaming at me by the time my rant ended.

I blinked at them. "What?"

Bruce's grin didn't waver. "That's a long list of things to manage. Is it possible you might consider cutting yourself some slack while you figure this out? Maybe think about the fact that there's no right way to deal with a situation like this and that talking to your *wife* and dear friend about some of it could help? That it's not all on you to manage alone?"

Those words broke through, finally penetrating the fog of self-flagellation and frustration I'd been feeling. I made a sound signaling I was listening, then gave them what they'd been waiting for.

"I get it. I'm not sure I buy it, but I get it. And yes..." My jaw clenched, and dread kicked at me, but I pushed on. "I'll talk to Winnie."

Bruce nodded approvingly. "Good. And what's the other thing you're not saying?"

My jaw clenched, annoyed he knew me well enough to tell there was something more. "When she's done here... it won't go back. If I lay it all out, we won't be able to go back to how it was."

Losing Winnie from my life for good, even the long-distance that would inevitably feel like table scraps compared to the feast of her in real life, would level me.

Adam settled his green gaze on me. "It's all risk. Whether you do tell her is one, and if you don't, that's another. You just have to decide which one you can live with."

Bruce's brows rose like he was impressed and agreed with Adam's insight, and I felt the truth of his words in my gut.

They both patted me on the back as we tidied up the table and exited. Their *attaboys* were appreciated, even if I didn't *feel* relieved like I wished I did. Instead of suggesting some higher form of self-control or distraction, they'd given me permission to be imperfect. They hadn't piled onto my guilt over these feelings for her... they'd done nothing to encourage me to lock myself down even further. To risk, one way or another.

Completely unhelpful. Frustratingly wise, I feared.

I didn't know how to navigate what would come next with Winnie... how I'd express myself without making things worse. But their point was well-made, and even though I hated to admit it, I'd been taking choices away from her. Almost as though it let me *not* risk telling her how I felt, I'd stolen the chance for her to decide.

So it was time to stop being afraid of pushing her and let her choose. It was time to man up and talk.

EMAIL

Seven years ago

To: Tristan Donnelly
    From: Winniechickendinny

Tristan,

I think it's time for you to get a dog. Probably a boy, though a girl would work for you too. I can see you being a sweet dog daddy to a girl dog. Something sturdy and that can keep up with you when you go for runs or walks in the woods—you'll end up somewhere with trees nearby, I just know it. And I'll come visit and we can wander around in the woods together. Maybe a Golden Retriever or something hearty and sweet.

I won't belabor the response to your last email. I'll just ask you this—are you okay? It sounds like that was a heavy night, but one worth experiencing. Thanks for sharing some of your thoughts, even though you didn't really plan to or mean to. I'm glad you sent it.

And I'm sure you won't like me saying this, but tough

luck, soldier—I'm sorry. I'm so sorry you've lost friends and that you've been so alone. I hope you know I'm here in any way I can be. I promise I'm here.

Sending you love,
Winn

CHAPTER NINETEEN

Winnie

I took a few steadying breaths, willing the gumption to exit my room and see what awaited me. Would Tristan be there, still apologizing for the best kiss of my life? Or would he be gone again without warning?

I was getting mad all over again just thinking about it.

Last night, Jo had driven me home because I couldn't stand to stay there and pretend things were normal. I'd been fuming, but I'd tried not to. I'd tried to slough off the obvious regret and disgust that had hit Tristan and worked to convince myself it was better this way.

Jo had made light small talk, and I'd summoned weak, uninteresting responses until we parked in Tristan's drive-way. She'd given me a kind look and said, "It'll be okay." She had no idea what was wrong, only that I'd gotten upset while I'd been outside with Tristan.

"I hope so," I'd said, my heart aching even as the sting of embarrassment still burned bright on my cheeks.

Right before I'd reached the door, Jo had hollered out to me. "If you need me to pick you up, let me know. I can be back here in twelve minutes, max."

That had made me smile, and I'd sent her a thank you before slipping inside. I'd let Juniper out for a minute after petting her and feeling a lift in my spirits at the sight of her excited greeting, then once she settled back inside, I'd retreated.

I wasn't proud of it, but I couldn't stand the thought of sitting on the couch waiting for Tristan to come home like some kind of angry parent. Or worse, a needy girlfriend.

As someone who hated confrontation and didn't put words together very well when stressed, I recognized the wisdom in giving us both time to think. I didn't purposefully do it so he'd have to wait to talk to me, but I also didn't know whether he'd *want* to talk to me, or when he'd get home.

When I'd heard his truck in the driveway less than half an hour after I'd shut myself away, I'd had a momentary flash of bravery where I imagined myself stomping out into the living room and demanding he tell me why he'd apologized. I'd stand tall and confident and know I had worth whether he wanted to kiss me or not. I'd have faith in our friendship and his years-long steadfastness, and I wouldn't mentally spiral out about all the reasons that wonderfully right kiss had gone wrong.

But it was another version of me who'd do this—maybe a future or past Winnie who had the energy to face down the one person who made her feel safe and peaceful. And last night, I'd lost any modicum of fight I might've had.

This morning, I hadn't woken with fight in me, but I'd

tossed and turned myself into feeling like it'd be a relief to face him, come what may.

He wasn't going to yell or be angry with me, I knew that. He wasn't going to make me feel small for kissing him back—at least not purposefully. Most likely, it'd be more of the same from last night—apologies and regrets etched in the lines of his handsome face that would ultimately crush me a little.

A lot.

When I finally did leave my room, Juniper was there with a giant doggy smile and her breathless energy that couldn't help but make everything better. I kneeled and nuzzled my head against her neck. For a dog who went outside fairly often, her fur managed to smell sweet, and she always looked brushed and cared for. I hadn't seen Tristan groom her yet, but he must've done it regularly.

"Good morning."

Tristan's voice startled me and prompted Juniper to trot over to the man who stood in the kitchen watching me.

"Hi."

I felt shy and awkward and so unsure, and I hated it. We'd been doing well these last few weeks, overall. Especially considering we'd never been near each other before a month ago. But this morning felt worse than ever...

"Will you look at me?"

His voice had a pleading quality to it that made my chest tight. When I raised my gaze to meet his, I could tell he hadn't slept. His eyes were shadowed and he looked bone-weary.

"Can we talk about last night?" he asked, his tone so cautious and gentle, it made me feel like a child.

"Yes."

"Good. Sit down and I'll bring you breakfast. We'll eat. And talk."

He bustled over to pull out a chair at the table I belatedly noticed had been set with his stoneware dishes and even some woven placemats.

"Okay."

So far, I hadn't figured out his mood, though he seemed... frenetic. His energy was high, and he had less of the steady, calm quality I'd grown used to.

In seconds, he returned with a bowl covered with a pan lid and a platter of pancakes stacked ten or twelve high. He came again with a plate of bacon laid in rows, and for the first time since lunch yesterday, I felt hungry.

"This looks wonderful. Thank you," I said, more than a little confused by the delicious-looking meal when contrasted with the odd events of last night.

"Do you want some orange juice? It's fresh squeezed." He held up a small crystal pitcher full of bright orange juice. It looked tiny and delicate in his large hands.

"Uh, sure."

My voice shook with a mix of humor and uncertainty and more than a few questions. Why did this giant, rough man have such a dainty little serving pitcher? And why did seeing him use it to serve me orange juice he'd evidently squeezed himself make my heart feel so full?

I dished out some piping hot eggs from the covered bowl and helped myself to a few pancakes and two slices of bacon. Juniper lumbered over to check out the goods while we served ourselves, but Tristan lovingly told her to go get back on her bed, which the best girl did without hesitation.

After a few minutes of nothing but the crackle of the fireplace and our forks and knives occasionally tapping against the stoneware, Tristan set down his utensils.

I froze, his eyes on me halting my movements, and swallowed. "Time to talk?"

"Keep eating, please. But yes... if you're ready, I'd like to."

I nodded, using the most recent bite of bacon to my advantage. I wondered how many times I could get away with a full mouth being my excuse for not responding.

Tristan's eyes shifted toward the fire, then came back to mine and gave me a heartbreakingly earnest look.

"I'm sorry, Winnie."

Any progress up the long ladder toward hope I'd taken swiftly vanished. My chest caved in and I instantly felt like a fool all over again. Somehow, I'd let the last fifteen minutes lull me into the idea that maybe he wasn't going to push me away and spread his regret all over the memory of last night.

"Don't mention it."

Eyes on my plate, I worked to ignore his stare. I didn't want him to realize how much it hurt to have him apologize *again* for kissing me, like it was some fundamental flaw of his that'd allowed it to happen in the first place.

"I am mentioning it because I have to. And I don't think you understand what I mean. I want us to clear the air, and to do that, I need to explain myself."

My gaze wandered back toward him tentatively, bracing against seeing any hint of regret in his face.

When our eyes met, the only expression there was intensity.

I exhaled and set down my fork, not wanting to let this draw out any longer than it had to.

"I understand you regret kissing me—that you feel it was wrong for some reason. I—" I didn't want to admit how much it hurt, but I also needed him to understand I didn't want his regret and apologies. "I don't really want to talk about it anymore. Can we just move on?"

His furrowed brow and flickering jaw muscle told me no, even before he spoke again.

"That's what you don't understand, though. I *should* regret kissing you because it means I've failed at prioritizing what you need in favor of what I want. That's not right and it's not fair, and it's not what I promised you years ago or before you got here months ago."

Hands clasped together in my lap, his words wound their way through my mind, but I could hardly make sense of them. I couldn't sit here and grapple with the huge implications—or what I thought might be implications but could very well be wrong about—of his explanation. I pushed back from the table and paced away, wringing my hands, until I paced back and steadied myself on the back of my chair.

"You—what do I need? What do you want that isn't what I need? What do you mean?"

He stood slowly, moving in that way of his that spoke of control and confidence, and also like if he moved too fast, he might spook me.

But honestly, he might've. Because I was on the edge of something—we were—and I needed him to make himself clear before those persistent little hopes ran away from me again.

"I promised you I'd be here for you. I promised you I'd put you first and do whatever I could to help you." His face was so, so serious.

"Okay. Sure."

The exasperation in my tone rang clear, and at the sound of it, humor flashed across his face, but he didn't give in to a full smile.

"You're in a stressful, complex situation. You've just

married someone you hardly know in order to help your family. You've been doing everything for them, and to top it all off, you were threatened and assaulted before you came out here."

Dread filled me up, up, up at the memory of Calvin's grip on my arm, and of what happened after. I shook it off.

"This isn't new. I'm sorry I brought all that baggage with me. I wish it'd been simple, like it was supposed to be initially—a long-distance thing where your life didn't have to change and you didn't have to have me underfoot and in your space all the time. I'm sorry I've imposed on you and—"

His hands were at my shoulders before I could finish, and he was pinning me with his gaze and shaking his head.

"No. *No.* I'm not saying any of that. Listen to me."

I swallowed, feeling chastised, and yet... what? It made no sense, but somehow, his stopping me from apologizing made me feel oddly cared for.

"What do you need me to know? Just... say whatever it is so we can get this over with," I begged.

His gaze tracked over my face and returned to my eyes.

"My only regret is I'm worried I pushed you last night—took advantage of you. That maybe, in a place of distress, you didn't really want to kiss me. Or, if you did, you didn't want it to become... what it was."

The faint color rising to his cheeks would've slayed me right there if his words hadn't. But oh, they did.

"I wasn't in distress. I was happy to see you after your trip. A little frustrated with you for never communicating with me about your schedule and not sure what changed between us in the last few weeks, if anything, but I was okay. I *am* okay."

At some point, I'd need him to understand that being

here had been so good for me, it was life-giving. It'd filled a part of me I hadn't realized had run dry.

I had friends here. I felt like a part of a community in ways I hadn't *ever* in my hometown, and I felt valued. Work was work, and I didn't love it. But I'd started to dream a little... to think about what my life might look like if I didn't go back to Kansas and let my family's needs supersede mine.

There were no plans set in stone, no real movement on options right now since going back wasn't even an option. But soon, the money would come in, and I could go back and wrap everything up and maybe... maybe have some choices to make afterward.

"*Okay* is not enough."

That low voice forced me back into the moment and my restraint broke. Any chance at simply taking his words and moving on fled, and I let loose the frustration and hurt that'd been building since he'd apologized after the kiss.

"How is okay not enough? I need some other level of emotional stability certification before I decide whether or not I want to kiss you?"

Heat flared in his eyes. "Yes. You need to be fully satisfied and happy and *then* you can decide. Then there's no way you're being coerced or manipulated or... used."

He practically spat the word, and it clicked.

I hadn't gotten it until right then that he wasn't trying to judge me for not having everything together. Instead, he'd judged himself. He worried he'd used *me* when, clearly, this entire situation was me using him.

I reached for him then, setting my hands on his shoulders as I stepped closer to him. His warm palms still rested on my arms.

"You aren't using me or manipulating me, Tristan.

There is no part of me that is worried you would. I have never felt that way, not for a second, and I can't imagine I ever will."

His throat bobbed as he swallowed, but the dark expression on his handsome features didn't waver.

So I pushed him a little, just a nudge with my hands. "What if what I need and what you want are the same thing?"

CHAPTER TWENTY

Tristan

She said it like... like it could be true.

What if what I need and what you want are the same thing?

Her hands on my shoulders, mine gently cupping her elbows now, I couldn't escape the determined resolve in her eyes.

"That's a big what if," I scraped out, heart pounding hard enough she had to feel it.

She studied me, her beautiful face so solemn and focused on mine, it made my heart clench. Was I so needy for attention—for *her* attention—that just standing here letting her look at me made me borderline dizzy?

"Are you fully happy and satisfied?" she asked softly, her hands flexing lightly on my shoulders.

I shook my head, trying to follow her logic. I was closer to those things now than I ever had been, but... "Is anyone?"

Her small smile sent a burst of heat through me. No one had addled my senses like this woman, and her reaction to my apology and reasoning for it had thrown me for a loop.

"That's kind of my point. Because if you're also not completely happy and satisfied—which I'd argue is not only *not* the point of life but a fairly unattainable axis of evaluation—then by your own metric, you can't be trusted to make your own choices about what *you* want any more than I can."

Her meaning settled over me and I felt the pull toward her stronger than ever. I wanted to capture her mouth with mine and kiss her until we were both drunk from the sensation. Was that what she needed?

She'd implied her needs were my wants, but she couldn't possibly know everything I wanted from her.

"It's not unreasonable to want you to be happy and feel safe," I said, channeling those last pieces of resistance.

We were still standing close. I could smell the soft scent of her—feminine and a little sweet. A lot alluring. One of her small hands rose to brush some of the hair that'd fallen over my brow back and my eyes shut reflexively, everything in me savoring the simple gesture.

"It's not. I want the same for you."

I released her and slipped out of her grasp, pacing away across the space and into the kitchen, turning back toward her to speak.

"So you're saying... what? Winnie, this is too important for me to guess. I'm a smart man, but I'll admit I haven't made an effort to—to—be with someone I care about in a long time."

And I'm not sure I've ever cared about anyone like I do you.

I knew I didn't. But I wouldn't pile that on top of the

already unwieldy tower of expectations and hopes here.

She moved toward me slowly, as though I were a wounded animal that might lash out at her. Guilt and shame swirled in my gut and I clenched my jaw, begging my sense to return and my clarity to help steer me in the way I should go. What was right here?

When she set her hand over mine on the counter, I met her gaze.

"I wanted you to kiss me, Tristan. If you remember, I enjoyed it quite a bit."

A brutal mix of wanting and guilt tore through me, but she was shaking her head before I said a word.

"I don't know why you're acting like that's wrong unless you don't want me or you're involved with someone else, but I'm assuming since you married me, the latter is not an issue."

My jaw flexed. "It is not."

One of her brows arched.

"So if you're not worried about someone else and you're going to agree that me being perfectly happy and settled before we... do anything differently is an unrealistic starting point since that's not real life, what is holding you back unless it's that you don't..." A small, pained smile flashed across her lovely face. "Don't really want anything with me?"

Her gaze dropped away from mine, but before she could pull her hand back, I grasped it.

"Haven't you realized? You will never have to worry about me not wanting you."

I think I've always wanted you, and seeing you unlocked that truth for me.

I definitely wouldn't share this last thought, but I couldn't have her standing here doubting herself—doubting my desire for her. Not just her physical body but that heart of hers, so tender and generous and persistent even when it was maligned and ignored. That heart, I realized more every second, had owned mine in one way or another since her first email.

"So..." She loosed an exhale, and her eyes hooked into mine, holding me hostage.

An incredulous, low laugh escaped me as I rounded the corner of the counter and stepped closer to her, unable to stand the distance between us for another second. "So all of that is to say, if anything is going to change, we're going to move very slowly."

She nodded and inched nearer to me, the hand not held in mine finding a grip on my shirt at my side. "That's wise."

Her eyes dropped to my lips, then met mine again. I breathed against the primal command rioting through me telling me to claim her now—right now—in one way or another. Kiss her, hug her, throw her over my shoulder, and run away with her.

Loathe to admit it though I was, the plan to go slowly made sense. We hadn't defined expectations, we hadn't clarified what either of us actually meant beyond that she didn't mind my kissing her. Well, hopefully, me stating that I wanted her and always would was clear enough, but I could acknowledge that, too, was fairly vague.

"What do you—"

Her phone rang out loud and jarring in the quiet space. Juniper's head popped up and she eyed us from her bed, but as Winnie fumbled for the phone in her pocket and gave me a regretful look, she dropped back down to snooze.

"Hello? Mom?" She answered the phone but mouthed *sorry* to me as her mother began talking on the other end of the line.

I shook my head slightly to indicate I didn't mind the interruption. Not entirely true, but I couldn't fault her for answering.

And it was just the reminder I needed.

As much as Winnie might believe she was choosing me in whatever way she meant when she'd been talking these last few minutes, when it came down to it, she'd choose her family. It was her default, and there was no scenario in which she'd choose me over them when the time came. She was only here by virtue of her needing me to help them.

I didn't judge her for this, nor did I feel sorry for myself when I thought of her leaving and going back to the life she'd committed to. I'd hate it, no doubt, and I'd be unlikely to find anything to fill the empty place she'd leave, but I would be grateful.

I wouldn't regret anything given to her while we were together just like I'd never regretted *not* giving much of myself to anyone else, especially not in the years since Winn and I had been connected.

She slipped out of the kitchen and into her room for some privacy, and I began cleaning up our breakfast. It was good we had time to digest the conversation. I had a few things to do before the self-defense class this afternoon. Then maybe we could watch a movie or read together on the couch.

Something simple. Small. Close.

Something that could bring her comfort and make her happy, and something I could remember when she went back to her real life.

Maybe she won't go back.

The words whispered through me and I grasped at them, but they dissolved like fog in my mind.

CHAPTER TWENTY-ONE

Winnie

With more than a little frustration, I sent off a text to Jeremy in response to the flood of messages he'd sent while I was at the self-defense class this afternoon.

Tristan drove me, and though we'd talked honestly earlier, it still felt like tension lingered between us. Not bad tension, per se, but we clearly needed to spell out what we each meant.

At least, I hoped he didn't feel we'd settled everything. I hadn't stopped circling his words except to stress out about the phone call with my family. My mom had been ecstatic to report that when she ran into the family lawyer at the grocery store this morning, he'd thought everything would be done by Tuesday at the latest. All the basic requirements would be fully met, and I'd have the money.

I didn't fault my parents for being eager about this

news. They'd known the reason I'd married Tristan was to gain access to the trust and help with the business. They didn't necessarily know I needed to escape Calvin because Jeremy was so deep in debt to a sketchy guy who had no problem threatening his sister, but they'd agreed maybe it would be better getting out of town for a while.

But the catch to all of this? The ultimate goal was me returning to Kansas and settling back into life as we'd all known it, just with more liquid assets and hopefully a debt-free Jeremy.

I hadn't figured out how to carve a different path here. I'd only just truly admitted to myself how much I didn't want to do any of it, let alone make a plan for an alternative.

I'd put thoughts of my family and Kansas out of my head for the blissful hour of the class. It didn't hurt that my gorgeous husband was an instructor and every time we made eye contact, my stomach did somersaults.

After wandering out of the training room and waving at fellow classmates, I enjoyed some fresh, crisp winter air before returning to the small room to wait until Tristan was ready to leave. I'd heard Jo attended the intermediate class and none of my other friends did, but I liked everyone I'd met so far and enjoyed chatting with them after class while Tristan cleaned up.

When I entered the training space, I heard people talking but didn't see them.

"You've got to get a better setup, Oak."

It was Adam's voice, and knowing he was talking to Tristan, I stopped short of rounding the corner and giving myself away. It wasn't the right choice, but something about the low tones of the comment piqued my curiosity.

"I'll be fine."

Tristan's short reply ratcheted up my curiosity by ten thousand.

"You need to ice and heat. Anti-inflammatories. Stretch your hamstrings and lower back. And last but not least, change up the sleep situation and make your life easier."

No reply from Tristan came, but footsteps did, so I jumped into action and barreled around the corner before they could discover me eavesdropping.

"You ready?" I asked Tristan, bright smile covering the newly rising concern.

He nodded, and after we'd both bid Adam farewell and waved at Bruce, who was still chatting with a small group, we loaded into his truck.

I debated whether to bring up the conversation I'd over-head. By the time we arrived back at his house, I'd waffled one way, then the other, and had ultimately not said much at all. Tristan had seemed content to drive in silence with only the radio humming low playing between us.

Once we walked in and he let Juniper out, he tossed his bag into his room and shut the door.

I'd never dared look in there. I'd gotten close, but it had seemed too invasive. If he didn't mind me seeing what his bedroom looked like, he wouldn't keep the door closed, so I'd decided, at the very least, I could respect this boundary. I'd foisted enough on him, he didn't need me nosing around in his things.

"Are you okay? Did your conversation with your parents go as expected?"

I forced a smile. "They're usually pretty predictable. Nothing new."

For whatever reason, I didn't want to tell him about the trust money becoming available.

"Good."

"Anything you want to tell me?" I asked, tilting my head to one side.

His eyes narrowed. "Why do you ask?"

Busted. Okay, maybe I wasn't as sneaky as I thought. Might as well come out with it. "I heard Adam telling you that you need to get better sleep and ice and heat and take pain meds. Are you okay? Did you get hurt?"

His jaw ticked and he moved around the kitchen filling two tall pint glasses with water, then handed me one. Instead of explaining, he guzzled the drink in a few long swallows. *Interesting.*

Maybe he was simply that thirsty. *Sure.*

"Tristan?" I asked, willing him to just tell me.

"My back is hurt. I have some degeneration in my discs from years of wear and tear. Halo jumps and—Army stuff. *Life.*" He ran a hand through his hair, but then let it rest at his neck, almost like he was holding a sore spot.

"I'm sorry. That sounds miserable. Is there anything I can do?"

He shook his head and let his hand fall, even though I could've sworn I saw something flash across his face before he replied.

"No. I just need to do a better job taking care of myself."

He didn't meet my eyes, though to be fair, he was checking the fridge for something, then the freezer. I didn't know what he needed, but he clearly didn't want to keep talking about this, so I moved on.

"If Adam says so, I guess you better. Is it okay if I hop in the shower first? I'll be quick and then maybe you can relax and let the hot water help you a little."

Tristan froze for a moment but restarted his movements seconds later. "Of course. Go ahead. I was thinking I'd just order pizza and we could watch something, if you want. Unless you have plans."

Relief and excitement exploded through me, and I beamed at him. "Yes, please."

I hadn't realized just how anxious I'd been about what would happen next. Would he retreat? Would he leave? Or would he stay and spend time with me?

By the time I'd finished my shower and blow-dried my hair, I came out of my room to find Tristan settled in on the couch with a cold pack on his neck and his feet propped up on the coffee table. He had a blanket over his lap and looked so cozy and gorgeous, it nearly made me lose my words.

"Pizza should be—"

A knock at the side door drew my attention.

"I'll grab it—you stay put."

"It's paid for already," he said from his spot on the couch.

The fact that he didn't seem to be getting up or insisting he get it and I take a seat spoke to just how much he was hurting.

A minute later, I set the box onto the counter and dished up two plates with pizza, each with our favorite flavors. This was one of those things we'd discussed years ago, and I'd never forget how our preferences differed. Thank goodness for being able to order half a pizza with certain toppings because I hadn't enjoyed ham and pineapple ever, and the fact he did was just so odd.

But as I was learning more and more, he was his own person. Sounded so silly to think so, but Tristan was just... himself. There wasn't anything he was trying to change or adjust to fit into what someone else thought he should be, and I admired that.

Envied it, even.

"Want to just eat on the couch so you can keep icing?" I found napkins, and when I heard his "sure," I delivered his plate to him. He had a tall glass of water on the side table next to him. "Do you want a beer or anything?"

His eyes flickered over me in a blink, then returned to meet my gaze. "No. I'm good with water."

"Mind if I have one?" I asked, already heading for the fridge.

"Of course not."

I padded to the kitchen and opened a beer, then poured it into a glass. I didn't love beer usually, but I really enjoyed the Silver Ridge Brewing ale and generally enjoyed the beverage specifically with pizza. As I angled the glass and slowly poured, a stark sense of pleasure hit me.

This was all so deeply domestic and normal for a Saturday night. He'd ordered pizza and we were going to sit on the couch and eat and watch a movie side by side. How many other married couples did this?

By the time I settled back in on the other end of the couch, he'd queued up a selection of options and made me choose the final one.

"Let's do *Mission: Impossible*," I said, then took a giant bite of pizza. My eyes shut as the delicious flavors of simple pepperoni and cheese hit my tongue and I chewed and swallowed before opening.

Tristan was taking a long drink of his water, though his eyes were on me.

A blush threatened to rise to my cheeks, but I attempted to brush it off. I gave him a goofy smile. "I didn't realize how hungry I was, sorry."

He shook his head slowly. "You don't have to apologize for enjoying your dinner. I'm glad it's so good."

That did... something to me. I couldn't explain what or why his repeated insistence lit a fire in my belly, or why his apparent desire to see me happy made me feel restless and excited, but such was my reality.

"It is. How's yours?" I eyed his pizza with wariness.

A smile flashed and he took a huge bite, then dropped his head back like it was so good, he could do nothing but. Then he groaned out an exaggerated but alarmingly sensual sound.

My mind teetered on a precipice. All it ever needed was a little nudge and it'd be slumming in the gutter where this man was concerned. I did *not* need to have a visual and auditory feast laid out before me because, for him, I feared I was constantly starved.

I forced out a laugh. If I weren't a woman currently thirsting after her husband, I would've laughed like a normal person. Honestly, who likes ham and pineapple pizza that much?

"Glad you're enjoying it."

He chuckled. "You're grossed out. Just admit it."

I glared at his pizza, then widened my eyes at him. "I just don't understand how such a strong, capable, handsome man can enjoy something so revolting."

This made him laugh in earnest, and he shook his head, then took another gigantic bite.

We settled in and let the movie play. I did not peek over at him from the corner of my eye every chance I got just to relish that we were sitting here together. I did not pretend to be revolted by his pizza even though I secretly really enjoyed how this very grown man ate a child's flavor of pizza with glee.

And I certainly did not let my mind circle around all

the things that'd happened today, especially some of the things he'd said earlier about wanting me.

No. I didn't do that.

Until he forced those thoughts on me and there was no escaping it.

CHAPTER TWENTY-TWO

Tristan

Winnie was laughing and clapping.

I thought I knew what to expect when it came to her love of spy adventures. She'd mentioned she loved romantic suspense novels—hence my reading Josie Wade books—and she had a deep and abiding love of the _Mission: Impossible_ franchise.

I'd never told her much about what we did in the EMU, but part of me wanted to tip her off about how some of the stuff in these movies wasn't altogether fictional. Of course, much of it was. But even in the military, let alone the CIA or Kappa sector, some of the trade craft and gadgetry wasn't purely made up.

"Here it is. Yes! Run on top of that train, Ethan! Runnnnn!"

She was bouncing up and down on the couch cheering as Tom Cruise's character ran at top speed. We'd had more than one conversation about how she always anticipated the shots of him running, because they cracked her up and delighted her at the same time.

So much of her was this light, happy person, and I hadn't seen but glimpses of it until this moment. Hopefully, it meant she was relaxing. We hadn't been over what the call from her folks was about, but I could tell she'd been in her head during the workshop this afternoon. I'd worried maybe she'd disappear into herself on me, so the joy of having her here going crazy over a movie I knew for a fact she'd seen at least twenty times had the pain in my back and neck quieting.

She continued watching the film and I watched her. Nothing on the screen could ever be as expressive and delightful as this beautiful woman fully engaged in watching something she loved. She was unburdened and free and so gorgeous, it had a new ache forming in my chest.

The credits rolled, the classic theme song playing, and she clapped and grinned over to find me looking at her. At another time, I suspected she might've blushed, but she was too keyed up.

"I love that movie. Can we watch the third one soon?" Her eyes were wide and bright.

"Uh... sure. Not the second?"

All joy fled and her face sobered. "Never the second. Please tell me you don't like the second one."

"I don't recall seeing it, but I may have. Definitely not a favorite or anything."

She flopped back into the couch cushion. "Oh, thank goodness. We were going to have to get divorced even sooner."

I coughed out a laugh, surprised by what she said, which she realized just after.

"I'm sorry. That sounded terrible. I didn't mean it to be

so callous. I just... there's slow motion in it, Tristan. *Slow motion.*"

I almost wished I had seen the movie recently so I could understand. "Noted. No *Mission: Impossible* 2."

She pressed a hand over her heart and nodded somberly as though it were an oath. This struck me just right and I chuckled.

"You're a little weirdo, aren't you?" I said, only grinning wider when her eyes flared at me.

"I'm a woman of taste, Tristan Donnelly. You should know this by now," she said, a haughty little tone in her voice that made me want to kiss the smirk off her face.

To be fair, most things made me want to kiss her, so I couldn't really blame her for it.

"Oh, I know. That's why you like Josie Wade's books better than the other romantic suspense authors you used to read, right?"

She beamed. "Exactly. She's just so good. Her heroes are..." She fanned herself.

Did she realize Josie Wade was writing books about, essentially, me? Not to flatter myself, but her heroes were always ex-military, typically ex-special ops, and usually working for some kind of security company. Me, Bruce, Adam, Kenny, Beast, Dorian, Jess, Cookie... so many of us fit the bill. And beyond that, we had other people coming from other branches of government like Eddie James-Williamson.

"They're decently accurate, too. There are some details no one would get right, some suspension of disbelief, but she gets much of it right. It's less grating to read than some stuff I've encountered."

Winnie had her chin in her hand, elbow leaning on her

knee to support her, and she was gazing at me with an expression I hadn't encountered yet.

"Can you give an example?" she asked.

Probably a hundred bad ones more easily than good ones. "Usually, the stuff that's wrong sticks out more to me, and there's not much of that in her books. She's probably married to someone in the service who helps her edit or something."

Winnie shrugged. "No one knows who she really is. Her author bio gives nothing away and it's a totally secret pen name. I went on a rabbit trail one day and looked all over the internet and never found anything." She gasped. "Wait, could *you* look into her? Could you find out who she is with the different background check stuff I'm guessing you guys use?"

"Maybe, but that's deeply unethical."

She made an embarrassed face. "Oh, right. Of course. I don't want to invade her privacy. I'm just a little obsessed with her stories... and her heroes." She sighed again.

It shouldn't have pained me how she kept mentioning how much she liked these fictional men, but for some insane reason, it did. "She's good."

"*Good* is putting it mildly, but yes. She is. And I love how you know that from experience and not just me telling you." She blinked down at her hands, now in her lap, then looked back up to meet my eyes. "It's really sweet of you."

Caught, I didn't look away.

"I wasn't trying to be sweet. I was trying to..." Hmm, what was the right response here? Because saying that, subconsciously, I'd probably always been trying to understand Winnie and what she wanted—in life and in a man— didn't strike me as the right low-pressure response. "Just trying to learn more about you."

She smiled and bit her lip for a moment, still gazing at me. "I've always had a little bit of a crush on you. You know that, right?"

I glanced at Juniper to give me an excuse to look away. "I guessed at it once or twice."

Saying *I have a crush on you now* wasn't about to happen, so I stood and gathered the now-warm gel packs I'd used for icing earlier and clicked off the heating pad. I didn't normally baby my back and neck like this, but Adam was right. If I wasn't going to correct my sleeping situation, I couldn't expect it to get much better, especially if I wasn't doing the things I knew I needed to do.

"How's your neck doing?" Winnie asked as she folded the blanket she'd used on the couch, then moved to fold mine.

I rubbed at it, frustrated it didn't feel all that much better and knowing it'd definitely feel worse come morning. "A bit better. It was good to relax tonight."

"I agree. It felt so normal."

I caught the edge of her smile before she turned away, and wanting pricked at my fingertips. I wanted to kiss her again so badly, and what was stopping us, other than maybe clarifying what we'd both meant earlier today?

"Normal?"

"Yeah, like what a real couple would do. Like it's just a normal Saturday night and my whole life isn't imploding." Her eyes flicked up to meet mine, and she gave me a small, slightly sad smile.

There it is. There was the reason I wouldn't kiss her or do... anything else with her. Anytime my brain lost track of that very sound logic, one of us would say or do something to remind me she was under incredible stress. I didn't even know the latest, but most likely, nothing had changed.

A few minutes later, after I'd let Juniper out and we'd finished tucking away dishes and cleaning up, we walked down the hallway toward the bedrooms. My stomach clutched with the desire to run my hands through her long hair or slide one under her T-shirt to feel the warm skin at the curve of her lower back.

"Thanks for hanging out with me and putting up with my love of Ethan Hunt, and thank you for the pizza. And the beer. And—"

"Winn, I got it. Thanks for letting me be a lump on the couch next to you. It was great." She had no idea how much I meant it.

Juniper snuck past my legs and pushed her way into my room right as Winnie opened her mouth to speak.

"Well, thanks—" Her gaze had tracked Juniper, and whatever she saw there was clearly alarming.

I whipped around, sure I'd see some nefarious force, but instead I found Junie lumbering around the edges of the deflated air mattress and settling on the corner of the comforter I'd laid over the top of it.

When I turned back to Winnie, she looked thunderous.

"Have you been sleeping on an air mattress?"

I'd never heard that tone from her before. It sounded a little like fury shook her voice, but that didn't make sense. "Uh, yes."

"Why?"

My eyes shifted from side to side. "Because you're in the main bedroom, and I don't normally have a guest bed. It's a workout room and office. I—"

Her hand came up in the universal sign for stop, so I did. Her lashes fluttered and she scowled at me, then brushed past and opened the door wide to look at the setup. Slowly, almost creepily slowly, she turned to me.

"That's what Adam meant earlier, isn't it? Is *this* why your back is so bad? Is this why you're in pain all the time?" She crossed her arms tightly in front of her.

"A little. It's not the only reason. I've got old injuries and issues after so many years in the Army and I'm sure they just... got aggravated."

I'd never seen her so focused and frustrated, so when she spoke next, I had no choice but to listen and plan to do whatever she said.

"Well, not anymore. You're sleeping in the bed tonight."

And then, she turned on her heel and marched away before slamming the main bedroom door behind her.

I hoped she realized that though I was kind and a little shy, I wasn't a pushover, and there was nothing she could say to make me take that bed from her.

CHAPTER TWENTY-THREE

Winnie

Fuming, I moved through bedtime prep at warp speed. How could this man have spent well over a month sleeping on the floor?

Okay, technically, he'd probably slept on a bed while away for work, so he'd had periodic reprieves while on assignment the last few weekends, but really? And worse, how did I not peek into his room and notice his setup? I would've put a stop to this nonsense weeks ago if I'd realized.

I'd wanted to give him a modicum of space I didn't invade. I'd taken over the bedroom, which now that I thought about it for even a second, I could clearly see was the primary bedroom and not a luxurious guestroom—I wasn't sure how long it'd take for me to forgive myself.

Maybe as long as it took for his back and neck to recover from sleeping on that poor excuse for a bed.

I'd move my things out tomorrow when I wasn't so mad and exhausted, but for now, I needed to make sure he realized there would be no getting out of this. When I opened the door, he stood in the hallway, leaning against the wall with his arms crossed and in jammies consisting of a different pair of jogger-style sweatpants and a crisp white tee.

My heart fluttered when he looked up through his lashes at me. *Goodness*, he was so brutally handsome, it wasn't fair. How was I supposed to stay mad at him when he had this tousled, sleepy air about him?

"I'm not taking the bed, Winn."

Ah. That's how.

"Yes, you are."

He shook his head.

I crossed my arms to match his stance. "You are. Your doctor literally told you to sleep in a bed hours ago. I'm not going to sleep in there like a queen while you're in here on the floor making all your problems worse."

His jaw ticked. "Adam isn't my doctor."

Lord, give me strength.

"I will sleep on the air mattress."

He shook his head again. "You won't. It's crap."

A frustrated laugh came out. "Are you kidding me? So you can sleep on the crap mattress but I can't? Need I remind you that I'm younger than you and don't have back or neck issues?"

He downright glowered at me. *Ooo.* Honestly, it was more than a little hot, but I couldn't enjoy the moment thanks to the fury rumbling inside.

"I'll sleep on the couch, then."

"No."

"Yes."

"*No.*"

This time, it came out with more vehemence.

"Tristan, seriously. At least let me see how it goes. If I wake up feeling bad tomorrow, we'll deal with it, right?"

I'd never seen the man look so thunderous.

"We will not deal with it tomorrow. This isn't happening."

I recognized the stubbornness in him, and it would only be matched and defeated by my own. That said, I did have a secret weapon and about now, I wasn't afraid to deploy it.

I set a hand on his arm and gripped his warm, thick wrist. "Please."

His blink told me I'd surprised him, so I continued.

"I know you'll never admit to this being an inconvenience, but it is. You can't pretend I haven't turned things upside down for you. And knowing you're sleeping on the floor or the couch and that's causing you pain or discomfort... I can't bear it, Tristan. I can't."

His lips thinned. "You're not taking the floor or the couch either. It won't do."

Victory was near, I could tell. "You'll take the bed, though?"

His eyes narrowed a little, and the look in them should've warned me, but I didn't see it coming when he said, "I will."

"Oh, good, I—"

"But only if you do, too."

My mouth dropped open and my mind blanked. Had he really just suggested...

"What?"

"I'll sleep in the bed, if you do, too. I'm not coercing you —if you're not comfortable with that, we won't change a thing. But there is no scenario in which you are sleeping on the floor, so I join you, or we keep things as is."

There was a set to his shoulders that hit me. He didn't think I'd go for it. He thought I'd shrink away or maybe decide that wasn't the right call, but little did he know, I kind of loved the idea.

Granted, it would be... new. Intimate. Kind of a huge deal. But neither of us was talking about anything more than sleeping, and the bed was truly big enough for both of us.

I stood straighter and leaned in so my lips were a few inches from his. "Which side do you prefer?"

His gaze darkened and he shook his head, but I turned and walked into the room. Juniper trotted in behind me and snuffed around the edge of the bed. I went to the side I'd been sleeping on and pulled back the covers, then sat on the edge of the mattress.

"Winnie, no. We're not doing this." He stood in the doorway, arms braced on the frame and dark gaze on me with more of that determination.

The sight of him standing there was... affecting.

What is it called when you're annoyed with someone but also want them so much you could hardly breathe? That's what this felt like. It felt like he was purposefully doing all these things—the dark looks and jaw flexes and this hot-guy pose in the doorway like he needed to hold himself back from entering his own bedroom he'd willingly given up to me for over a month—just to mess with me.

But that wasn't Tristan. He was steady—he was Oak. And this was really him trying to get out of an agreement we'd just made.

"We are. You said you'd sleep in here if I did and here I

am, settling in with my book"—I held up an e-reader—"and ready for your stubborn butt to join me."

I patted the bed next to me and raised a brow.

He just stood there for another minute, then let his arms drop and crossed them over his broad chest again. "Really, Winn. It's not happening. I appreciate it, but—"

I shoved out of bed and stormed toward him, grabbed his hand, and marched him inside and around to his side of the bed. I took him by his shoulders, fully acknowledging he was letting me manhandle him, because if at any point he didn't wish to be moved, I wouldn't be able to budge him. When he faced me and his back was to the bed, I shoved him a little until he sat down.

Hands still on his shoulders, I stepped between his legs. "You are going to sleep here, Tristan. You know I mean it when I say I will rest easier, and I know you will."

"*Right.*" He'd mumbled the word like a curse.

"Adam said you need to sleep better. I now understand what he meant was you need to sleep in an actual bed. This is the bed in your house."

I waited for more verbal protest, and sure enough, it came.

But not before his large hands rose and braced on my hips over the thin material of my pajamas and sent my heart fluttering and every nerve ending in my body on alert.

"I'm worried you won't say no to me."

The somber tone and genuine concern etched in the lines of his handsome face spelled it out clearly, but it shot fury into my spine.

"Tristan, I need you to hear me right now." His focus didn't waver, so I pressed on, my body shaking with adrenaline. "I might be in a challenging place in life, but that doesn't mean I'm not capable of consent."

His mouth dropped open, like it finally hit him what his comment meant.

"I didn't mean to imply you weren't. I just... I don't want to do anything wrong."

It felt like *anything wrong* might have more loaded behind it, but right now, I just needed to get through that thick, stubborn skull of his.

"You are a very smart man, but you are being so dumb right now," I said, tenderness settling some of the frustration.

He was still worried about me being able to decide—it all went back to that. I loved him for this worry on one hand, but on the other, it gnawed at me how he wouldn't trust me to tell him what I did or didn't want.

I dipped my head and slid my hands so they were sifted into the hair at the back of his neck, holding him so he wouldn't look away, not that he would. Our eyes locked and, bodies close here at the edge of his bed, he needed to understand.

"I trust you. I need you to trust me."

"I do trust you," he said instantly.

"Not enough, though. You don't trust that if I wasn't comfortable, I would tell you."

He exhaled, and I could see the defeat.

"I won't do anything to hurt you."

Indulging in a desire I'd had since I first saw him, I ran one hand through the strands of his hair. His eyelids drooped in pleasure, and he got this lost, almost desperate look.

"I know you won't," I said, my words slightly louder than a whisper.

And then, because there was no other choice at this

moment, after he'd been so frustrating and considerate, I leaned down and offered my lips to him.

Our eyes connected at nearly point-blank range. Only one heartbeat thumped in my chest before he tilted his chin and captured my mouth in a slow, sensual slide that nearly melted me on contact.

Far too soon, he pulled back and set me away a little, though he didn't let me go.

"No more of that now."

"What? Why?"

I might've sounded desperate. I might've *felt* desperate.

Fire in his eyes, his gaze dropped back to my lips and his hands flexed on my hips.

"We still have a lot to talk about, and I'm not... strong enough for this right now."

I went liquid inside, any solid in me turning to absolute mush at the insinuation that this man who had such control and circumspection might feel a little unsteady. At the same time, I wasn't going to assume.

"Because..."

His throat bobbed and his gaze fell to my mouth again. "Because you have no idea how much I want you, and we haven't talked. And we're going slow because this will... change things. And we both need to sleep."

Heat practically boiled my blood. "I'm not that tired. I swear, I—"

"Winnie, please." He crushed his eyes closed and his grip on my hips was nearly painful, though not actually.

"Tell me. Anything," I said, absolutely breathless.

His hazel eyes opened, and he seemed to war with himself before speaking again. "We haven't even been on a date. We haven't... done anything. I know maybe it's old-fashioned, but I—I want more for us."

Even as a slight pang of disappointment hit, the rightness of what he said rang through me and I didn't bother trying to hide the smile it brought to my lips. "You want to take me out on a date?"

A low, rough laugh escaped him and he gazed at me, his hands still firm and delicious on my hips. "Yes, I do, Winnie. Will you go out with me?"

It shouldn't have thrilled me so much, but hearing those words in his sleepy, sexy voice just about made my heart explode with excitement. He'd admitted so much—we both had—and yet, the simple excitement of a date with him felt like a gift.

So much of my time with him felt like a gift, in truth.

Not wanting to leave him hanging, I ducked my head and stole a quick kiss, then grinned when he shook his head and a smile tugged at one corner of his mouth.

"Yes, I will go out with you, Tristan. And tonight, I'll sleep next to you, too."

Three years ago

To: Tristan Donnelly
   From: Winniechickendinny

Tristan,

Do you ever look at your life and wonder how you got to where you are?

Probably not. You're so purposeful about everything, I wonder if you've ever doubted yourself for a second. I admire that. I truly do.

I've hit a roadblock, and I'm starting to worry I've been bending over backward for my family for nothing. Or, if not nothing, then something I don't even want.

I think I want to get a master's degree. And I want to travel. I want to see more than just what's drivable in a few hours from my hometown and I want to make a life for myself that feels significant. I don't need to be the one rescuing kidnapped Americans in far-flung places—I'll leave that to you, if you don't mind. I just...

I feel a little like Belle at the beginning of *Beauty and the Beast*, running into a field with arms thrown wide and begging for adventure in the great wide. Except my ask is smaller. It's less about adventure and more about having something that's mine.

Gosh, selfish much? Sorry. I shouldn't focus on the negative when I have so many positive things in my life. And you certainly count as one of those, even though you've been quiet lately. I know you're busy, but I'd love to get an update. Is that Kenny guy okay? And Dorian? I'm so sorry they were hurt and so thankful you weren't.

I'll let you know what I do about the master's. What will it even be in? I'm still figuring that out. Can it be in romance novel–reading? I guess I don't really need an official degree in that—I've probably earned an honorary PhD by now.

Sending love,
Winn

CHAPTER TWENTY-FOUR

Tristan

I'd never been someone who woke slowly.

Years of training and stealing sleep in the corners of hours and airplanes meant that when I did wake, it wasn't through a sleepy haze, but rather with an instant awareness and readiness for whatever lay beyond the veil of unconsciousness.

This morning was no different, except it wasn't a threat I needed to guard against, I found upon waking. At least not one overtly perilous.

Instead, it was Winnie's softness pressed against me—maybe not an actual danger, but a reality that indeed threatened me on several levels.

After talking and willing her to understand how my setting her away hadn't been to hurt her, but to save her—though I hadn't used so many words—we got into bed.

My bed. Both of us. In the bed.

And even though we'd agreed nothing would happen, and she appeared to accept my reasoning, even if it'd only included part of my justification for not taking things farther physically, sliding into the same set of sheets hadn't exactly relaxed me.

Thanks to the size of the bed, we weren't touching. We'd both taken a side, and she had tucked into a book on her e-reader while I stared at the same paragraph in the Josie Wade novel I'd been reading right up until I realized what was coming—a kissing scene.

I could not be sitting here next to this woman, sharing a bed, reading about people getting close like that... and survive it. Nope. Couldn't do it.

So I'd rolled away from her, turned out my lamp, and wished her goodnight, and then she went ahead and terrorized me with more of her sweetness.

She'd reached over and run a hand over my back and said, "Have a good sleep, Tristan."

I'd turned back to see her and our gazes had connected. "You, too, Winn."

I'd known I was in love with her before this moment, but it burrowed into me, inescapable and everlasting. As she turned out her light and we lay next to each other, as her breathing deepened into sleep, and as the peace of midnight descended, it burned through me.

I loved Winnie Delmonico. I'd always loved her in some way, but this closeness, this brush with intimacy, both emotional and physical, stirred a new level of devotion and desire in me.

What I didn't know about the way forward could've filled volumes. I'd been thinking this all had to come to an end, and it did... but some part of me resisted accepting it. At the same time, whatever I wanted had to take a back seat to what would be best for her—what *she* wanted and needed.

My arm ached from staying on my side too long, but I didn't want to roll over. With my body curved around Winnie's, even though we weren't nearly as close as I would've liked, I could breathe in her scent and watch her back rise and fall as she slept.

Despite how hard it had been to stop kissing her and simply go to bed, it'd been the right choice. Winnie and I had known each other in some ways for well over a decade, and yet in others, we were brand new. I'd never done anything on impulse, and I wasn't going to start now.

Even if that impulse told me to trace the hem of her shirt where it rode up at her lower back and feel the soft, warm skin there. Even if it said she'd welcome my touch, that she wanted it as much as I did.

Even then, I wouldn't indulge in what was a soul-deep desire for her—this woman who had long been my best friend and who was now my wife.

Couldn't think like that, though. That way lay madness.

"Are you awake?"

Her whispered words were almost too quiet to hear, except I was awake and fully attuned to her.

"Yes. Are you?"

She snickered and rolled over so she was facing me, but her head remained on her own pillow. Our bodies were a foot apart, and still, this quiet conversation was something I'd never shared with anyone.

"Did you sleep okay?" she asked, her eyes still smiling.

"Yes."

"Better than the floor?" One eyebrow raised and her lips turned up at the corners.

"Yes."

She grinned, and my heart kicked.

"Can we take Juniper for her walk together? Would you mind if I join you?" she asked, so sweet and unassuming it almost hurt.

I'd worried how, in person, I wouldn't be able to suss out whether she was doing things to make me happy and appease me or do things she wanted to do. But seeing her now with her hands clasped together and gazing at me with little begging eyes, I could see plainly how much she wanted this simple thing. And I couldn't forget her demand that I believe her when she told me what she wanted. I could do that. I would.

"We don't mind." Junie probably already loved her better, and as for me? I couldn't think of anything I wanted more than just to be with Winnie always.

Breaking eye contact for fear she'd see that all too vivid thought broadcasting across my face, I sat up and got out of bed. No sense lingering here in the calm and lazy perfection that was this quiet morning, with wintry light spilling through the shades and a still-snoozing dog in the corner.

Maybe there'd be more of this, but for now, we had to allow ourselves time to grow together. Make memories together. *Enjoy the time we have while we're together.* And maybe, just maybe, there'll be more of it after all of this...

Shaking that off, I left her room and all its temptations.

"Meet you in the kitchen in ten."

Juniper bounded ahead in search of the stick I'd just thrown, her paws disappearing into the six inches of new snow blanketing the walking path through my back yard and into the wilderness my land abutted. The natural beauty stretched endlessly and made me feel the expansive freedom I'd longed for after years in a suburban area near Fort Liberty where we'd been stationed with EMU.

Something wet and cold pelted my side. My head snapped to the left to find Winnie with wide eyes and a matching grin, and I only barely jumped out of the way of her next snowball.

"Really? Hitting an unarmed man?" I asked, kneeling to pat some of the powdery snow together. It was bitterly cold this morning, so it didn't make for very good snowballs, but it'd suffice. I tossed one at her, and it broke on her back as she ran away laughing.

"I'm just as unarmed as you, plus you just hit me in the back. Isn't that ungentlemanly conduct or something?"

She peeked at me from where she crouched, then sent another ball flying at me. I ducked, then threw one at her, but she shimmied out of the way just in time.

We went back and forth until I saw the perfect opportunity and took a slowly lobbed snowball to the face.

Winnie gasped and, through laughter, said, "Oh, no! I'm so sorry. Although I feel like you kind of headbutted it..."

I took off my sunglasses and squinted against the blinding white landscape, shook the melting snow from the lenses, and replaced them.

"Aren't you going to come make sure I'm okay?"

I bent and took the stick from Juniper's mouth, threw it again for her, then held my empty hands out to my sides to show I was unarmed.

She shook her head, slowly backing away. "I don't think so."

"No? Even after you injured me?"

I wasn't hurt. She knew it. Still, I'd hoped my plan would've worked a bit better.

She laughed. "I don't think you're injured."

Hand pressed over my heart, and my shoulders drooped. "You wound me."

"Ha!" she cackled, then started running. "I'm not falling for it."

Well, if she insisted on me chasing her, I wouldn't resist. I took off running, following her down the path a ways, then into the taller snow that had accumulated over the last few weeks. Her steps slowed a bit, but she was still remarkably fast. All her morning walks must've gotten her used to the altitude in the last few weeks.

"Just give up now and I'll go easy on you," I said, not quite winded but getting there.

"Never."

She glanced back to see I'd gained on her, and her eyes went wide, then she yelped and tried to keep her momentum backing away from me, but that slowdown gave me the advantage I needed.

I barreled right to her, ducked my head, and hauled her over my shoulder without stopping. With her weight on me, I had to slow down a bit, but we still moved along at a decent clip—having spent a fair amount of time in my career training to carry heavy packs and even people for miles out of enemy territory and in various situations, a giggling, flailing Winnie in my own back yard felt like pure joy.

"Put me down, you madman! You are not jogging with me over your shoulder. Your back! This is not—"

I shifted her weight and brought her into my arms in a cradle hold and kept her there. She was breathing hard and I was, too, admittedly, but our eyes were locked together.

"What's my punishment?" she asked, trying to see through my opaque sunglasses.

Probably trying to read me, but she'd have no luck.

"It'll have to fit the crime." I squeezed her tighter so she wouldn't slip, enjoying how comfortable she seemed to be right here in my arms.

She made a face at my words. "Oh, great. Good thing I didn't put on makeup yet."

She really thought I'd hit her in the face with a snowball? I shuddered to think what this meant for the men she'd dated, or maybe it came down to her brother being a general idiot. Either way, I relished the opportunity to show her an alternative.

I kneeled in the snow and set her down. For a heartbeat, I thought she'd run away, but when I shook my head and patted her leg, she got the message that I could easily catch her again and relented. She flopped back into the powder and closed her eyes, cringing against what she must've anticipated being a snowball to the face at point-blank range.

At her side, I leaned on one hand next to her head and with the other now free of its glove, I crushed a small ball of snow into shape and then gently touched it to her lips.

She sucked in a breath, and her eyes opened to mine staring down at her. Her lips parted just a touch, her warm breath coasting across my chilled fingers as I dragged the ice across her bottom lip, then traced the shape of the cupid's bow of her top one.

She just watched my face, evidently rapt. I couldn't deny I felt the same, or something like it, because soon enough, I tossed the melting snow away and indulged in simply taking in her beautiful face and those eyes looking at me like she'd never wanted anything more than she wanted to kiss me right in this moment.

"I'm not sure that was much of a punishment," she said, a little breathless still, despite having been lying there for a minute.

"It was for me," I admitted.

The wrinkle between her brows asked the question for her.

"Being this close to you and *not* kissing you is getting harder by the minute."

Heat flared in her eyes, and in an instant, her hands had reached up and pulled me down to her. Her lips were still cold, but she deepened the kiss in seconds and the contrast of her warmth and the chill of everything else had me groaning audibly. Nothing was ever as good as I imagined except this—except everything about Winnie.

Lost in the frenzy of the kiss, it took a minute before Winnie jerked and pulled back, then started laughing. Juniper blinked back at us from where she stood with the pompom of Winnie's hat in her mouth and expectant eyes. She dropped the hat and her head swiveled back and forth between our faces, ready for more fun.

Winnie's face was full of humor and joy, and I very reluctantly stood and pulled her up after me. As we walked back toward the house, she wrapped one arm around my waist.

"See? We don't really need to worry. Juniper's the perfect chaperone."

I agreed gamely, but inside, I had my doubts. I hadn't lied when I said not kissing her was becoming harder. Keeping any amount of distance had ballooned into a monumental task and all those determinations and promises

I'd made about putting her needs first seemed to have dissolved in the snow.

But that wasn't the only reason I'd held back, and she'd made clear my insistence on her needs was misplaced. I believed her, but worry over potentially losing her if we kept moving forward, at how irreversible all of this was becoming, still loomed.

Even so, I wasn't sure I'd be able to go back. And if I couldn't—if we couldn't—then what was the way forward?

Two years ago

To: Tristan Donnelly
    From: Winniechickendinny

Tristan,

Life is looking different lately. I'm stepping up my hours at work, so I'm going to have to withdraw from my classes this semester. Dad had a heart attack, and you can imagine how scary that was. He works too hard and doesn't rest or eat all that well, but he's still decently healthy. None of us saw it coming.

Jeremy was going to come work too, which I think I've mentioned, but I guess not anymore? I'm trying not to be angry with him but dang, it's hard.

You know, sometimes I wish we could meet. Don't worry, I'm not proposing we actually do that—I honestly don't know when I could manage time away right now anyway. But I just... sometimes I wish I could just hug you.

You've got better things to do than listen to me whine, I

know. I hope your last mission went okay. I haven't heard from you in a few months, so please update me when you can.

Sending love,
Winn

CHAPTER TWENTY-FIVE

Winnie

After getting cleaned up—and mentally recovering from the devastation that was kissing Tristan Donnelly—I wandered into the book store to meet Jo. Instead of finding her at the desk, she was helping someone in the non-fiction area, and I spied Jess slumped into one of the comfy chairs near the romance section.

Jess could've won a Miss America crown or modeled or become a leading lady in film if she'd had the desire. She just had this grit to her that said she'd worked until she got what she wanted, and yet she was easily one of the most beautiful women I'd ever seen in an athletic, natural way. She wasn't soft and feminine like Dove or a little wild like Elise. She wasn't quiet and a bit mysterious like Catherine or friendly and overtly loving like Jo. She was just... awesome.

"Hey! Are you coming to coffee, too?" I asked her right as she looked up and gave me a barely there smile.

"Nah. I'm hiding out here." She tipped the book toward her chest so I could see the cover—a historical with a man in a kilt on the cover.

"Oo, looks like a good one. I haven't ever really gone for historicals, though."

She closed her eyes and rested her head against the chair's arm. "I love them. I don't mind contemporaries, and I can get behind a good romantasy, but what I love best is a Scottish hero and a woman who's rising above cultural constraints to find her happiness and agency against all odds."

Huh. That did sound nice. "Maybe you should make me a list of your favorites."

Her smile came in fully grown this time. "I'd love to."

It dropped away almost immediately, though.

"Are you okay?" My tone was tentative because while I did think of her as a friend by now after weeks of meeting at Craic on Fridays and our book club plus the group text we had running, I didn't know her all that well. She struck me as fairly private, and I didn't want to pry.

Her lips thinned. "I'll be fine as long as the utter carrier group of testosterone-addled coworkers at my job will listen to me at my meeting tomorrow morning."

My brows rose and I wondered if Tristan was included in there—probably so since he was a key player at Saint Security, though I didn't think of him as particularly *addled.* Masculine, overprotective at times, stubborn as all get out....

Okay, so he could definitely be one of the ones she was referring to. "If you ever need someone to listen, I'm here."

She nodded. "Thanks. I'll see you next weekend for book club, if not before, right?"

I confirmed and saw Jo notch her head toward the back room and hold up a finger, so I moved to the front door and stepped outside to wait for her. A minute later, she shuffled out in an adorable matching hat, scarf, and glove set.

"So ready for coffee and a pastry. You?"

"Yes, please."

The temptation to tell her I'd kissed Tristan, or that we'd shared a bed, almost bubbled over, but I focused instead on the adorable shops lining the street. We turned the corner from Silver Street onto Snow and found the coffee shop, Joe, a few doors down. I hadn't explored much over here, but I immediately knew I wanted to.

"This place is going to be a little bistro restaurant, and down there, a chocolatier is going in. Down at the far end, there's a spot that has sat empty since I've been around, but I heard the other day that someone is going to put in a wine and cheese shop."

We both made excited faces and my heart squeezed at the reality. "That's amazing. This is such a special little town."

If I stayed on my current course, I wouldn't be here to see all of those plans come to fruition.

After the last twenty-four hours, I couldn't think of much I wanted less than to leave this place and the people in it—most especially the man who'd given me a soft kiss on the cheek and told me to have fun with my friends.

It was such a simple thing, but it filled my heart up to bursting. There was no sense that I should hurry back, no pressure that I should really be doing something else. And searching inside myself, I didn't feel the anxiety over whether he secretly thought I should be doing something else like I so often had with my parents.

In a matter of weeks, my perspective had shifted

enough to shine a light on just how warped my ability to function independently had become. Not that I needed my parents to tell me what to do, but how I was so used to considering their needs and perspectives over my own that I became unable to do anything other than what I thought they would prefer in order to keep them happy.

"It is. I didn't really expect to live up here, but after the bookstore was settled and I saw how supportive the community is, I couldn't resist making my way here for myself once I finished my master's." She reached for the handle and held the door.

I stepped through and the scent of coffee enveloped me in a lovely, warm hug. Patrons chatting and sipping coffee filled several tables, all from emerald green mugs of varying shapes.

"What'd you get your master's degree in?" I asked as we shuffled into place in line.

Several people greeted Jo like an old friend and anyone who met my eye smiled warmly. It wasn't as though people in Wichita, Kansas, weren't friendly—they were. But there wasn't this instant willingness to meet a person's eye. Maybe it was because I'd walked in with Jo, who was clearly well-known around the area.

"There she is," a shockingly handsome man in a green and cream flannel plaid shirt said from behind the counter.

Truly, what was in the water here? This guy had a close-cut beard and a hat turned backward with pleased features and a charming grin aimed directly at Jo. *Hello!* Could this be the guy who'd stolen her attention away from Bruce a while back?

"Hey, friend. How's the crowd today?" Jo asked as she approached the counter.

"Booming until about ten. I let Nan go around then and

Dina around noon—you just missed her." He waved behind him as though she'd literally just stepped out.

"That's good. Hopefully, it keeps up after the weekend."

Their dynamic had shifted to something far less flirty and far more... businessy. But like, colleagues. And I had a hunch I wanted to follow as soon as we sat down. We ordered and the man—who Jo then introduced to me as Ethan—told us he'd bring our order in just a few.

Jo waved to someone as they exited, and once she turned to me, I couldn't wait anymore.

"Can I ask..." I tipped my head toward the front where Ethan was busy making our drinks.

She hesitated for a second, then ducked her head. "We're friends."

I waited. There had to be more, especially with that hesitation.

"Okay, we—" She reached up and her smiled broadened.

I turned to see Ethan delivering two steaming mugs, one with a narrow bottom that widened out and featured a mountain in the foam and mine in a large cappuccino bowl with an incredibly detailed snowflake in it.

"This is gorgeous. Thank you so much!" I eagerly took mine from his tray and set it down, then eyed the small plate of scones he nestled between us and two circular porcelain disks.

"Enjoy, ladies." He winked at Jo, gave me a nod, and disappeared back to the counter.

More than one set of lunching companions followed his movements with their gazes—I couldn't blame them. He was an incredibly handsome man, also charming, and could apparently drizzle foam into art. If this tasted even halfway decent, I'd pledge my devotion to the man... or, I would've, if I wasn't one hundred and fifty percent in love with Tristan.

"You were saying?" I prodded, cupping the giant mug and taking a first, delectable sip.

She swallowed and set her cup down, then slid one of the disks on top. When she noticed my look of mild surprise, she explained. "I hate cold coffee, and at this altitude, it actually cools down slightly faster. So we like to include these lids for people who stay. Otherwise, everyone would need disposable cups and lids, and that's just a waste."

"So you say *we* as though..."

A demure little smile shaped her lips. "Yeah, I'm part owner here."

Delight filled me. "That's amazing. I—I am confused, though."

She grinned. "I get it. I mean, I got my master's in communications. When we first moved here, I thought I wanted to stay in Salt Lake and live in a city. It was a nice step away from Seattle where I'd been, but once I got to know Silverton... it just had my heart. Plus, my dad's here, the Saints are here, and they've sort of become like family..."

I'd heard her dad had married the Saints' mom, hence the reference to family, I supposed.

"And Ethan?" I asked, curious if he was part of this puzzle.

"Ethan is a great friend and business partner. We went out twice and I—" Her voice dropped low. "I think he was more interested than I was." She made a regretful face.

Ah. So all that joy at seeing her on his end wasn't feigned, and I hadn't read it wrong, if I had to bet. But it also made sense that she saw him as a co-owner. But dang. What a mess. "Sounds tricky."

She nodded. "Yep. Especially because he's Adam's brother."

I blinked and watched as a blush bloomed on her cheeks.

"Wait. Adam like Saint Security Adam?"

She nodded.

"Ethan is—*oh my gosh, I totally see it now.* They're from here?"

"No. Adam retired from the Army last year, and Ethan knew he planned to come work at Saint—even before Wilder moved out here, he and Bruce had scouted everything and found investors. So most of the people in their old unit knew it was happening because so many of them were near retirement and needed to be able to make plans. Ethan was looking for a fresh start after getting out of the Army a few years before—he didn't stay in until retirement. Anyway, I guess, yeah, he came out here even before Adam and when he and I went on our first date, he mentioned his plan for a coffee shop. Even though we didn't have sparks, I loved the idea."

"Wow. That's... amazing. And I have so many more questions."

She shook her head. "No. No. We're done with me. I need an update on you and your gorgeous faux husband."

My mouth dropped open. "Faux?"

She gave me a soft smile. "I don't mean to pry, but I just thought... maybe it would be good to talk to someone?"

I couldn't think between the blaring alarms and the stark sense of relief butting heads internally, and more than that, the trickle of fear.

If she knew, who else did?

CHAPTER TWENTY-SIX

Tristan

I stood staring out at the night sky and stars winking high above while Winnie finished getting ready. She'd rushed in an hour ago, apologizing up and down for being late.

She hadn't been late. I'd told her we should plan to head into town around six thirty and it was only now six. She'd also texted me more than once to say she was sorry for how late it'd gotten and she'd make it up to me.

Nice thought, but a worrisome one since she had nothing to make up for. That tendency to prioritize everyone else but herself had crept back in and though I loved her, I wanted to crush it.

Maybe not *crush* it. Some of the qualities making her so warm and loving were also those that ended up creating this sense of obligation. I wouldn't want to change her. But I did want her to see she didn't owe me anything. She'd gone to see her friend and, I assumed, had a wonderful time that lasted longer than anticipated. Nothing at all wrong with that and a lot right with it.

"Sorry I'm late. Just need to grab my jacket and I'll be good to go."

I turned, ready to chastise her for apologizing yet again, but my words stuck in my throat. She wore slim black pants that stopped a few inches above her ankle and bright red pumps with murder weapons for heels. On top, she wore a soft-looking red sweater with a neckline that—well, was it even a neckline if it didn't touch her neck? It seemed suspended as though by magic, revealing her shoulders and decolletage, but covering her arms, chest, and back with the cozy fabric.

My gaze brushed the bare tops of her shoulders before she slipped on her puffy black winter coat, and I wondered if she could read the destruction she'd caused on my face.

Ideally not, because she seemed to like knowing when I found her attractive and if she did *anything* to indicate she'd like to sit down and stay a while and, say, let me run a hand over the soft arc at the curve of her shoulders or taste the stretch of skin—

No. Absolutely not.

The whole point of this evening was to develop our relationship in person and while yes, I very much looked forward to developing the physical aspect of things, I didn't want to do that at the risk of everything else.

I wouldn't. No matter how much I hungered for her in every possible way. Because she deserved more and I wouldn't lose her to lust or greed.

Losing her in any way would wreak havoc on my life when the time came—*if the time came*—but losing her completely because of some foolish need to rush into things? I would never forgive myself, nor would I ever recover.

Winnie had filled a part of me that'd been empty since my parents died. Maybe I'd become too dependent on her, particularly considering how infrequently we were in touch at some times. But even in those more spare phases of our relationship, she was still there.

Losing her altogether couldn't happen, and it was one more reason I'd keep a leash on myself tonight and indefinitely.

So I muscled my eyes from the alluring view of her collarbones and the delicate sweep of her neck and said, "No need."

"What?" she asked, bending to stroke Juniper.

Now she was bending over. In those pants. Trying to test the will I'd summoned last night and apparently still very much needed a tight grip on. "Just that…"

Her smile flashed, and she nuzzled her forehead against Juniper's.

What was I even saying?

She straightened and pinned me with an expectant gaze.

"Just that you don't need to apologize. You're not late. We're on time."

Her dark eyes found mine, and my insides did all manner of things to alert me. *Yes. Helpful. Thank you so much.*

"I'm working on it."

I reached for her, instantly disliking the tone of her words. "I don't intend to be hurtful when I say this, but I realize that regardless of intent, words can hurt. Please forgive me."

She faced me fully and set her hands on my chest, over the jacket I wished I hadn't put on yet.

"I don't mean it like that. I just mean... I'm trying to recognize when I have actually done something wrong, or even inconvenienced someone, and when I'm functioning on autopilot. It's surprisingly hard, although I guess it's not when I really think about it."

This woman was a marvel. She was strong and smart and gentle, even with herself. At least, she was trying to be, and I now realized her consternation a moment ago had been with herself, not with my words.

"It's a process. Any change is." I tucked some of her dark hair behind her ear, then indulged in sliding my thumb along her jaw before I let my hand drop. "You're dealing with a lot, and on top of all of it, you're growing. Most people hunker down and just grit it out during hardship, but here you are trying to grow."

Her eyes took on a glassy quality, and her hands slid up and around to the back of my neck. She rose on her toes, tilted her head, and pressed a kiss to my lips.

"Thank you. I know you don't want me to say it, but *I* want to."

She grinned and I couldn't resist stealing another kiss before we both seemed to know now was the time to go. The night was brutally cold when we moved to the truck, and I worried about her feet, her ankles exposed to the chill... suddenly, everything that had been sexy now seemed like a needless risk.

"You probably should've dressed warmer."

Her head snapped to me, but she didn't say anything, so I took the chance to clarify. "You're going to freeze just walking into the restaurant."

She still didn't speak, and I couldn't decipher what was

happening, because she kept her gaze forward once I also got in.

I'd obviously said the wrong thing—not a shock since I hadn't been in a relationship in years and I certainly hadn't been in one with Winnie. The drive went quickly as I internally scrambled. Did I sound like an overprotective, controlling jerk?

I cringed at the thought as I parked the truck and immediately launched into an apology. "Listen, Winn, I—"

"I wanted to dress this way, even knowing it's cold outside."

"I shouldn't have said anything. You look gorgeous and I shouldn't have said a damn word."

She was studying me in the darkness of the cab, and I waited, wondering if I'd just ruined the evening, then added one more thought. "Please forgive me. I don't know how to do this and I'm trying. It's all... new to me."

"How to do what?"

Love you. Need you. Want the best for you and want you for myself at the same time.

"Find the balance of protecting without being overbearing. I'm afraid I'm just plain overbearing sometimes, and I'm trying to figure out where that line is."

She reached for my hand, and we knitted our fingers together. "I can cut you some slack on that."

I chuckled. "Yeah?"

She nodded. "You've been great, and honestly, it's kind of refreshing to have someone worry about me. I just have to figure out how to let you do that without trying to appease you."

"We'll work on it."

We both squeezed our linked hands like some sort of business agreement and finally exited the car.

"Hey, can we—" She stopped herself as I offered my elbow to her and she took it.

"Go ahead."

She glanced at me, then back down at the sidewalk. It'd been salted and looked dry, thank goodness.

"Can we not talk about... everything? Just act like this is really just us, on a date, without all the other stuff behind it?"

I knew what she meant—not the history of our friendship, but could we avoid spending time hashing through updates on the money and her brother and her parents?

I hoped I didn't sound too eager when I said, "Of course."

I'd found a spot close to the restaurant, thankfully, and we shuffled inside Basta a few seconds later.

She shuddered and looked at me. "Okay. I'll say it. You were right. It's f-freezing."

I wrapped her in my arms, and she snuggled into me, seeking warmth. I didn't mind this at all. In another minute, the hostess led us to seats by the windows looking out at Main Street, though mercifully, it was comfortable enough to remove our jackets and not get the ambient chill from the glass panes.

Our waiter greeted us and poured waters in the glasses set at the table, then excused himself while we opened our menus. There were small candles flickering in a glass vase, and dim lighting set the romantic mood. White tablecloths and gleaming silverware would've made me feel out of place in jeans and a plaid shirt, except we were in the mountains. "Mountain Chic" had its own definition, and though there were probably some Hollywood starlets floating around dressed to the nines, we weren't out of place here at Basta.

"Everything sounds good. I'd meant to have actual

lunch, but I filled up on coffee and scones with Jo, and then got wrapped up in chatting until it was too late to eat for fear of ruining our first date." She took a sip of her water, then glanced around the room full of packed tables brimming with the hum of conversation.

"Nothing can ruin our first date." I couldn't tell if she'd gotten nervous, but the way she'd been talking, it felt like maybe she had.

"No? In my experience, there can be any number of things that ruin a first date." She tucked her napkin in her lap and set the menu aside.

I chose not to display the displeasure I felt at the thought of her on first dates, particularly in the wake of my idiotic display in the car. Also, her insinuation seemed to imply those dates had been not good, and therefore in theory, the person hadn't gotten a second date.

I couldn't imagine her doing anything to put me off. She had flaws just like I did. She was a pushover when it came to her family, and she cared too much what people thought. I was too used to being on my own and could be a touch stubborn.

We were imperfect people who knew a lot of the rough stuff about each other. That was miles ahead of almost any relationship of any kind I'd ever had save my former EMU team, and even then, that only applied to some of them.

Instead, I leaned my forearms on the table and spoke in a low voice. "Well, Winn, I'm a sure thing."

EMAIL

Eighteen months ago

To: Winniechickendinny
From: Tristan Donnelly

Winnie,

How's your dad healing up? And Jer? Is he showing up yet?

I don't want to sound like I'm anti-Jeremy, but it's time he grows up and shows up. You can quote me on that should it be useful.

Attached you'll find a photo of my puppy, Juniper. She's a yellow lab and is supposed to be a pretty sturdy lass when she grows to full size. Right now, she's waking me up at all hours of the night, and my next-door neighbor and her kids are helping during the days when I'm at work. Fortunately, I'm home, likely for good barring majorly unforeseen changes, until I retire later this year. She's... well I already love her like crazy. Kind of pathetic, right? I knew she was mine the minute I saw her, though.

Do something nice for yourself, okay, Winn? You're awesome.

Sending love back,
Tristan (and the pup)

CHAPTER TWENTY-SEVEN

Winnie

My mind short-circuited.

What was I supposed to say to that?

What *could* I say to this gorgeous man giving me a smoldery-hot look setting me on fire and had some serious double entendre going? Or was it just the one entendre? Honestly, I didn't know. He wasn't saying he was a sure thing like I could have my way with him.

What are you even thinking here, woman?

I exhaled slowly and reached for my water, ducking my face into my glass as the words really took root. By the time I swallowed, I was laughing.

"Okay, Tristan Donnelly, coming at me with a *line*."

Inevitably, his amused smile was heart-breaking and thrilling. He shook his head like he was erasing the words.

"I just mean, we don't have to stress. Like you said,

we're just going to have fun and enjoy being together instead of updating on all the *stuff*."

I nodded, appreciating the confirmation we were both on the same page there. "Okay, then... tell me something about yourself you've never put in an email."

He thought for a moment before leaning back and fiddling with the blunt end of his knife, his eyes focused there as he spoke. "I never told you this because I didn't want it to be a big deal but... for a while, you were my beneficiary."

I froze, wondering if I was understanding correctly. "What does that mean?"

His gaze flicked up to mine, then back to his utensils. "If I'd died, you would've gotten my SGLI—my life insurance policy payout and everything."

My mouth dropped open, and I kind of lurched forward but didn't say anything, because what could I possibly say to that? Good grief, it felt like my heart was in a vise and emotions pressed in on every side.

He'd been so alone that a woman he'd never met had been his beneficiary?

He'd done it because he had *no one* else, and though I'd always known his parents had passed when he was nearly out of high school, I didn't register until right this moment just how alone he truly was.

He'd given everything he had, in that awful scenario, to *me*?

He never told me.

And then, maybe the most terrifying part of it was the reality that he'd had to make those plans. What twenty-something has plans like that? So few, I'd wager. I certainly never had. But that was what his life had been—risking his actual life and knowing he very well may not make it back from whatever mission he was sent out on.

I launched out of my seat, rattling the table and drawing attention from others no doubt, before grabbing his hand as he turned to me and hauling him out of his seat and into my arms. I crushed him to me, desperate to just... just hold him and remind myself he was fine. He was right here in front of me, perfect and beautiful and so freaking wonderful it hurt.

"I'm so sorry you ever had to even do that," I whispered, knowing it didn't make sense, and yet I had to say it.

"I'm not. I couldn't think of anyone more deserving. I probably should've told you, but I didn't want to upset you."

Throat tight and barely holding back tears that would absolutely destroy my mascara, I looked at him with lips pressed tight together. He let out a soft, affectionate laugh and cupped my cheek.

"None of that. Let's order."

I hadn't noticed the waiter standing to the side, but of course he had, so we sat back down and I composed myself quickly while the waiter reviewed the specials. A few minutes later, when we were alone at the table again, he caught my eye.

"Now you tell me something you never put in an email."

His expression was light and happy in a way that astounded me right now.

I was still reeling from his confession, and he seemed like he'd just taken a lovely Sunday stroll through town or something. Of course, his news hadn't been news to *him*, only to me, so I supposed it made sense I was the basket case.

I cleared my throat, still feeling raw from this vulnerable discovery about a man I'd viewed as indomitable. "Uh, let's see. I hate wheatgrass? I'm allergic to almonds? I—how do I match that?"

He stretched out a hand, palm up, and waited for me to take it. I did, instantly easing at the contact.

"You don't match it. You don't have to. You just... be yourself. I don't need anything from you. I only want what you want to give."

This. Man.

How could he be so closed off to his own pain—and he definitely was—and so sensitive to mine? We had never talked about his family and the loss there. I knew what happened in the most technical terms, but this recent confession had been a bigger insight than anything to this point in our relationship.

I'd said we shouldn't talk about the mess back in Kansas, and I didn't want to, but his honesty made me want to share something more than just a factoid I might've overlooked in years past.

Squeezing his hand for strength, I exhaled and gathered my words. "I don't think I want to keep running the business."

His attention stayed riveted on me. He didn't remind me I'd said I didn't want to talk about Kansas. He just waited, patient, listening.

"I honestly don't know if my parents even want me to do that. While I was talking with Jo today, I had this moment where I realized maybe I've done this to myself. Maybe I assumed they wanted to keep the business afloat, and because I was so eager to figure out the problem and then *did*, maybe they thought that's what I wanted. But I can't bear the thought that all of this comes down to me being unable to tolerate a hard conversation with my parents."

I gasped, the words having fallen out so rapidly, I had to catch my breath. My heart pattered inside my chest and I took a drink of water, then reached for the wine that had appeared on the table at some point.

"Can you talk to them about it?" he asked, his voice calm and without judgment.

An exasperated laugh tripped out of me.

"In theory, yes. In reality, it's something I should've done a long time ago. And I'm just—" I sniffed hard, forbidding myself to break down in tears. *Two* instances of nearly crying on one first date was not a good look. ' I hate the idea that I'm so weak I couldn't even *ask* them if this is what they really wanted."

Or ask myself the same question months ago.

He was shaking his head before I'd even finished. "You're not weak, Winnie. You love your family and you've all been through a terrible few years."

"That's true. And I'm trying to remember to cut myself some slack, but I hate this default in me that says I have to be the one to solve everyone's problems. I honestly don't know if it's something I dreamed up, or if they made me feel that way at some point, and now I've adopted it as my mission or something."

He gripped my hand tighter, reassuring and strong. "This seems like something a therapist would help with. I've been to therapy on and off over the years. I know a few people who've used someone here, if you're interested. No pressure, because I think you're working through this as best you can, but sometimes, we need access to tools we don't have within ourselves."

"I've been thinking that, too."

For a long time, the thought of needing outside help had made me feel even more inept, but he'd described it perfectly. I didn't have the tools to sort out these years-old habits developed during traumatic family events. It'd become frustrating enough I needed a change—more tools than I possessed. And that was okay.

Even accepting *this*—the truth that it was okay I didn't have all the answers for myself—was a small victory.

"And as for the business, which I realize is a more immediate issue... I'll support you, whatever you want. You can go back and live your life however you want. You don't have to pour your inheritance into a business that isn't something you care about. You can sell it or—I don't know what the other options are, but we'll figure it out."

We'll figure it out.

My heart fairly glowed with those words. "Thank you."

I wanted to say more. Maybe admit the other truth that had been burning through me lately, more and more and the strongest it ever had all day today—I didn't want to go back. I didn't want to go back for the business or my family or *anything*.

I want to stay here with you.

"Well, well, well, what do we have here but a romantic dinner for the Donnelly family?"

We looked up to find Kenny hovering over our table with a delighted smile. I rose and hugged him, and he pressed a friendly kiss to my cheek.

"Don't you look lovely, Winnie," he said, eyes wide with appreciation as he stepped back and beheld me dramatically.

A grumble came from Tristan's direction, and Kenny and I turned to see his glaring.

"Unhand my woman, Barbie."

Pure liquid thrill shot through me at the tone, the look, the words... wow. I didn't mind Tristan being a little possessive of me, firstly because I was technically his wife, and second because we both knew darn well Kenny wasn't actually coming on to me. He was a flirty, friendly guy and he would never encroach on one of his friends' partners.

"Easy there, Oak. Just giving her a compliment. Let's not get too caveman on her. She might realize her mistake and come looking for other options." He winked at me and dug his own grave.

Tristan just shook his head. "You are a child, aren't you?"

Kenny preened. "If by that, you mean I'm startlingly young and handsome compared to your old ass, then yes. That is correct."

I chuckled and Tristan did, too. My heart flipped at his smile and the way he rolled his eyes. Kenny ate up every bit of the attention.

"What are you doing here? Out on a hot date with some lucky lady?" I asked, craning my neck to see if anyone was lingering nearby we hadn't noticed.

"Nah, just getting takeout. I like to keep it fancy. Saw you two through the window as I was walking by." He held up a brown paper bag with handles and the Basta logo printed in bright red stylized font on the side.

"I hope it's delicious," I said, patting his arm as he nodded at Tristan and bid me goodnight.

The heaviness that'd settled between us during our conversation had been banished by Kenny's cheery, flirty arrival, and by tacit agreement, both of us seemed to want to maintain it. So we shifted gears to talking about my day with Jo and the next book I'd read. He told me about his upcoming work at Saint Security.

And I tucked away the truth about not wanting to leave,

praying I'd have the boldness to bring it up again sometime soon.

Because if I didn't, I'd be back in Kansas before I knew it, feeling just like I did now, but having lost even more than I'd ever imagined.

EMAIL

Seven months ago

To: Winniechickendinny
    From: Tristan Donnelly

Winnie,

I've settled into Silverton, and so far, Juniper and I are really liking it. She got used to the altitude faster than I have. It helps that Bruce somehow already knows everyone, and he's encouraging me to tag along. The people here are great, and even those who haven't served seemed to respect it. Sounds kind of silly, but that's not always the case.

I think you'd like it here. The property I found has trees all around, and right now, the field out back is covered in purple and white and yellow wildflowers. It's gorgeous. I attached a pic so you can see. Oh, and Junie sends her love.

I hope you're doing okay. Is Jeremy around at all? Your dad okay? Catch me up when you have a minute.

Tristan

CHAPTER TWENTY-EIGHT

Tristan

Juniper greeted us, then burst past us outside. She'd want back in as soon as possible, so I waited by the door while Winnie removed her gloves and coat.

We'd lingered over dinner, neither of us wanting the evening to end. Well, I didn't actually know what she wanted, but she didn't seem to be in a rush. We'd shared a molten chocolate cake and laughed together. It'd felt like a dream.

In truth, it was a dream I'd clung to more than once in my life since she'd started writing. I'd never admitted to myself that what I wanted with Winnie was something romantic, but it clearly had been over the years. When we'd first met, she'd been a kid—it hadn't even occurred to me. But she'd grown up and at some point, that'd changed.

Locked in a cage too small to lay down or even sit for SERE training, in the dead of night on watch in a faraway place, in the wake of a narrow miss with death, after a draining therapy session processing loss… I'd thought of her.

I hadn't planned to tell her she'd been my beneficiary, mostly because I always felt it made me seem more tragic than I was. I'd lost my parents when I was seventeen, but I'd had seventeen years with them. Seventeen years with loving, engaged, thoughtful parents who loved each other, too.

After learning about Bruce's upbringing and more than one of my other friends' pasts, I'd absolutely embraced how I'd been deeply blessed by the time I did have. My parents had left an indelible mark on me.

Therapy had helped me see that losing them had pressed into me the idea that I would lose anyone I loved. I didn't like admitting it because, logically, I didn't buy it. Logically, I knew I had people. After joining EMU and becoming a part of a team with Adam and Kenny and Dorian, and getting to know Bruce and Wilder and so many others, I knew what it was to be loved in a way.

But it was Winnie who showed me I could have someone lasting… at least a version of a person. Words on a screen or on a sheet of college-ruled notebook paper. Sometimes in pen, with ink smudged from her left-handedness, sometimes with little stickers to seal the envelope, often with song lyrics for subject lines in emails, I could have her.

I wouldn't overwhelm her by telling her she was still my beneficiary—she'd receive everything I had if I died, especially now that we'd married. But even before, I'd never changed anything. Retiring from the Army meant I had to review all of the information, then signing on with Saint Security, again. And there was not another person on this Earth I'd want to have everything I had to show for my earthly existence save her.

Acknowledging that, it made my feelings for her obvious. But I couldn't have admitted it to myself before seeing her, before knowing her in technicolor, because I wouldn't have survived not knowing when I'd get to be near her if I had.

"Tristan?"

My name from her lips snapped me back to the moment, and I heard Juniper whining at the door. I yanked it open and she bolted inside, a brutally cold gust following her before I could shut the door. She made right for her bed, circled it a few times, then snuggled down into the cushion.

"You okay?" Winnie asked, approaching me with concerned eyes.

"Sorry. I spaced out, I guess. Must be getting tired."

My smile felt a little false. I didn't know why the realization I'd just had in that mundane moment had hit me with such a burst of melancholy, but it had.

Actually, of course I knew why—because ultimately, she had to choose a path for herself. I wouldn't do anything to influence her or try to win her to my way of thinking. I wouldn't expect her to give up her own desires for the sake of mine. She'd had too much of that already.

And in the end, you'll lose her anyway.

There was the deep-seated fear I didn't want to hear, but it kicked the tires of my heart, testing me for a stronger voice. Just now, I didn't have one, even if I desperately wanted to believe it wasn't true.

"Do you want to go to bed?"

The innocent question felt loaded down with every manner of weight tonight. Body armor and ammunition and weapons piled high over the simple words.

Yes. More than anything.

But I knew she was asking the simpler question. "Probably should. I have an early meeting tomorrow."

We moved down the hallway together. I wanted to touch the stretch of her shoulder left uncovered by her sweater—to brush aside her long hair and kiss her neck.

As though she could hear my thoughts, she slowed, then stopped and... waited. Ahead of us, the hallway and bedrooms were dark. Behind us, the fire lit the living room and one kitchen light remained on until I shut things down later. Here in between, it was dim and quiet.

The space between us pulled taut. She still faced away from me, and apparently, all my determination to let her decide and lead the way had evaporated in the heat of this moment because I stepped close and did what I'd been imagining.

I slid her long hair to the side. Her breath caught.

I pressed a soft kiss to the place where her neck curved into her shoulder and exhaled sharply.

"Tristan." It was all air and consonants.

"Yes, Winn." She hadn't asked a question. I hadn't answered.

I'd walked in the door intending to share a few more moments of conversation with her and then lightly try to talk her into agreeing I should sleep on the air mattress again before acquiescing and sleeping on the far side of my bed with her.

No touching.

No sliding my lips against her skin, my hand still tangled in her hair. No whispering, "Tell me to stop."

"No."

Not a whisper, but definitive and full-voiced, especially when she leaned back into me, and her hand came up to grasp the back of my head and hold me in place.

I indulged in pressing into her, routing my kisses along

the smooth line of her neck and behind her ear, my free hand not in her hair finally sliding over her hip and pressing over her belly so we were locked together.

After another kiss to the soft space at the curve of her jaw, she turned and wrapped both arms around my shoulders, pulling me down to her, commandeering my mouth with hers.

The demand in this contact detonated any restraint either one of us had been clinging to, and all sense of time and space ceased to exist in this hallway as we sank into the oblivion of pleasure from this connection. Our kisses became hungry, our need ravenous, the futility of pressing closer together becoming both a thrill and frustration.

After some amount of time still standing in the dimly lit hallway—could've been a freeze in time, could've been minutes—we stumbled backward toward the bedroom, legs tangling until I slipped my hands down over the curve of her backside and picked her up. Her thighs locked around me, arms at my shoulders, lips against my jaw, now my neck, and I barely made it to the bed before I turned and sank to sit on the mattress.

The bounce of impact jarred us, rattling our senses enough to press pause on the play-action of the moment.

"Sorry. You okay?" I asked, running a hand from the back of her head and over her hair in an effort to soothe any possible hurts.

She grinned. "I would say better than okay."

A burst of pride and pleasure filled my chest. "That's good news."

She chuckled. "I never really thought about whether we'd be... physically compatible."

"No?" I coughed, surprised at the comment.

"No. I just sort of assumed that since we've always been

able to talk through things, even if it was in writing, we'd figure out how to talk through any other issues."

I registered the flicker of nerves in her gaze. "Anything. We can talk about anything, Winn."

She had something in mind—something she very much wanted to discuss, but it was like she'd shut it inside a safe and had forgotten the combination. Her mouth opened to speak, but she closed it and locked whatever she needed to share back behind her soft lips.

"Can we get ready for bed and then... cuddle a little? Maybe?"

A short, airy laugh came out as I surrendered to the subject change. Whatever she had in mind wouldn't be coming out tonight, but I hoped she'd feel she could tell me soon.

As for cuddling her... "Of course."

We'd been wrapped around each other, and the intensity between us felt like a bonfire, but I didn't regret the slow down. Especially now knowing she had something important on her mind, I wanted her trust before we took anything further.

And more than that, I needed to know this wasn't fleeting for her.

I needed to know I wouldn't lose her.

I didn't know how things would work, but maybe we'd be long-distance for a while. Maybe... well, maybe I could look for work in Kansas. I hated the idea of moving again, but would I do it for Winnie?

Yes. Absolutely, I would. And every person at Saint Security would support me.

So for now, I'd take her closeness however it would come. And I'd wait for when she felt safe enough to tell me everything.

CHAPTER TWENTY-NINE

Tristan

After parking in the Saint Security lot Monday morning, I turned off the truck and gave myself a minute to sit and absorb... everything before the interior got cold.

Winnie had slept in my arms for most of the night.

It still felt like a dream, and certainly one I had no desire to wake up from, but the reality of life would crash back in as soon as I stepped out of this vehicle. So I shut my eyes and let myself remember the sweet scent of her hair and the warmth of her body. The pleasing weight of her next to me, her soft, steady breaths in the night.

Mostly, I'd slept. I'd never slept so close to someone save teammates in a few dire circumstances over the years, and it was never particularly restful and absolutely not peaceful sleep. This had been nothing short of magic.

A sharp knock on my window sent the memory flying.

"Come on, sleepy head. Wife keep you up late?" Kenny waggled his brows and gave me a wolfish grin

Yes, but not in the way he was thinking. If we got there someday, I wouldn't mind it. *Okay, understatement.* But I couldn't find anything to regret about last night—the date, the time together, the simple blessing of sleeping next to her. Even if she was still holding something back, waking side by side this morning had given way to a new closeness.

Maybe it'd been the date or the softening of boundaries between us—certainly touching in bed, even in the largely cozy, comforting way we had, hadn't been on the table before. We'd chatted over breakfast before she took Juniper for a walk and I left. She'd kissed my cheek before I got into the car, then started down the path with my dog, and I'd darn near choked up.

A normal day in a life I'd hardly dared dream for myself. A portrait of a fantasy made real.

Kenny glared at me from the walkway leading to the Saint door, so I shoved my truck open and got on with it. We made it inside to the currently empty reception desk— Nikki had recently started up with the accountancy for the season and we hadn't replaced her. Sarah Saint hadn't decided to come back to work, but that was entirely under- standable considering her baby was the cutest thing to ever exist.

"You in the meeting this morning?" I asked Kenny, not recalling his name on the list.

"Nah. I have some paperwork I didn't finish last week, and I head out to relieve Cookie later so wanted to wrap it up." He twiddled his three fingers at me in a doofy farewell, then turned down the hallway toward his office while I headed to the conference room.

Kenny would be replacing Cookie, who'd been on

assignment with movie star Jenna Halter, along with Hijack. Unfortunately, Cook's grandparent had just passed, so he needed a swap. Kenny had volunteered, and I was grateful to him for being willing to go. There were plenty of us who still liked to travel, but I found myself... less interested in the prospect these days.

Inside the conference room, Wilder Saint sat at one end of the long, polished table. Jess Korbel sat squarely in the middle, arms crossed and energy buttoned down. Adam sat across from her and glanced up at me when I entered.

"Hey, Oak. Just waiting on Jaws to finish up a call."

Bruce jogged in from behind him and we both took seats, Bruce next to Jess and me next to Adam. The clock struck nine right as Bruce said, "Okay, Jess. Ready when you are."

Jess's previously buttoned-up calm slipped a bit, and her jaw ticked before she spoke.

"As you know, I agreed to come work here under the provision that I would be able to function independently and with a guarantee I would *never* be partnered with *him*."

We all knew she meant Jude Rawlins, aka Beast, though I couldn't recall a time she'd used his nickname or addressed him by his given one. Still, there was no one else it could be.

"Correct. And we have maintained that without issue. We've got enough staff, this hasn't been a problem, but we're here for a reason, so clue us in so we can help fix it."

Bruce's ever-accommodating tone belied no hint of frustration or impatience. He genuinely cared about the staff here, as did Wilder, and we were lucky to have them at the helm.

Adam and I served as auxiliary leadership since we were the next most senior employees, having signed on nearly the instant Bruce and Wilder had spread word about the endeavor, and now Eddie James-Williamson also functioned in a leadership role after coming on board early last summer. She brought experience and a wealth of contacts we didn't have, plus a general take-no-crap attitude everyone responded well to.

For her part, Jess seemed to be hesitating, gritting her teeth so hard she couldn't speak.

"Whatever you've got for us, Pop, we're ready to listen. You're a valuable member of this team and if you're not happy, we want to fix it." Wilder had become much softer in the wake of leaving active duty and becoming a husband and father.

With an exhale, she nodded, almost like she was willing herself, then lifted her eyes to meet Adam's across from her, then mine, then Wilder's, and finally Bruce's.

"I have a great deal of respect for you all. I am grateful to be a part of the team and I never want to seem anything but. I understand there are many moving pieces and we're all in this together, working for coverage and expansion. Working to be the best at what we do. I love that."

She let her statements hang there, and I knew without looking that each of us had the same low-level dread thrumming through our minds. She'd set this meeting up for a reason and here it came.

"I can't be around him. And I won't be. You need to send him or me out because having both of us stationed here isn't going to work."

A flush had risen to her cheeks, but otherwise, she still looked perfectly calm.

"I'm not about to leave because you got your panties in a twist, *Pop*."

Everyone's eyes shot to the doorway, which Beast literally darkened. At six foot six, he was the tallest and broadest of all of us. In many respects, he was simply too large for the teams in special operations—being on the smaller side had its advantages, and all of us who were taller had to work around that. There was no working around six feet six inches and well over two hundred and sixty pounds. Still, he had skills and he'd used them well.

His face was set in that unperturbed mask he wore whenever he interacted with Jess and many others. He could soften up a bit around the guys, but the history between these two never ceased to cause drama.

Bruce rose to his feet. "Can't have you talking like that, Rawlins, or—"

"*My* panties in a twist? Am I the one who walks around grunting like I can't summon words from one of the *several* languages I happen to know every time I'm in the room with other human beings?"

Jess had shot from her chair and rounded the table before Bruce had risen fully to his feet, but I'd seen her movement and stepped in front of her.

Beast just looked at Jess for a beat, then loosed a pointed grunt.

Jess let out a sound of pure frustration between clenched teeth and then turned to Bruce and Wilder. "Me or him. I do *not* want to be this kind of person, but it's that, or I go job hunting and I will be honest and say I *really* don't want to do that."

"Easy way out," Beast mumbled.

Jess's jaw flexed so hard, I decided it must be reinforced with steel not to shatter under the rage.

"Gentlemen, I'll leave you to your discussion and expect to hear something by the end of this week."

When her fiery gaze met mine, I stepped out of the way and she marched up to Beast, who still blocked the door.

They faced off for a heartbeat, his gigantic frame towering over her small and charged one, before she said, "Well?"

He grunted, absolutely just to spite her based on the little smirk that slipped before he covered it up with that bored mask when she practically stomped out of the room.

The four of us *not* a part of the problem glanced at each other and Beast sauntered into the room and posted up in the corner where he could see the exit and crossed his arms, legs braced wide. He wasn't about to sit down at the table.

I'd seen him use this intimidation tactic with all manner of terrorists and bad guys, and here he was employing it with *us?* No better way to join a conversation amongst friends. Still, those of us standing took our seats because at least some of us would act like mature adults.

"I don't think we need to fill you in since you invited yourself to the meeting. So... you going or is she?" Bruce sounded impressively unrattled, though any one of us would've done the same.

"Not it."

Adam shut his eyes as though he were praying for patience. "Come on, man."

Wilder leaned back in his chair. "Why not?"

Beast's flippancy receded and he squinted a bit, then his gaze flicked to Adam. "Family stuff. I can't go international."

In a military unit, that kind of vague excuse wouldn't fly. But this was one of the beautiful realities of being *out*. We had freedoms we never did on active duty, and this was one of them. We could simply *talk* and potentially avoid getting sent on an overseas assignment. We didn't have to draw up paperwork or justifications why, and still face the potential of a deployment or long TDY.

Wilder nodded. "We'll find something for her for now. You may need to take a turn depending on how she feels and how... long this lasts."

Beast didn't nod or give any discernable reply. Instead, he stalked off with his usual brusqueness and left us to discuss.

Bruce dropped his head back in his chair and swiped a hand over his face. "God save us from the drama. I have a teenager. I do not need more of it here."

Wilder seemed deep in thought, and Adam was shaking his head like he was disappointed—whether with Jess or Beast, I couldn't have said.

"Someday, they're going to have to talk about it. We're not going to be able to juggle them forever. I honestly thought they'd be over it by now." Bruce was leaning on his forearms, talking mostly to Wilder.

"I'd hoped, but I guess we didn't realize..."

Adam sighed. "I was honestly surprised she agreed to work here knowing Rawlins was already on staff."

Everyone's attention shifted to him. When Wilder and Bruce asked him to explain what he knew they didn't, he did. He'd been privy to some of their past, and now, as he explained what he knew, the need for them to stay apart made perfect sense. The fact that Jess ever agreed to come work at Saint or that they could stand to be in the same building together, seemed more than a little miraculous now.

We dispersed and went about our days, the details of Jess's trip taking shape—she'd replace Kenny on the personal security assignment with Jenna Halter and leave immediately. After running out to do a security check for one of our home security clients toward the end of my day, Bruce caught me in the hallway before I reached my office.

"Got an update from a contact in Wichita you should know about."

I straightened, senses instantly on alert. "What?"

"Jeremy Delmonico was found severely beaten in his vehicle, which had also been virtually destroyed. He's conscious as of this morning but not talking to the police."

Which meant, without a doubt, all of this had just escalated. Because they'd not only attacked Jeremy and from the sounds of it nearly killed him, but they still had something over him enough he was too scared to tell the police.

And just like that, reality came back in full force.

EMAIL

Four months ago

To: Tristan Donnelly
From: Winniechickendinny

Tristan,

Jeremy's in trouble. Like, major trouble I don't even understand what he's done, but apparently he owes a ton of money. I haven't mentioned this because... I don't know, I guess I was embarrassed? I know you don't love how he's been acting and I don't either, but I thought he'd bounce back. All this time, since Thomas and then especially since Dad's heart attack, I thought he'd figure himself out. That my parents retiring and selling off part of their business and maybe even Jeremy getting his trust would somehow help him.

Apparently not.

Ugh, I'm just sick to my stomach about it, and I cannot let my parents find out how bad this is. The last thing they need is more stress coming at them.

Sending love,
Winn

CHAPTER THIRTY

Winnie

When Tristan walked through the door, I was practically floating on air. I'd spent the day researching everything I needed to know in order to present my parents with alternatives to my keeping the farm running. Everything from allowing someone else to manage it for them to selling it to a current employee to dissolving it entirely... truly every avenue.

But one look at his face told me he hadn't had such a good day.

"What is it?"

He set his coffee mug and water bottle on the counter along with his keys, then held out his hand without a word.

Not good. His expression wasn't angry or sad so much as... curated. If he'd had a normal day, even before the last few of our growing closer together, he would've given me a small smile or flashed his brows. Instead, here we were, him leading me to the couch and me with my heart nearly pounding out of my chest.

"Tristan, seriously. What is it?" I asked as I sat down next to him on the couch.

"Bruce has a contact in Wichita, and we asked him to keep tabs on the situation with your brother. He called Bruce this afternoon to report that Jeremy was attacked and is in the hospital. He's in stable condition now."

My heart stopped for a few seconds, then restarted at a sprint, my mind whirring just behind the breakneck pace. "He's stable—does that mean he wasn't at some point?"

Tristan's steady gaze didn't waver. "We don't have all of the details, but it appears he wasn't conscious for at least a while and was in surgery. This all happened sometime overnight, and we just got word."

I shot to my feet. "I need to call my parents. How come they haven't told me anything? Wait, do you think they don't know? I need to get out there."

Juniper trotted over to pace back and forth with me.

Tristan rose and took my hand again. "You can absolutely do that, and if you want, we'll have a plane ready for you within a few hours. But I would like to ask you to consider *not* going back right now."

My brain felt crowded, too many thoughts packed into a small space, and I shook my head to clear it. "What? Why?"

His strong hands came to my shoulders, and he waited until I stilled and gave him my focus.

"Because Jeremy was attacked. Supposedly, he's not talking to the police—not saying who did this, but we're pretty sure it's Calvin and his goons. And this means you going back there puts you at greater risk."

"Me? No. I'm—I'm—I'm not a part of this. I need to see him.

I need to make sure my dad's okay. I—" I choked on the words, the need to solve this problem and the truth that I couldn't. Because Tristan was right—more than likely, I'd be more at risk.

"If you want to go, I'll go with you. We'll bring Adam or Kenny for backup. But at this point, I think we need to focus on talking to your folks and ideally Jeremy before we put you in a higher risk situation."

My chin wobbled and I pressed my lips together to stave off the tears, but it didn't work. They came hot and heavy, and I dropped my head into my hands. Tristan pulled me to him and wrapped me in his arms, unfazed by my rapidly increasing breakdown.

Juniper whined like she was in pain—poor sweet girl probably was with that empathetic heart of hers. Tristan soothed me with gentle hands pressed against my back, slowly sliding up and down, until all my tears had fallen and I was cried out.

I pulled back and got out a watery, "Thank you."

He swiped a thumb under one eye, then the other, cupping my face tenderly. "Of course."

Juniper's head nudged my leg, and I went to my knees, hugging her and welcoming the little embrace she offered with her head and paw. If I'd had any more tears in me, her sweetness would've drawn them out, but instead, I savored her comfort before crawling up onto the couch and slumping down. Tristan took his place next to me and set a hand on my leg, squeezing as though to reassure me everything would be okay.

Maybe the oddest part of this whole situation was that I did feel some certainty everything *would* be okay. It was such a different sensation than I'd had before I'd gotten here, before I'd connected with Tristan in real life. I'd felt utterly alone in the work of protecting and helping my parents and handling my brother's mess.

Now I had reinforcements, even if I hated how his being there for me would put *him* at risk, too. And Adam or whoever else came with us.

But his steady reassurance and presence, his willingness to let me choose what I thought was best, made me more comfortable relying on him. *How odd.*

"Do you think he'll be able to talk? I mean, is there any way to know?" I asked him.

"Maybe start by messaging. See if he can respond. We'll take it step by step."

Hours later, I'd spoken with Jer enough to know he was okay on the most basic level and for him to tell me not to come back. I'd also gotten my parents on the phone, and after they'd rushed to the hospital and seen to Jeremy, they'd call me back. Bruce's contact had found out first, so I'd known before they ever heard a word, and I'd been the one to break the news. I hated to think how long it would've been before anyone knew what'd happened if Bruce hadn't been keeping tabs on him.

I'd been an anxious mess all evening, but Tristan had been steady at my side—feeding me a snack and nudging cool glasses of water in my direction. Juniper came to check on me every so often, offering sweet paws for shaking and more than once, a hug.

Everything felt like it was happening to someone else. I'd cried earlier, but now, I felt a remoteness as my parents spoke from their home after leaving the hospital when visiting hours ended.

"I just don't know how to help him. Whoever did this…" My mom sighed, grief and genuine confusion in her voice.

She hadn't guessed this had to do with Jer's debts because he wouldn't connect those dots for her, and thus far, they didn't realize just how terrible it was or just how dangerous the people he owed were.

I'd wanted to protect them from this awful reality, but had I just made everything worse?

"Why won't he talk to the police? I don't understand it." My dad sounded equally baffled.

And he would, because they didn't realize the guys who beat Jeremy up were bad guys, and more and more, it looked like Jeremy had been involved with something illegal. I believed him when he said he didn't realize how dangerous Calvin and his people were, but that didn't stop the situation from being very sticky.

"I'll see what I can find out," I said, because what else could I say at this point? "Are you feeling okay?"

My dad grumbled. "I'm fine. Just tired now."

The pause on the other end of the line made my ears prick up like a deer in the woods.

"Winnie, if you know something, you need to tell us." My mom's voice had a slight shake to it, like nerves or adrenaline propelled her.

I shut my eyes and sank back into the couch, lost for what was right in this situation. Should I tell them? Should I keep them ignorant of the larger issue now that everything had escalated?

Tristan sat at the other end of the couch messaging on his phone periodically and checking on me. I caught his eye, and he gave me that steady look of his that somehow grounded me. It said something like, "I'm here with you and believe you can do this." Maybe it was just him looking back at me with no thought behind it, but it felt like he was bolstering me with the connection.

"I'm not sure what to tell you." That was purely true.

"How about you tell us everything you know, and we'll go from there. Keeping information from us isn't going to make anything better."

The edge in my mom's voice made my hackles rise, that tender place in me ready to do whatever needed to be done to appease it.

"I think the guy he owes money is the one who beat him up."

There. Said it.

Tristan watched, clearly tracking the conversation. He'd asked long ago if I wanted privacy for these conversations, but I didn't. I needed him close by.

"How could you keep this to yourself?" My mom's tone had risen to one of deep upset.

"This is irresponsible, Winnie. It's important information. We'll need to go to the police with this."

My dad's censure stung, but I understood it.

"I'm sorry. I was trying to do what's best for everyone."

"Jeremy's been in danger and you've said nothing? That hardly seems like the best for *him* or *us*."

Months ago, this comment from my dad would've hit differently. It would've made me rush to apologize and figure out what I'd done wrong. But today, after distance from them and the situation, after patching up some of the holes in myself, I heard something different.

Not a true statement that I needed to accept as fault. Instead, I heard the blame.

A fire lit in my gut, and I took a slow breath, attempting

to remind myself they were probably in shock and deeply upset. They were looking for someone to blame, and apparently, their daughter was easier than the people who actually perpetrated the crime.

"We both downplayed how serious this was because we didn't want you any more upset than you already were. Between this and the business, it felt like too much."

A disbelieving laugh through the phone made my heart thud heavily in my chest.

"Please don't pretend like any of this has to do with the business. You're out of town living with some man you barely know, and we're just now finding out your brother has been in severe danger all this time? How could you fail to tell us? How could you leave?"

My mouth fell open, and out of the corner of my eye, I could see Tristan sit up and lean forward, watching me carefully.

"How could I?" I asked, my voice deceptively quiet and masking the cataclysmic levels of hurt and anger brewing in my chest.

"Yes, Winnifred, how could you be so selfish as to leave *and* leave us in the dark about what's really happening?"

The air rushed from my chest in a frustrated, disbelieving woosh before I gathered my words.

"I'm here because we all agreed it was best I left. I married Tristan—not a man I don't know, by the way, and someone you encouraged me to marry—to get the trust. You are fully aware of that and pretending like you have no idea what I'm doing in Utah is... is... just a lie. On top of that, pretending you had no idea something was going on with Jeremy is utter nonsense. You knew he needed a ton of money and helped him by selling off part of the company *and* that he used his trust money for the same. You also knew there was enough pressure on him about this that he suggested I leave town and *you all agreed*. I apologize for keeping the gravity of the situation from you, but I would also suggest that maybe your son, the person who is in this mess in the first place, should've been the one to tell you the truth."

I hadn't even realized I'd reached for Tristan's hand, but I held it now, fingers laced and clutched tight in the silence that followed my tirade.

After a moment, my mother spoke. "It's been a difficult day. We'll talk tomorrow." And she hung up.

I looked at the phone for a moment, equal parts stunned and not at all surprised that instead of responding to what I'd said, they'd simply ended the call. But why would I be stunned by this?

Wasn't this the way they'd handled every disappointment or point of friction over the years? And wasn't this one of many reasons I'd always rushed to appease them, to make sure I was doing what they wanted so they wouldn't shut down and shut me out?

I'd worked so hard to keep them happy—to keep that unending well of grief from burrowing so deep into the foundations of our family that it broke us. I'd convinced myself I could stop it, that entropy from pain and loss, by staying, by being faithful to what they wanted, by doing anything I could to be what and who they wanted.

But I couldn't reverse time. I couldn't go back and save Thomas—I couldn't patch up the hole in his heart we'd never known about until it was too late. I couldn't stop this twisted, heartbreaking reality our relationship had become, and I couldn't keep Jeremy from his mistakes.

I could only make choices that honored what I thought was right *now*. I saw with harsh clarity the mistake of trying to wring myself out for them, to push away any opportunity for myself in favor of cowing to what I *thought* they'd want. Maybe sometimes I'd been right, maybe occasionally it'd helped, but it'd also hurt. Them. Me. All of us.

As much as this crushed me, I also felt strangely relieved. Because I wouldn't keep trying for them. Now, I would try for *me*. I had reasons of my own for changing and they were worth the pain of growth.

"What can I do?" Tristan asked in that low, slightly rough voice I loved.

"I don't know. I think I'm..." The truth lay heavy in my chest, somehow both unbearable and freeing at once. "I think I'm done."

CHAPTER THIRTY-ONE

Tristan

I ran Winnie a bath and led her to it. She'd been staring into space, mind somewhere else, since she'd said she was done. There was a hollowness, a chill to her, that had me worried.

The bright lights of the bathroom and the scented soap from the tub were a stark contrast to the dim living room and the hours of waiting, and finally, the cruel conversation with her parents. I'd done my best not to react to her side of the conversation, but I didn't need to know what they'd said to know it'd crossed a line.

In all our years of communication, she'd never complained about her parents. Never said a word against them beyond wanting to help them, care for them, how she understood they were different now after they'd lost Thomas and had been mired in grief.

I suspected they'd never pushed her like they had today,

but she also hadn't ever gotten so much perspective. She'd never been away from them—her plans to go away to college canceled because Jeremy had left and she didn't want them to be all alone. Her dreams of overseas vacations forestalled until Jeremy was in a better place or wasn't so busy or they didn't need her help.

They'd kept her tethered, and now that she'd gotten free, she saw the rope.

I was glad for it, but whatever came next wouldn't be easy.

I'd poured her a glass of wine, set her book nearby, and lit a fancy scented candle Sarah Saint had given me as a housewarming gift on the edge of the tub.

"Take some time. We'll eat dinner when you're done. No rush."

She caught my hand just before I left.

"Thank you."

My heart squeezed painfully in my chest and I stepped close, hands on her shoulders. "You're going to be okay. I'm with you."

Her eyes glistened instantly and she nodded. "Thank you."

I wouldn't stop her from saying thank you now, though she didn't need to. I didn't need or want her gratitude. I simply needed her to believe what I said. She would be okay, and I wasn't going anywhere. She could count on me to ride this out, however it went.

I wanted to kiss her, maybe distract her from all of this for a while, but I didn't want to risk that being the wrong thing. I didn't know what she needed at a time like this yet, so I pressed a kiss to her cheek and pushed her hair back from her face.

"See you in a bit."

I left her to the bath and started on dinner. I didn't know if she'd have an appetite, but I wanted her to eat if she could. I hadn't made it to the store since I'd come straight here to tell her about Jeremy, so I relied on frozen meat and some tortillas I'd left in the fridge from last week. I browned the meat and seasoned it, warmed the tortillas, and smashed the last decent avocado with a squeeze of lime and some kosher salt. With cheese, sour cream, a jar of salsa, and chips, it was nothing fancy, but it would do.

Forty minutes later, she emerged in sweats and her hair pulled into a bun on her head with little wings sprouting from all around. Her face was flushed and scrubbed clean, and remarkably, she didn't appear to have spent the whole time crying. I wouldn't have blamed her, but I was heartened to see her eyes weren't quite so red-rimmed as they had been when she went in.

"Smells good," she said, wrapping her arms around my waist.

My heart pattered, mimicking Juniper's pleasure when Winnie looked at her. I hugged her to me, pressing a kiss into her hair.

"Pretty basic, but it'll get the job done." I resisted asking how she was. It would be a useless question, and what could she be beyond heartbroken?

We prepared our tacos with music playing low in the background and the occasional pop from the fireplace as accompaniment. Juniper bustled around hoping for spills, and soon, we sat at the table across from each other.

After a few bites, she wiped her hands and shook her head. "I feel like I just stepped out of the Twilight Zone. Like I've been living in an alternate universe, and that conversation just shoved me into a different dimension."

"And how is it, in this new dimension?"

She gave me a soft grin. "Disorienting, but... I don't know. Kind of freeing."

Hope and relief welled up in me, glad she felt anything beyond despair. "Freeing how?"

Her eyes searched around the room before meeting mine.

"It's like I have permission now. I know this will sound silly, but there are a lot of things I've wanted to do over the years that I've never been brave enough to because I worried if I did, things would go wrong for my family. You know I wanted to get a master's degree—I'd actually taken a few online classes before my dad's heart attack. I've been so obsessed with this idea I had to keep them safe and do whatever I could to protect them, but what good has that done? Jeremy's still a basket case who's basically destroyed his own life, and my parents are going to find out anyway."

Her hand shook as she reached for her glass and gulped down some water. After another minute, she met my eyes and the expression in her face was so full of heartbreak, it gutted me.

"Have I been a fool? I mean... I'm realizing they've been like this since after Thomas died. I thought it was good that they relied on me—I was happy to help, and mostly, I've felt it was a duty I was proud to bear. But I think today, I saw the truth for the first time and I'm..." She swallowed hard. "I'm hurt and so embarrassed."

I covered her hand where it rested on the table, hoping to offer comfort as I spoke. "You have nothing to be embarrassed about. Loving your family, sacrificing for them, is valuable. They are the ones who should be ashamed of how they treated you—how they've expected you to be their foundation when they were crumbling."

A wry look entered her gaze. "I appreciate the support,

but I know I've made choices. You've even tried to get me to see that, haven't you? That I could take a little more space for myself and it ultimately wouldn't change things for them?"

I pressed my lips together, wondering how best to explain what I'd seen.

"I have. Not because I think you're a fool, but because it has always seemed like they were taking advantage of you—whether consciously or unconsciously done. They may not have intended to saddle you with the feeling that Jeremy is the one who needs to be protected, or that you had to compensate for his lack so they wouldn't feel it so keenly, but they did. And intentions can matter, but they don't stop people from hurting us even when it wasn't their intent."

She absorbed this as she took a bite, so I resumed eating, too. After a few minutes, she touched her napkin to her lips and leaned back in her seat.

"I think you're right. I think that's what has kept me from getting angry with them at times, because there have definitely been moments where I've seen it for what it is—their seeming to need me but not admit it or whatever. I recognize they were broken about Thomas's death, and it changed who they are and how they function. And I know not everyone who loses a child is affected in the same way, but for them... it changed them in some really complex ways, and I don't think they ever got help for processing in healthy ways. And now... what you said is right. I don't think they mean to intentionally hurt me, but they do."

I gritted my teeth, hating her admission even though I'd known it. I'd always known her parents were selfish and ignorant of how their unwillingness to free Winnie had kept her tethered to them.

"So, what now?" I asked, not wanting to pressure her but wondering, because it felt like she was on a precipice.

After a long exhale, she gave me a small smile. Such a simple thing shouldn't have lit me up, but it did. The flash of her white teeth and those lovely lips curving just a touch sent a ripple of heat through me.

"Now I do what I can to support them from here until Jeremy's mess is truly cleaned up. And soon, I get honest about not wanting to continue the business and let them come to terms with that. And—" Her gaze searched mine in a way that told me she was looking for something. Everything in me hoped she'd find whatever it was. "And I'll go from there."

I could've sworn she was going to say something else and pulled it back, just like the other night, but maybe that was my hopeful heart running away from me.

Instead of prodding or begging her to tell me what she really wanted to say, I nodded and vowed I'd be patient.

"Good plan. I'll be right here with you every step of the way—just let me know what you need from me."

And eventually, I hoped she'd finally take me up on that.

CHAPTER THIRTY-TWO

Winnie

I woke with Tristan's heavy arm over my torso and his words bouncing around in my head.

Just let me know what you need from me.

Oh, the pages I could fill with responses to that.

Because more and more, I'd realized I don't *need* Tristan in the way I felt I did when I first got here. Considering the dire circumstances of actually needing him to marry me for the trust *and* keep me here so I could avoid the drama and danger in Kansas, I'd felt almost wholly reliant on him.

Innately, I hated this. Not that I didn't trust him, because clearly, I did. I never would've gotten on the plane or reached out to him in the first place with this wild plan, if I hadn't. But now that I'd been here for a while, I could see I didn't need him in a fundamental sense. The terms of the trust had been satisfied, and the money would be coming through this week—but even now, so late in this process, I'd decided I didn't want it for the family business and therefore if something happened to halt all of it, it'd be okay.

As for the danger in Kansas... I didn't plan to go back. Not now, not ever, for anything longer than a quick visit. I loved my family, but the last twenty-four hours had drilled home a lesson I'd been on the verge of learning for what felt like a decade. My family had gotten used to me being the one to take the blame, solve the problems, and bend over backward to satisfy their expectations, and that wasn't healthy for any of us.

I didn't know how everything would shake out between us, but right now, I was more glad than ever to have space. I needed to figure out how to convince Jeremy to tell the police what'd happened so he wasn't in even more danger, but other than that and a few hard conversations with my parents, I felt free, just like I'd told Tristan.

I was building a life here—I had friends and people who knew me. I loved this town and the mountains and the people here, even the tourists with their goggle tans and their ridiculously overpriced parkas. It all felt like a life I'd dreamed of, like freedom I'd assumed I'd never really have a chance with.

And that freedom made me shift from *need* to *want*.

It'd been coming a while now, but here in the quiet with another crisp wintry mountain day dawning outside and snuggled up with this man I loved and had loved for so long, I wanted more. More time with him, more options for the two of us, more from my own future that hopefully involved him.

He kept himself tucked away enough I couldn't be sure if he wanted the same, but I thought maybe he did. I hoped...

Tristan's arm tightened around me, pulling me to him

and nesting us together. His large hand spread out over my belly and sent every butterfly in existence fluttering inside me. This intimacy in sleeping next to each other had only increased my awareness of him, and frankly, my desire for much more between us.

"We slept in," he said, his voice rumbly and low and utterly delicious.

"We did." I arched my back to stretch a little, and his arm tightened around me.

My stomach dropped low.

We breathed together, on the verge of something as our chests rose and fell in time with each other. Bodies previously warm and sluggish from sleep were fully awake and alert now, and I waited...

Maybe his hand would dip under my shirt, or he'd drop a kiss to my shoulder. Maybe he'd do anything at all and I'd let him.

He squeezed my hip and rolled away, a rough exhale coming from the other side of the bed, where he'd already exited. My eyes shut and I gathered myself, reeling from the heat and connection of just... what breathing together had felt like.

Good. Grief.

I didn't know what to say, some confusing mix of thrill and disappointment and maybe a little embarrassment edging its way in until he spoke.

"I hope it's okay I did this, but if not, I'll cancel it."

I turned to look at him as he slipped a fresh T-shirt over his head. *Darn.* Just missed a glorious view. I'd only caught glimpses of him and he was utterly, mercilessly beautiful. Probably best I didn't get the full show after our little cuddle episode just now.

"What is it?"

His gaze coasted over my face and slipped down over the rest of me before jumping back to my eyes, and with a small smile, he explained. "You've got brunch with your girls in thirty minutes."

Jo wrapped her arms around me and crushed me to her.

"Are you okay? Can you tell us what's going on?"

Dove, Elise, Catherine, and Nikki sat in the back room at All Booked Up, all watching me with concern in their eyes. We were only missing Jess, who'd shipped off on assignment suddenly. I wasn't sure if it meant things had or hadn't gone her way at the meeting with the Saint Security leadership, but I hoped it meant something good for her.

I'd mentally prepared for this conversation on the drive into town, and after dropping Tristan at work, I'd given myself a little pep talk in the truck leading to this moment.

"Yes. I can tell you. But let me tell you everything before you ask questions, okay?"

They agreed, Nikki giving me an encouraging nod, which I took to mean she supported this move. I appreciated that because part of me felt so selfish for what I was about to do.

I sat down and told them about the family business struggling, the trust, asking Tristan if he'd marry me so I could access the money, the drama with Jeremy that led to me traveling out here, and the latest with Jer's hospitalization and the argument with my parents.

When I sat back, they all stared at me, wide-eyed. Even

Nikki seemed a little overwhelmed despite knowing some of the story.

"So wait... *wait.* You and Tristan are married but not *really* married?" Elise asked, voice as jam-packed full of incredulity as possible.

Oddly, it hurt to admit now, as though it wasn't actually true anymore. "Yes. We married for the sake of the trust. I only moved out here because of the way the guys after Jeremy were escalating things."

Guilt spiked in me and proved old habits die hard. But I wasn't culpable for the attack on Jeremy, nor was it my job to figure all of that out for him.

Elise shook her head slowly. "Please... and I mean this with the utmost sincerity, *please* tell me you've enjoyed the marital benefits afforded you by the great state of Utah. *Please* tell me you are not living with that absolute bonfire-hot man and not doing something about it."

I laughed, taken aback by her plea. Nikki did the same, and Jo and Catherine giggled into their hands. Dove was the only one who responded right away.

"Elise! That is none of your business. None of any of our business." She sat there primly, back straight and hands folded in her lap over the skirt of her dress, then pinned me with a look. "Even so, I do hope you've celebrated your union properly."

At this, we all cracked up, and my cheeks were flaming red. It was all in good fun and a perfect distraction from the nerves that'd nearly swallowed me whole on the way here.

"Seriously, though, how are you handling that? I mean, I assume you've seen the man?" Elise asked, the same disbelief shading her tone.

"Honestly, it's only recently become an issue." I

couldn't stop the grin, especially when the *oohs* and *ahhs* started.

Jo had been on the quiet side since she knew all of this thanks to our coffee-turned-afternoon together a week ago.

"I also want to apologize to all of you. I wasn't honest about this early on, but I didn't think I'd be staying. It didn't feel fair to tell you when I would be leaving and Tristan would be dealing with the potential fallout by himself if people found out it was all for some trust. But now... whatever happens with Tristan, with my family, I'm staying. I don't know exactly what that'll look like, but I want more Silver Ridge Romance Readers Club and coffees at Joe and... everything.

That's what it felt like—everything. The possibilities had opened up to me, and I could choose—and I had every intention of doing so.

"That's wonderful, and you don't need to apologize for not baring your soul the minute you met us. That's all so personal, and we're honored you shared with us now."

Dove smiled at me with such kindness, my heart swelled.

Jo agreed. "Exactly. We don't expect you to spill your secrets right away... but we're glad to hold them with you now."

Catherine, Nikki, and Elise echoed her sentiments, and I was nearing the point of tearing up.

"Thank you so much. It feels impossible that I'd feel so close to you and so cared for after just a few months, but... here you are."

Jo grinned. "Here we are. And here *you* are." Her face softened and brows knit. "It sounds like you're settled on staying here, but with everything going on with your brother and your parents right now, have you told them?"

Elise nodded and pointed at her. "Yes, have you told them, and more importantly, have you told Tristan? What did he say?"

My stomach dropped. As much as I dreaded telling my parents the many truths I needed to share with them, the larger looming task was Tristan. Because even though I felt sure he returned at least some of my feelings for him, I didn't know if he truly wanted to share his life with me indefinitely. He'd made space in his home, but did he want to do that forever?

There was no way to know except to ask.

CHAPTER THIRTY-THREE

Tristan

Two days later, Winnie paced the living room floor with her phone to her ear when I got home.

Since the attack, Jeremy had continued to improve, her parents had been largely out of touch, and the two of us had been... basically roommates.

No more tense moments like the first morning we'd woken up after her call with her folks.

And that wasn't something I could think about right now, especially considering how she seemed to need space, and reminiscing about being so close to her would only make me want a lack of space between us.

"I just told them the plan, and they aren't exactly happy, but they seem resigned to it. I don't know how much you still owe—"

A shocked expression took over. "*Jeremy*. How the—you know what? I don't want to know. All I need to know is that you will do the right thing with that money and get yourself out of this hole. And this is it. I am not doing anything else—I can't. I have to live my life, and honestly, you have to live yours."

She sank into the couch and gave me a look that said she was over this conversation. Then she shot to her feet again and the pacing continued.

"You know I love you. I want you safe and happy and free of all this mess."

She nodded, eyes flickering over to mine as I piddled around in the kitchen. It was late and I'd eaten at work during a late strategy session we had with a few international team members, so I knew she'd eaten, but I wanted to do something for her. After a minute, I started the kettle while she wrapped up the call. When she did, she tossed the phone away from her and slumped into the couch with a groan.

"How'd it go?"

She peeked at me with one eye. "As well as it could've, I think."

She stared up at the ceiling while I poured water over a tea bag and set it on a saucer with some shortbread cookies she liked.

"Here. Sustenance after the battle is essential." I set the small plate and teacup on the side table, then took the hand she lifted and pulled her upright.

She looked exhausted, but not in a bad way. Not drained and muted like she had when she'd first arrived in Silverton.

"My parents took the news about not wanting to infuse the business with the cash poorly until I told them I wanted to use some of it for Jeremy. Now that they realize what a deep hole he's dug, they approved of that. And they said more than once we'd 'revisit' my plan to leave the business and my offer to help them figure out how to sell... I don't think they believe me. Pretty sure they plan to talk me out of it."

She exhaled a world-weary sigh, then noticed the cup.

Eyes wide, she gave me an amazed little smile that sent my heart into my throat.

"Did you make me tea?"

I nodded, heart fairly thundering. "Thought you could use something calming."

She picked up the saucer and took a cookie in hand. "Do you drink tea?"

"No."

She lifted the cookie and dipped it in the tea, then took a bite. Her low moan of pleasure made my stomach tighten, and I forced my gaze away from the bliss on her face.

"This is perfect, thank you."

Satisfaction like I'd never known permeated my senses. How had this simple thing made her so happy and offered me so much at the same time?

Had I truly been so cut off from relationships that such a small gesture brought me joy? Or was it that I got to see *her* happy?

I already knew the answer before I finished the thought. While I'd lived alone, I hadn't isolated myself from friendships or affection in every regard. This blooming sense of rightness in my chest as I watched her sip the apple cinnamon tea came from her.

In truth, it came from finally being able to see her, touch her, do something simple for her beyond answering an email that may or may not help whatever situation she'd describe in her last correspondence.

The immediacy of communication paired with getting

to see her in color, in three dimension, and in all her human glory, was a gift.

"I'm sorry I've brought all of this to your door. I know the idea was that it'd all be sorted and I'd be out of your hair sooner than later..."

My gaze snapped to hers. "I'm not sorry. And I don't want you to be."

"It just feels like this has spiraled out of control. I knew he was in trouble, obviously. I knew Calvin was absolutely no good, but he's going to be recovering physically for months. And what I'm giving him is apparently only going to make a dent. He's... I don't know when that's all going to be resolved."

I could no longer sit here and stay detached, stay separate from her, when she was only inches from me. Setting a hand on her arm, I mentally pleaded with her to understand and believe what I said. "I have no regrets here. I am not in a rush for you to leave."

"What if—"

She tucked her lips together like she had to restrain herself from saying whatever it was she needed to say, and that just wouldn't do. Not again.

"Tell me."

Her dark eyes met mine. "What if I don't want to leave at all? Ever?"

Only years of training and practice kept me sitting calmly and not hauling her to me and kissing her until neither of us could breathe.

"Then you'd be welcome to stay."

If that wasn't an understatement, I couldn't imagine what was.

She shook her head slightly. "No, I mean like, if even after Jeremy's mess is sorted, I want to stay."

I took the tea from her and set it on the side table, then clasped her hands in mine.

"You would only need to tell me what you need from me, Winn. You can stay here in Silverton and make a life you want doing whatever you dream up. I'll help you in any way I can, and I guarantee Jo and Nikki and the others will, too, let alone everyone at Saint you've already charmed."

She smiled softly, like this idea pleased her, and I willed myself to proceed—to be bold.

"Or, if you wanted, you could also stay here with me and Juniper. Keep... doing what we've been doing. Or... some version of it."

I sounded like a stuttering fool, but the catch of her breath and the flutter of her lashes made my whole body freeze in anticipation of her response.

"You—you'd want that? To have me stay? With you?"

A low, incredulous laugh rushed out of me. "Yes. Always."

Her mouth dropped open. "Really? Like... you want..."

I gripped her hands. "I want whatever you want. Truly."

She absorbed this, her eyes flickering back and forth between mine. "What if I want you to tell me what *you* want?"

The insistence in her voice left me no choice.

"More than anything, I want you to be happy and cared for and living a life *you* choose." She squeezed my hands, demanding more. "I refuse to tell you something that will influence your choices."

Her brow furrowed. "That makes no sense. How can I make the best choice without all of the information?"

"There's also the issue of the circumstances. I don't want to sound—"

"Please don't finish that sentence if it has anything to do with me being incapable of knowing what I actually want." Fire in her eyes reinforced her words and the shake of vehemence in her voice.

"I would hate myself if you felt pressured by what I want. I couldn't stand it."

I couldn't stand it if my wanting you to stay with me ends up with you leaving.

She leveled me with her stunning gaze and gripped my hands with hers.

"I need you to trust that I know myself and can navigate this. Because I already know what I want, but I don't have any idea what you do because you refuse to tell me out of some misplaced sense of honor. I love that you want to respect me, but you're not doing that if you're not listening to me *now* and believing me *now*."

My head dropped so our foreheads pressed together, and her hands threaded into the hair at the back of my head.

"I'm sorry. I—God, I guess I'm more of a coward than I thought."

But with her so close, her cinnamon apple tea scenting the air around us, I continued, braving every fear I'd ever had. If this sent her running, I only had myself to blame, but like she said, I had to trust her. I sat back, speaking softly through a heart pounding so wildly, it was a wonder it didn't rattle the room.

"I love you, Winn, and I want you with me for as long as you'll stay."

She laughed and grinned so wide, it made a new sun rise.

"I love you, too. And I want to stay as long as you'll let me."

We beamed at each other as elation washed over me

and the atmosphere shimmered with joy and relief and... heat. Like a match lit in a darkened room that bloomed into a steady flame stoked by so many trials and experiences knitting us together, sparks and fire exploded between us.

We were kissing, grasping, gasping, needing each other in every way a couple who'd known each other for years and married each other and *loved* each other could. Loving each other in those ways, in three dimensions, in full color.

Winnie loved me, and she wanted to stay, and there had never been a luckier man on earth.

CHAPTER THIRTY-FOUR

Winnie

The early light of the morning slanted in through blinds we'd forgotten to close the night before. We'd forgotten nearly everything except each other, ignoring the outside world and reveling in the newfound truths between us.

Tristan loved me, and he'd listened to me and believed me. He'd trusted me with his love, with what he wanted, and it'd been the best gift I'd ever received.

But the man was nowhere to be seen as I rolled toward his side of the bed and found it cold. It had to be early, but Tristan had clearly left more than a few minutes ago. I refused to sink into worry and instead pulled on sweats and padded into the living room.

The sight of the man in his T-shirt and sweats with socked feet sent my heart fluttering. He turned just as I entered, and Juniper rushed me, swirling around and dancing in that way I recognized. I let her out with a pet to her head and watched Tristan sliding omelets onto plates.

"That looks delicious," I said, leaning a hip against the counter a few feet from him.

He turned, the hunger in his eyes clear enough it had nothing to do with breakfast. "You look delicious."

My cheeks flamed but I didn't break the connection between us, instead giving in to the pull of his messy hair and hazel eyes and... well, really everything.

"How'd you sleep?"

His voice soft, eyes probing, my stomach did flips.

"Very well. You? You were up early."

"Wanted to feed you. Keep your energy up." He winked.

I giggled because it was too much, and yet I couldn't deny I enjoyed this playful side of him. He'd loosened up a bit, like sharing our feelings and allowing the intimacy between us to grow had freed him.

"Thank you."

We ate omelets and talked softly about our plans for the day. He found any excuse to touch me, and I welcomed the contact, indulging in the same—a brush of our hands, wiping a fallen eyelash from his cheek, resting my knee against his and soaking in the thrill and comfort.

It was another day before I spoke to Jeremy again, though I'd checked in with him about every twelve hours. I'd had a few text exchanges with my parents as well, and I'd requested a formal meeting tomorrow. Anxious to make them understand I wasn't going to change my mind about leaving the company, I needed them to come to the table in a more official capacity than talking on the phone as family members. I hoped this approach would help.

But it was the call with Jeremy late Thursday afternoon that solidified everything for me.

"Hey, sis. You heading back this way soon?"

He sounded tired and... something. Weird, but I couldn't tell exactly how. Maybe it'd just been a bad week, which would be accurate, to say the least.

"No. I'm not planning to come back until everything with you is settled. Then I'll come out and pack up my apartment and I'll be done with Kansas."

Maybe that was a harsh way to put it, but at this point, I was ready for a new phase.

"Done? What does that mean? You're just riding off into the sunset with some guy?"

"Tristan is hardly some guy. You used to write to him, too. And it's not exactly riding off into the sunset because I have a lot to figure out still, but I am really happy here."

Recognizing this was like seeing a rainbow for the first time in years. Each instance gave me such a deep sense of gratitude, I was finding my frustration and anger over this situation with Jeremy dissipating because it'd brought me here.

Jeremy was quiet for a minute before he spoke again. "That's good. You do deserve some happiness."

"Thank you. You do, too, though. Did you get the money to Calvin?" I almost hated to ask, but there would probably always be a part of me that would worry about him digging a deeper hole instead of filling it in.

"Uh, yeah. I actually wanted to ask you..."

Dread and frustration hit.

"You have more money from the trust, right? You only gave me part, and since you're married now, you have two incomes."

My stomach clenched with a mix of disgust and hurt. "I set aside a little from the trust to give myself options."

Maybe I'd go back to grad school or do something else. Either way, that money was supposed to give us options. It'd been a gift to each of us from our long-dead grandparents, and he'd blown through his within days of turning thirty-two and gaining access.

"I can't give you any more money. I'm sorry."

He was silent, and my heart squeezed. I hated saying no, and a few months ago, this would've nearly killed me. Actually, I probably wouldn't have been able to say no to begin with, let alone a second time with his pleading.

"Seriously? You won't do this for me?"

I blinked, petting Juniper, who'd nestled next to the couch and rested her head by my leg. "Seriously. I've done everything I can, and at this point, the rest is up to you."

Juniper's eyes opened and studied me like she could tell how this conversation stressed me. I ran a hand down her smooth coat, seeking the comfort of her nearness. I'd definitely need a hug after this.

"You're comfortable leaving me to get beat up again? That's what you're saying?"

My mouth dropped open in disbelief, but I recovered thanks to the anger that zipped up my spine. "No. I'm not. But if it were up to me, you'd talk to the police. You'd take—"

"I can't go to the police, Winn, or I'll go to jail. Don't you get that?"

Fear struck me then. "Why? Why would telling them—"

"Just trust me when I say I can't do that. My only way out is to get the money. And if you have the money, and you're refusing to give it to me then... I guess we have nothing else to talk about."

Words wouldn't come. They simply wouldn't find their way out of my mouth, and if they had, I wouldn't have been able to guess what they'd be. What could I say to that?

He muttered something under his breath I didn't catch, angry and mean based on the tone, then said, "Have a nice life, Winnie. I hope you're happy with yourself."

I stared at the phone and blinked a few times, begging this to be a dream instead of reality, where my brother had just drilled home every gut-wrenching conclusion I'd been coming to these last few months.

"What did he say?"

Tristan's low voice reached me, and Juniper and I moved toward him instantly.

I recapped the conversation, resisting tears. I didn't even feel the desire to cry—more like I wanted some way to expel this emotion, to rid myself of the truth I was facing and couldn't stand.

Tristan's jaw flexed and he cupped my face.

"You are not wrong for saying no. It's not your responsibility to dig him out of this, and his choice to guilt you is a reflection of where he is now. He's in trouble and he's overwhelmed. It's not okay that he spoke to you that way, but you are not wrong. It doesn't mean you don't love him or care about him."

He was saying things I knew to be true, and yet hearing them from outside my own mind was a balm to the ragged edges in me. Eventually, I hoped I wouldn't need the reassurance, but I welcomed it now. "Thank you."

Saying no may be a small thing, but it was a monumental one, too. It would be the first of many moments to stretch me, to test this new mettle, and as Tristan gazed at me, his rough palms gentle on my face, I believed I could handle it.

The next day, the conversation with my parents went marginally better.

"I don't understand why you're doing this. You've always wanted to work in the business, and now all of a sudden, you want a different life?" My mom's voice was strung with hurt and genuine disbelief.

It helped a little that it wasn't pure criticism.

"I haven't been honest with you, and that's my fault. I'm sorry, truly. I haven't wanted to stay for a while, but it felt like the right thing."

It was too cruel to explain I'd never really wanted to work for their business, but I'd felt obligated when Jeremy didn't—that I'd taken on what they'd thought would be his role in an effort to spare them more grief over not having one of their children follow in their footsteps.

"I wish you'd told us. You could've avoided this whole mess. You could've waited to get the trust in a few years and not had to move away."

The hurt in my dad's voice gutted me.

Because the truth was, I'd made mistakes. I'd tried to protect them and take care of them, but that had resulted in a fair number of lies, and those were hurting them now. What I'd thought would help in my misguided mindset at the time was coming to call now.

"I know. I'm sorry. But I can't regret coming here. I..." I

exhaled, because this was the part I hadn't mentioned yet. "I'm going to stay here."

"In Silverton?"

"Yes. I'm making a life here."

And what I didn't explicitly say but they might've realized was, I had space from them here in order to do so. I hated the idea that if I returned, I might fold right back into the balled-up little version of myself trying to placate them and keep the peace between everyone, but how could I be sure?

This was me drawing a clear boundary—saying no to my brother, saying no to the family business, and saying yes to making my own choice to stay here.

As good as it felt, my whole chest ached with grief. I didn't want to hurt them. I wanted them to be safe and happy and fulfilled, not so worn down by the blows life had dealt them. I certainly didn't want to be another moment in their lives they needed to mourn.

"If this is what you think is best, we'll support you. I'm just sorry it's coming in such a dramatic way."

My mom's voice still held that tinge of hurt, but no devastation. Maybe it always would be a little drawn, a little sad. I was sure I'd need to work on handling their disappointment or really any negative emotions since I'd been so paralyzed by them in the past. Therapy would help, and I'd get started at my first appointment next week.

"Thank you. It's the best decision I've ever made."

Coming here to start with and staying here to end the long chapters of my life where I let fear and complacency rule me. In some ways, maybe I did have Jeremy to thank for all this since I never would've left Kanas if it'd only been about the money.

We hung up not long after they agreed to let me send

them the information I'd put together on different courses of action they could take with the farm. I didn't know which one they'd choose, but I deeply appreciated I didn't have to be the one to decide.

Later, when Tristan walked through the door looking like everything I'd ever wanted wrapped in a flannel shirt and a beard, I couldn't decide whether to laugh or cry.

"Ready to head to Craic?" he asked, dropping his bag and coming straight to me after giving Juniper some attention.

"Ready."

And I meant that with every bit of me.

Ready to move forward with my life. With him. In this town.

Ready for whatever came next.

CHAPTER THIRTY-FIVE

Tristan

We'd planned a get-together to coincide with the girls' book club—a kind of working brainstorming session. Completely voluntary, this would become a standing bonding and planning time for the company. No reports or scheduling needed, we could sit around the space we called the team room and relax.

I didn't particularly want to be here. Lately, any time I was away from Winnie, she filled my mind. That'd been true for much longer than the time she'd lived here, in truth, but at least tonight, I knew she was doing something she loved—talking about books with her friends.

And so, I sat here with my friends. We were missing Eddie, who was with Bri somewhere, and Jess, who'd taken Kenny's place on the UK assignment to help create space between her and Beast. At least there was no animosity floating around the room, waiting to rear its head.

In our EMU days, the team rooms had small bars with fridges stocked with food and drinks, chairs for relaxing, and sometimes a pool table or card table, sometimes both. On the walls and hanging from ceilings would be various items from missions completed by that team—trophies or tokens to remind the members of the team's history. The amenities largely depended on the team's leadership over the years and what they brought in, but the space was a respite, a place to circle up, and a haven for mentally straightening out after a mission.

We'd designed a larger version of a team room in the new building starting construction this spring, but for now, we'd created an iteration of it where we held our self-defense classes. At ten after seven, Bruce, Wilder, Kenny, Adam, Beast, and even the illustrious Dorian sat around sipping beers.

"We have three new people onboarding locally in the next few months. Eddie's bringing on Caleb Hale from her husband's security team this summer. I can't believe it's grown so fast." Bruce had the most pleased expression on his face.

I couldn't fault him. He'd been directly responsible for building the business while Wilder focused on nailing down local contracts and equipment.

"Proud to be in business with you all," Wilder said, holding up his bottle.

Everyone raised theirs in acknowledgment, some verbalizing their agreements, Beast grunting as usual, and Dorian staying completely quiet.

He hadn't come around in a while, so I was glad to see him here. We never knew when he'd show, but we'd all agreed he'd be invited to everything, every time. Even if he said no ten times in a row, or ignored the invitation that many times, we'd reach out an eleventh just in case. And here he was, proving the method valid.

Wilder snuck out as we began discussing some of the outfitting plans for the new building, and I couldn't blame him. His wife and child were at home, it was a Saturday night—where else would he be? But he'd promised he would come for the initial part this week, and that in the future, it was highly possible Sarah would try to spend time with friends so he wouldn't be missing out on time with her.

A few years ago, I wouldn't have imagined him saying anything of the sort, but there he went, practically skipping out to his car to get back home. Bruce was here because Nikki was at the book club, and none of the rest of us had steady partners.

Well, except me. And Winn was at book club.

There was another miracle. I didn't have to go back years to feel astounded by the changes in myself—not only externally, but internally. I wouldn't have said I had no hope of marrying or having a life with someone. On one level, I'd always wanted what my parents had. Seeing Wilder with Sarah and baby James, and these last few months seeing Bruce and Nikki… it'd made me want that kind of partnership for myself.

In my gut, even if it sounded a little wild, I'd always felt a pull toward Winnie. There was a reason beyond coincidence we'd not only connected years ago through a seemingly random assignment of her family to be my pen pals, but that we'd stayed connected. That through her brother's death and multiple challenging deployments and hardship after hardship, life milestone after milestone, we'd stayed connected.

I'd never opened myself up to anyone before, but I was learning to do it with Winnie. Slowly, and probably frustratingly for her, but I was letting her see more of me than anyone else had. She already knew me better than any other person on earth, and that was only deepening.

"Stone, how's it been?" Kenny asked the solemn man sitting nearest the door when we took a break.

Stone, aka Dorian Forrester, just nodded, his dark brows arching in as relaxed an expression as I'd seen in a while.

"You—" Doc looked down at his phone. "Sorry, I just got like three texts from Jo." He frowned down at his screen. "Was Winnie going to book club tonight?"

My senses instantly went on alert, and I pulled out my own phone to check our message history. "Yes. She drove in earlier to pick up some drinks at the market. Beast gave me a ride."

Adam was already calling Jo before I finished and I'd dialed Winnie, but no luck. Bruce had his phone to his ear before either one of us had ended our calls.

"Jo, she should've been there. Do me a favor and just go lock up, okay? You guys stay put. I'll be there in just a few minutes. Nope—everything's fine. Just precautionary. See you soon." Adam's voice was soothing and calm, betraying none of the urgency all of us felt.

Bruce swore as he hung up his call. "Our contact in Kansas got taken down with the flu. He resurfaced today and was just about to let us know that Jeremy's guy's gone missing, and so has Jeremy."

I'd already tracked her phone—we'd shared our locations early on for security purposes, and I'd never been more thankful—until it showed her at the bookstore. But if she was there, Jo would've called back. Or Nikki. They would've let us know.

"Phone says she's at the bookstore." I dialed again on speaker and it rang and rang until it hit voicemail.

Everyone's eyes shot to me for a beat, and then we were all moving, even Stone. He might be slower now after his injuries, but he wouldn't opt out on this.

Bruce yelled as we ran, "Three two-man teams. Report back on the fives. Grid search. Oak, text us what she was wearing if you've got it. Doc and Stone, you're at the bookstore."

No need for reassurances that we'd find her. No attempt at quelling the worry that everything was fine. Just action.

Because we would find her.

And she would be okay if it was the last thing I did.

CHAPTER THIRTY-SIX

Winnie

I'd thought I was scared when I first encountered Calvin. I'd thought that'd been a genuinely terrifying moment in my life—*the* most terrifying.

I wished that was still true.

I'd been feet away from All Booked Up when a hand clamped down on my shoulder and something hard poked into my back. I'd never had a gun pointed at me, let alone touching my back, but I instantly knew what it was and that I was in trouble.

None of my sessions with Tristan and Bruce or Adam or anyone had prepared me for someone holding a weapon. It'd all been for situations where someone was trying to physically attack me or restrain me. My mind blanked and I froze.

"You're going to keep walking, and if anyone has questions, you smile pretty and keep moving, or you die."

I knew the voice from the last time I'd seen him when he'd squeezed my arm so hard it'd bruised.

I hesitated for a moment because my phone was in my hand. I'd been about to text Tristan that I was heading into the store. But before I could type the second one in 911, Calvin snatched the phone and tossed it under the car parked on the street in front of the bookstore.

So I walked, mind scrambling for a way out, begging for Tristan or one of the girls to see me. One of them would know something was amiss since I hadn't gone into the shop. Maybe they were calling Tristan or the police right now.

Around the corner, a man with a face mask waited by a running car. When we approached, he yanked the door open and Calvin shoved me into the vehicle. I crawled to the other side of the car and grabbed the door handle, but before I could open it, Calvin gripped my arm and pulled *hard*.

Pain raced through my wrist, and fear locked me into place.

The other man had started driving, and Calvin fumed next to me, reaching into the front seat for something.

"That wasn't very smart, Winnie. I've got a gun and you're outnumbered, but you're going to try to get right back out of the car?" He swore violently like I disgusted him for trying to escape, then pulled a roll of duct tape out and grabbed my hands.

"What do you want? Why are you here?"

We were driving now, fast but not enough to get pulled over. Calvin wrapped the duct tape around my hands, around and around, then glared at me.

"Am I gonna need to shut you up, or can you do it on your own?"

I shook my head, praying he wouldn't cover my mouth or eyes. My heart hammered and my wrists burned where the duct tape bit into my skin.

We were on the outskirts of town, and I prayed they weren't going to take me down the canyon. Mercifully, the driver pulled into the back of a warehouse-looking building, and soon, they were hauling me out of the car.

This wasn't too far away. This was... someone could find me.

They pushed me into a seat, and the other man produced a computer.

"You're going to transfer the rest of your pretty little trust fund into my account. You're going to do it without my having to wait, or we're gonna have a problem."

His words jumbled in my head, the fear and adrenaline cranking so hard in me I could hardly take a full breath, but I told him the truth. "I can't do that on this computer. I have to have my own. I don't know my passwords."

"You stupid—"

"I swear. I don't know it. It's a different account than my usual banking, and I don't have it memorized."

He sneered and swore again, then kicked the folding chair next to me and it tumbled to the concrete floor in a noisy crash. "Where is it?"

"At my house."

And hope bloomed then. Because if I could get to the house, maybe I could alert Tristan somehow. He had security cameras and an alarm system.

In a matter of minutes, we were back in the car and heading in the direction of Tristan's. But the hope I'd be lucky enough to come back and find Tristan waiting was foolish. I knew it, even as my heart sank at the sight of the little house all dark from the outside.

In a few minutes, they'd wrangled me out of the car and fished out my keys so we could open the door.

"There's a dog in here. Please don't hurt her." I could hear Juniper on the other side of the door, anxiously anticipating someone coming in.

They burst through the door violently. I was trying to calm Juniper, who'd instantly started barking and looking for a way to lunge at the men who held me in front of them.

"It's okay, Junie. It's okay—"

The other man kicked her, and she made a horrible sound, then Calvin shoved me hard enough that I stumbled forward. A cacophony of barking and yelling ensued, but by the time I turned around, they'd managed to get Juniper out and slammed the door.

My sweet Junie still barked, and I saw her jumping up on the door, trying to see in, to get in, to help me. My heart ached for her, but I was relieved they'd gotten her outside instead of doing something more drastic.

I wouldn't forget how they'd kicked her.

"Let's get this over with and dump 'er," the other man said.

Calvin grabbed my arm and led me to the table, where I'd left my laptop. "Do it, Winnie, and this'll all be over."

"What do you need me to do?" I wasn't about to fight them.

Calvin sat across from me while the other guy paced, looking out windows. Juniper continued to bark and jump, and my heart clattered around in my chest.

"I'll give you the routing and account numbers when you get in. First, I want you to sign in and show me you've still got the money."

Through the stress of the last... however long it had

been, I only just now realized the true heartbreak of his words.

"Did Jeremy tell you?"

His smug expression answered for him, but when I started shaking my head, my mind rejecting that my brother would do such a thing, he explained.

"He might not've done it all that willingly, but you've got money and he doesn't, so what other choice does he have? In the end, what other choice do *we* have but to come here and get it?" His eyes skated over me and lingered at my chest.

I folded my arms awkwardly so I covered myself, though my hands were still taped together.

"And maybe after you've transferred the cash, we'll think about celebrating."

Dread like I'd never known coated every inch of me. "Just tell me what to do."

I signed into my account but moved slowly, knowing that once this was done, all bets were off. They had no reason to treat me decently after I'd done what they wanted. That said, maneuvering the keyboard when my hands were taped together, wrists facing each other, was slow going.

"Get it done. The longer you take, the worse this gets for you."

He was literally breathing down my neck, and I shivered with disgust.

Would anyone know I was missing yet? Tristan didn't have a clock on this wall but—yep, it was half past seven now, which meant I was a full half hour late for book club. They'd try to call me, and maybe Tristan?

Please, God, let them call Tristan.

If they told him, he wouldn't hesitate. I knew that like I knew my own name.

I must've taken too long to react, or maybe he didn't like how I'd craned my neck to see the clock on the stove. Whatever the reason, Calvin shoved my face down to the keyboard and pressed it into the keys, arching over me and whispering into my ear with a cutting snarl of a voice that sent the hairs on the back of my neck rising.

"Stop stalling. Sign in. Transfer the money. Live to tell about it. If not, I'm going to have to escalate this, and I don't particularly want you hurt when I have my fun later, but I'll do what I have to."

He forced my head down farther, enough that my cheekbone pressed painfully into the surface, until he let up and I slowly straightened, clarity overcoming the rampant fear with one thought.

My job now was to survive. To last as long as I could until Tristan got here. To go just slow enough that it ate up time and not any slower so I drew attention.

If I could do that, I might make it out of this alive.

CHAPTER THIRTY-SEVEN

Tristan

We parked at the end of the long drive, tips from pedestrians and some help from our Saint Security IT specialists helping us narrow down the direction they'd gone, and finally, my very own security system revealing they'd brought Winnie back to our house.

Our cars would be covered by the forest surrounding the house, and hopefully, Juniper would ease up on the barking, though if she did, it might alert them. The darkness provided by the early March night helped quite a bit with our ability to approach the house without being detected like we certainly would've a few hours earlier.

Four of us were moving quickly and silently spread out over the road with me at point. I'd hope to intercept Juniper and Beast would keep her calm while Kenny, Bruce, and I entered the house and got Winnie to safety. Adam and

Stone were at the bookstore, though we'd ascertained there was no safety issue there.

The police weren't far behind us, but we weren't waiting. If we were anyone other than former career-long members of the best trained hostage rescue team on the planet, we would've waited for them. But no amount of training on a police force could begin to add up to our expertise, and so we'd move now and let them come clean up. If they had issues with that methodology, they could take it up with me after Winnie was safe.

Ideally, everyone would make it out, Winnie safe and sound and the bad guys with cuffs on.

But for now, I honestly didn't care about a damn thing other than getting Winnie to safety.

I signaled and we sped up, racing at a sprint now that we'd be in view of the windows facing east. Juniper's bark shifted and she came bounding around with a snarl, until she realized who we were.

"It's okay. We're here. Stay with Beast, okay?"

I kept moving, knowing she would. She was obsessed with him, and he'd brought a leash to clip to her collar just in case.

We lined up on the right side of the door in a stacked position, me first, then Kenny, then Bruce. As the second man, Kenny was breacher and tried the door, pulling it open with force once he felt it'd been left unlocked.

And then we were moving. I was in first and instantly attacked the man standing in the kitchen, whose eyes went wide when he saw us entering as he took a giant bite of an apple. With a quick chop to his neck to cut off his airway, I swept his legs and rolled him, leaving him for Kenny to zip tie.

Bruce was already talking and holding his hands up, weapon included. "No need for that now."

"Drop your weapons or I shoot her."

Calvin Smith had his arm around Winnie, pressing his palm to her mouth so she couldn't speak, the muzzle of a handgun jammed into her temple.

Rage, and something I didn't normally feel on the job— fear—hit like a club to my face, but I funneled it all down, down, down into the depth where I locked everything up on mission and raised my hands as well, surveying Winnie.

Her eyes were wide and she was looking around, trying to see what else was going on in the room, but Calvin held her so tightly, she couldn't move her head.

"What are you doing here? You're a long way from home, right?" Bruce asked, sounding downright conversational.

"You're going to set your weapons down and turn around and walk out of here like you never saw a thing. And because you're idiots and you've taken me down a guy, I'm definitely taking her with me."

Over my dead body. And more likely, over his, though we had yet to need lethal force since leaving the military. We rarely did hostage recovery anymore, and most of our bodyguarding and security work didn't get this heavy.

In the movies, we'd have dart guns we could shoot into bad guys' necks and put them to sleep. In reality, if you shot a dart gun into someone's carotid, it'd explode and kill them in a near-instant bleed out.

So, no dart guns to be had here. But there were other options.

"Why would we do that, Calvin? What incentive are you giving us to cooperate? How about you let Winnie go and we let you go. That sounds fair to me." Bruce's tone continued to convey friendly cooperation.

"Totally fair," Kenny echoed from behind.

I didn't need to know he had his hands raised, as well. He might be a jokester and a bit immature, but he knew the stakes here, knew the rules.

In any other situation, this guy would've had a bullet between the eyes the instant we walked in the door, but again, we weren't law enforcement and we weren't dealing with terrorists. He was threatening Winnie's life, so in theory, we could take him out and be justified, but if we could get out of this without shooting a man in my living room, a place I desperately hoped to spend a great deal more time with the woman he was threatening, that'd be ideal.

Calvin shifted, adjusting his grip on Winnie, and then he yelped out a curse and dropped his hand just long enough.

"You bit me!" he yelled, pawing at Winnie to get a grip on her again despite his now bleeding hand.

She dove away from him, and while his attention was on her, I pulled the gun from his hand and passed it off to Bruce, who switched on the weapon's safety instantly while I wrenched on Calvin's shoulder hard enough to cause him pain. Eh, maybe a dislocation. Certainly enough to change his trajectory and lay him out after dodging one wild attempt at a punch.

And then she was in my arms, and relief came rushing through right as the police yelled into the room from the entrance to alert us they'd arrived. I caught Bruce's eye and he nodded—he'd take care of it. They were welcome to come in now, and we'd all holstered our weapons.

Calvin was screaming something about lawyers and

payback, but I blocked it all out and cupped Winnie's face, which already had a bruise on her left cheek.

"Are you okay?"

"I'm... I think so? I'm so glad you came." She gripped my wrist, her eyes welling with tears of relief.

"I will always come for you. Always."

She leaned up on her toes and pressed a kiss to my mouth. Gratitude for her, that she was safe, and for my team, rushed to every extremity.

"I love you, Tristan. I need you to know that. I really, really love you."

Relief gusted out of me even as I wondered at her urgency. "I know. I know that. I love you, too, Winn."

"Okay, good. I know we've said it, I just... I didn't really think I'd die, but I did have this thought like, what if I'd stayed in Kansas? What if I'd cowed to Jeremy and even Calvin and just... given up? Stayed there and never gotten the perspective of being here? And what if I'd never gotten to be with you? To see what could be between us? It was an awful thought."

Her eyes were so troubled by the memory of those thoughts, I pulled her close and held her.

"It's too late now. We already know how good we are together. There's no going back."

"Promise?" she asked, so sweet and hopeful.

"I promise."

CHAPTER THIRTY-EIGHT

Winnie

Four women burst through the door an hour and a half after the madness had cleared out of the house.

"Okay, honey, if we didn't already know you need a good therapist, I think abduction officially qualifies you," Elise said, opening her arms to me.

I laughed, grateful for the desire to laugh instead of cry or simply stay silent, let alone a friend so honest and funny. "Don't worry. I already have an appointment with Dr. Corrigan next week. This will definitely be top of the list to discuss."

Oddly, I didn't feel traumatized by what'd happened. I felt... numb about it. The strongest emotions coursing through me right now were love and certainty about Tristan, and a deep sense of betrayal for Jeremy.

"How are you, though? Did they hurt you?"

Dove's hand was soft on my arm, but firm enough to tell

me she was in nurse mode as she looked at my eyes, noted the abrasion on my cheek, and took in the rest of me.

"I'm okay. Bruised cheek and exhausted from adrenaline overload, but he didn't really have a chance."

I swallowed, that thought being one that might end up plaguing me. Toward the end, before the guys came for me, I could tell he'd decided he wasn't going to just get the money and go. He wanted to punish Jeremy, or maybe me, or maybe he was just a sick jerk, but he'd planned on more.

I'd said thank you to Bruce, Kenny, and Beast, who'd taken Juniper to the emergency vet once the police had hauled Calvin and his goon out of the house. Apparently, Beast had disabled the vehicle while minding Junie and had also been positioned to intercept anyone exiting the house until the police came and everything was determined to be resolved.

A few police had lingered, taking my statement because I'd said I wanted to get it over with, and Tristan's, and then Bruce, Kenny, and Beast had all agreed to head to the station to complete theirs. It seemed the local vet was a friend, and Junie had already been seen and brought back by the time my friends arrived. My sweet dog would be sore and clingy, but didn't have any lasting damage physically.

Adam lingered by the front door, but I went to him and hugged him. "Thank you."

"I wasn't even here."

"But you were at the bookstore. You were protecting my friends. Thank you."

"So was the other one," Dove said, some kind of... something in her tone. "The quiet one."

I blinked, trying to think of who that would be.

Adam filled in the blank. "Stone—Dorian. He was there, too. He left a little while ago."

The only thing I knew about Dorian was that he kept to himself and didn't do crowds well. It made sense he wouldn't have come here. A part of me still felt amazed that Elise, Dove, Catherine, and Jo had come at all, but I'd also started accepting this was what community was. This—showing up—was it. Nikki had actually already come and gone, having been the most aware of what was happening thanks to Bruce's updates. I completely understood her need to be with Bruce. He'd never been in danger, not really, but even the possibility of it would have me wanting time alone with my person.

I wanted that with Tristan, because I had been in danger, and so had he. It would take time before I could shake off the feeling of Calvin's hands on me or the worry over Tristan getting hurt coming after me.

"I'm just glad they got to you and that you weren't hurt too badly. I can't believe this happened," Jo said, hugging me to her.

"It feels like a Josie Wade novel, though I'm guessing everyone was fully clothed?" Elise asked, eyes jumping from Tristan to Adam, who stood talking in low tones in the kitchen.

I chuckled. "All of them were fully clothed, if you can imagine."

Dove giggled and Elise muttered something about what a shame that was.

Jo and Catherine laughed as well, and all of us found ourselves watching the men.

"I heard Tristan was quite heroic."

My stomach flipped when I caught his eye across the room.

"That he was. They all were, really. Bruce was all charming and conversational, Kenny seemed totally at ease, and Tristan... he was focused. Steady. And in what felt like seconds, he'd taken the gun and Calvin was on the ground. It kind of drilled home the kinds of things they must've done in the Army to be that calm in this situation."

All of our attention shifted to the men still talking, who must've sensed our gazes and looked over.

"Everyone okay?" Adam asked, ever the doctor ready to assist.

"All good, thanks, Adam."

He and Tristan turned back to their discussion and Elise fanned herself.

"Every single Saint man is just... too much. How did we end up with them all in our little town?"

Dove sighed. "I'm not mad about it, even if it's a look but don't touch situation."

All eyes turned to her, but Jo spoke first. "And who would you be looking at but not touching?"

Dove's lashes fluttered and her eyes went wide. "Oh, me? I just mean, like, you know, Bruce is taken, Wilder's taken, Tristan's taken. Adam's such a nice guy, and Kenny's a wild flirt, and that Beast isn't really a social type, and Stone..." She swallowed convulsively. "He doesn't seem to like people very much. So we just admire them from afar."

"Dorian did seem pretty much nonverbal, but I felt better having him there, so it wasn't just Adam against however many possible bad guys." Jo folded her arms close against her chest. "We were so worried about you."

"Thank you. And thank you for texting Tristan. I'm sorry I scared you guys."

Catherine shook her head, and the others intoned their agreement as she said, "It's not like that was your plan. If you'd had a choice, I bet you wouldn't have gone with that guy."

I loosed a laugh, the tightness in my chest still easing by degrees. "Very much true."

They all gave me hugs and Adam did the same before he walked them out, leaving just me, Juniper, and Tristan alone for the first time since earlier tonight, before so much had happened.

We'd hugged and held each other, yes, but we hadn't been alone, between other Saint Security personnel, the police, and friends checking in. The quiet that settled around us now felt like a long-awaited relief.

"You okay?" Tristan said, sliding an arm around my shoulders and pressing a kiss to my temple.

"I think so. I'm not even sure what to think except it feels like a combination of relief and exhaustion and disappointment." My composure wobbled for the hundredth time tonight, but I held the tears at bay, thankfully. "I'm so angry with him."

Tristan sighed, knowing exactly who I was talking about. "I am, too. I think you have every right to be."

"I tried to help him. I even went against my better judgment and didn't call the police because he begged me not to, and now this happened *and* he's going to jail. I mean, they're not going to let him go, right?"

I turned to look at his face, finding him watching me intently.

"If he gets assigned a decent lawyer, maybe he can make a deal to testify against Calvin in exchange for a decreased sentence, but he's implicated in some bad stuff."

He didn't need to rehash all of the charges Bruce had listed hours ago when his contact had called with an update. Not only had Calvin and his guy gotten arrested here, but the Silverton police had contacted the Wichita police and given them several other names Calvin had apparently listed, including Jeremy's.

And whether Jer had done the things Calvin claimed he had or not, I didn't know any more. Five years ago, if someone had asked me, I would've told them it was impossible he'd get into so much trouble. But the years hadn't been kind to my brother, and more and more, I was feeling the reality that my choices had only enabled his wayward wanderings.

"I feel so foolish for having protected him for so long, and after all of that, my parents are having to learn about it in an arguably far worse way." I sighed out the grief and frustration, wondering if I'd ever be able to forgive myself.

Tristan pulled my chin toward him. "You did what you thought was right. You'll learn from this—you already have. You've been honest with them about your own needs and plans, and that's progress. Isn't it?"

I nodded. "Yes. It is. I hope they can forgive me." I hadn't spoken with them yet.

My phone buzzed and I glanced at it, then held it up for him to see the *Mom Calling* flashing across the screen.

"Speaking of, guess I should face the music here." He kissed my forehead, and I answered the call. "Hey, Mom. I—"

"Winnie, you need to get home. Your father's in the hospital."

Four months ago

To: Winniechickendinny
From: Tristan Donnelly

Winnie,
Please call me.
Tristan

Tristan

She refused to let me go with her.

Within hours of her mother's call alerting us to her father's condition, Winnie was on a flight out of Salt Lake City to Wichita. Julian Grenier had offered his private plane, but his crew was on rest and the commercial flight got her in sooner than his plane could've.

She'd been quiet. So, so quiet. Like a flashback to those first hours here. She'd been scared and upset, and though I hated it, feeling guilty. She had to know her father's condition wasn't her fault, but when I tried to say it, she wouldn't hear it. She begged me not to try to reassure her, and I could read between those lines.

She felt deeply. Even through email, I knew this about her, and now I'd gotten to witness it, I wanted to spend my life giving her reasons to feel more joy and happiness and peace. I'd thought we were nearing the end of the stress and worry and guilt and shame, but everything turned on a knife's edge yesterday, and here we were.

Separated by a thousand miles again, and it felt harder now. Far worse than before. Because now I knew what it was like to be near her, and being apart chafed. It was wrong.

We'd been moving ahead together, or so we'd planned before the events of the last twenty-four hours had happened. I believed we would find a way to do that still, and yet this distance between us felt heavy and worrisome.

I cared about her father, and I hoped he'd pull through, even though I felt he had a lot to apologize to his daughter for. I had to honor the way Winnie showed up for the people she loved, and no part of her hesitated to do whatever she could to get to Kansas and be by her father's side.

What I couldn't abide was how any part of that came from a motivation out of guilt or obligation. She'd embraced her own choices and desires these last few months, and she was so proud of herself, I prayed to God she wouldn't allow her kidnapping, then her brother's arrest, and now her father's hospitalization to pull her back into a life of placing herself last.

It was after ten o'clock when she called me.

"Hey. Sorry it's so late."

"It's fine. How are you?" I sounded eager enough that Junie perked up and trotted over to check on me where I sat in our bed.

Our bed. It would always be our bed now, wouldn't it? Would I ever sleep alone here without missing her?

Never.

"I'm okay."

Her words knifed through me, her voice small and exhausted. "You'll be okay, Winn."

"They caught it in time again. It's just going to be another recovery. It's..." She sniffled, and my heart squeezed, the knowledge she was crying and alone at her apartment threatening to gut me. "It's going to be a long recovery."

My stomach dropped and dread rushed in. "I'm sorry. I know that's hard for all of you to hear, especially your dad."

"Yeah." Her voice sounded shaky and she was likely still crying.

I yanked a hand through my hair. "I can get a flight out tomorrow. Come take care of you so you can take care of them."

She was so quiet, I glanced at the phone to see the call timer ticking away. She hadn't hung up. Did she need that long to consider the offer?

"Thank you, but I think I need to just... be here."

By myself.

She didn't say the words, but I could hear them in the silence between us.

Without you.

My protective instincts and the love I had for her—the longstanding love of a friend and the newfound love of a lover—roared in me with a need to go to her. I could surprise her, force her to let me cook for her and do her laundry and whatever else anyone needed until things were okay again.

But wasn't that another version of what I'd said all along I didn't want to do? She was choosing to handle this her way, and though everything in me disagreed with her methods, I had to respect it. Didn't I?

Wait, did I?

Yes, idiot, you do.

Even in crisis, after everything, I had to prove I could

trust her to know her own mind. She needed me to trust that, as painful as it was right now.

"Okay, Winn. Whatever you need." I hesitated, wondering if even this was too much, but in the end, my heart pushed the words out my mouth before I could stop myself. "I love you."

It pounded inside me, rattling my whole body. If I had neighbors nearby, they might come knocking, wondering what that racket was, but it was only this heart of mine trying to beat out of my rib cage, trying to be nearer to this woman who owned it.

"I love you, too."

Quiet, but clear, her words soothed the wild thing in my chest in a way I hadn't realized I so desperately needed until the pounding, drumming pace steadied, and I shut my eyes. "Get some sleep, Winn. Keep me posted when you can, but take care of yourself."

We hung up a minute later and I sighed, my hand finding Junie's warm head nudged next to my hip on the bed, eyes watching me dolefully like she could feel my heartache.

"She'll be okay, Junie. And we will, too."

She would.

We would.

We'd be back together again when she was ready. And I'd be waiting.

CHAPTER FORTY

Winnie

Seventeen days.

I hadn't seen Tristan in seventeen days. My dad's heart attack had been relatively minor but still enough to send all of us reeling. Paired with Jeremy's incarceration, it felt like a gaping chasm separated me from the life I'd gotten so excited about in Silverton.

What I'd feared hadn't happened, though. I'd worried I'd step back into the state of Kansas and every bit of progress I'd made would evaporate into the flatlander air. I'd feared, especially with the guilt that'd hammered me during my flight and on the way to the hospital, that I'd fold up my plans and hopes and I'd surrender to the life I felt obligated to lead for my family's sake.

And while it'd been painful, I could happily say that hadn't happened.

I'd met with the therapist over video call twice now. We

were digging into challenging subject matter, but she was helping to reinforce all the reasons I'd left. And she'd already helped me wade through some of the guilt and shame I felt for having bent myself so far out of shape in my attempt to keep the peace.

"You know, you don't have to stay here."

My mom's words cut through my thoughts. I'd spaced out, gazing out the window in front of the sink, where I stood scrubbing a stubborn casserole dish one of their neighbors had brought by a few days ago. Food was in no short supply here, particularly of the casserole persuasion.

"I'm here to help."

I was working on keeping my responses simple. My therapist had helped me see how I'd gotten into a pattern with my parents—one where I told them what they wanted to hear, not necessarily what was true. Keeping my responses simple and factual was one small tool I was using to help retrain myself.

My mom huffed. "You've been very helpful, Winnie. But you've been here for weeks, and your father is recovering well. He didn't even need surgery this time, and they've got his medications figured out."

I rinsed the glass dish and set it in the drying rack while I worked to find the words that would explain why I was still here. She'd been asking me every day when I'd be leaving. I tried not to let it sting or make me feel even more guilty.

My mom's long sigh made me turn and face her fully, temporarily abandoning the last few items in the sink.

"I don't know how to say this except to just say it." Her voice shook a little, and she clasped her hands together.

"Okay."

My heart climbed into my throat and I braced. We'd

had some terribly frank conversations the last couple of weeks, and it always took time to recover and parse out what I felt and how to move forward. It'd been exhausting, but admittedly, healing.

That said, I was tired from a long day, and I wasn't sure how well I could take her arrows if she shot them tonight.

"I'm sorry." Her voice wobbled and she firmed her lips, her brows knitted in a pained line. "I'm sorry you felt like you had to move away in order to have a life—that we made you feel like you had to lie to us."

My heart pinched. "I'm sorry I didn't just tell you everything going on with Jer—"

Her hand waving off my words stopped me, and she continued. "I don't mean that. I'm not trying to guilt you. I am genuinely sorry your father and I became so comfortable with how things were... with you trying to make up for your brother's missteps."

Missteps was a mild way of putting it, but I nodded, appreciating her words more than she would ever know. "Thank you for saying that."

"It's not enough, I know. *We* know. And as much as it pains me to think of you all the way in Utah with that man..."

"Tristan is a good man, Mom. He's the *best* man." There was no other way to say it.

Her expression softened. "I hope so. I'd like to believe you wouldn't choose to be with someone who wasn't wonderful, but I worry we drove you away..."

I took her hands, holding them firmly with mine.

"In the end, I'm grateful for the push to leave. It's been hard, but essential. I know myself better, and though I wish Jeremy wasn't..." I was being more direct these days, but I still couldn't really stand to say *in jail*. She knew the truth, as did I. "I wish it hadn't happened that way for him, but I'm grateful to have ended up with Tristan. If I could go back, I would only want to undo the hurt between you, me, and Dad. I wouldn't change being with him."

Her expression morphed into one so genuinely happy, it was almost like seeing a different person—maybe the version of her before so much grief had hounded our family over the last decade.

"I'm so glad. And I hope maybe, once your dad is a bit farther out from all of this, maybe we can come visit you. Get to know him a little. See what your life is like there."

I swallowed down the welling emotions. "I'd love that. I know he would, too."

Or, I hoped.

In truth, I'd held him at a distance these last two weeks —I was polite and informative about the facts, but I couldn't offer more. I'd felt so overwhelmed with confronting what was happening with my family, I'd kept our connection minimal. I'd worried that if I let myself lean on him, I wouldn't be doing what I needed to do for myself. I would fold myself up again, but for his sake. I wanted to talk to him, but I needed the time with my own thoughts in this place I planned to leave and didn't really imagine I'd come back to except to visit.

"I think it's time to look at flights," my mom said, squeezing my hands and letting them drop.

My pulse picked up in recognition of that truth.

I'd helped my family, and now it was time to go back to Silverton—back to my husband and to the life I'd only just started really embracing.

It was time to go home.

CHAPTER FORTY-ONE

Tristan

Juniper watched me pace the living room and around the kitchen island for the hundredth time.

"I know. I should sit down. Or go for a run. Or do literally anything other than drive you crazy with my nervous energy, right?"

I crossed to her and took a knee by her bed, drawing comfort from her yet again. I'd gotten many Junie hugs in the last few weeks, and now with Winnie due home any minute, I could hardly handle the anxious buzz in me.

So much for being Oak. I was more like an acorn with its little hat popping off.

Or whatever that little thing attached to the branch is called—all this just pointed to the fact I wanted Winnie back and she was on her way and she hadn't let me pick her up and I wasn't sure why.

We'd barely talked, and when we did, I could tell she

was exhausted, and I didn't want her spending her emotional energy on me. I would have her back as soon as she could get back. That kept me going. She'd apologized for not having more to give, and I'd promised her I understood. I did. We sent text messages and a few exchanged selfies for proof of life. Not nearly enough contact, but I would never have enough of Winnie.

I'd never thought of myself as an emotionally needy person. If anything, I'd become used to a lack of that kind of connection. Of course my friends talked to me and checked in with me, but it was all within the realm of the routine—at work, on Friday nights at Craic, on the weekend for whatever it was we had going on.

But this? This desperation to know how she was doing and feeling and what she needed and whether she was taking care of herself? I'd never felt less calm or steady than I had in the last two weeks.

I was trying to give her space. I didn't fully understand the distance between us, but I also knew it wasn't a punishment or game. That wasn't who Winnie was, and it wasn't who we were. So I resisted the pull toward worry, toward the fear that nipped at my mind as I drifted off in my bereft bed alone, and I waited for her. I didn't want her emptying herself out and then trying to still pour into me. I didn't need that, even if deep down, I was yearning for any piece of her I could get.

But she'd texted each day—a simple good morning and good night. She wouldn't have continued this if she planned to stay in Kansas.

More than that, she wouldn't have texted yesterday to say, "I'll be home tomorrow afternoon."

Home.

I had never wanted something more than I wanted for

her to feel at home here, to feel loved and cared for and like she belonged here, with me. And if she was calling this home, if her return to Silverton was her returning to a place she felt was home...

I'd never thought of myself as a dreamer, but maybe I'd been dreaming of this all along. Maybe loss didn't follow in my wake, after all. Maybe all these hopes I'd only recently dared acknowledge weren't those of a fool.

Juniper jerked in a hop, pulling out of my arms and bolting for the front door. That canine hearing had detected the very thing I'd been waiting for all morning—or in truth, for weeks.

Voices outside sent my heart into my throat, a jumble of feeling and anticipation clogging up everything in me beyond the stumbling need to get to the door and set eyes on her. She hadn't reached the door yet, so I flung it open and Junie went barreling out to find our missing piece.

And there she was, reaching for a suitcase while Jake, one of the drivers who provided rideshare service seasonally, unloaded a second one. She'd only left with one small case.

Every bit of me wanted to run to her like Juniper, who was now swirling around and Winnie was laughing and talking to her as she bucked but didn't put her paws on Winnie, because she was just that good. The best girl.

"Thanks, Jake. Have a great day," Winnie said as he slipped back into the driver's-side door, and then she finally looked my way.

"Hi."

It was almost all breath, but I heard it, even with the sound of Jake's car crunching over gravel in the driveway, even over Juniper's wound-up loud breathing, and even through the thundering of my own heart.

"Hi. Welcome home." I stepped forward, tentative but ready, and held my arms open just a touch.

A smile burst over her face, and she dropped the bag in her hand and sprinted across the space between us, shutting it down forever and launching herself into my arms. I caught her up, held her close, and pressed my face into her neck, inhaling the sweet scent of her and knowing... knowing that as much as I'd always longed for a place of my own, this is what I'd wanted.

A person. A family. Someone who embodied the very idea of home because she carried with her my heart and brought along so much goodness and peace and joy.

It hadn't ever been about loss. It had been about belonging again. And I had never belonged to anyone like I did Winnie.

"I missed you," I said, my voice rough with emotion.

"I missed you, too. So much. So, so much."

Tears in her voice clawed at me, and I pulled back.

"Are you okay? That's a dumb question, but... is everything okay?"

I had tried not to worry, and the Saint Security team had done their level best to keep me busy and distracted so I didn't go out of my mind with thoughts of her, but that only went so far.

"I am. I'm sorry I wasn't good at keeping you in the loop. I was trying to focus on making choices for the right reasons... I just needed to work through some things."

Her eyes held so much love and affection, there was no time to doubt she might end all of this.

Months ago, I would've assumed we wouldn't last—couldn't last. That this happiness was doomed and that she'd never choose me over her family. I'd had the thought more than once early on—that when it came down to it, she'd choose them.

But even before she'd left to take care of her dad, I'd felt in my gut we had something that would stand up to the test.

"You don't have to apologize. I just wish I could've done more for you." I tucked some hair behind her ear, savoring the pleasure of such a simple action.

"You were amazing. You didn't shut me out, but you gave me space. You did what I asked, even though I know it was difficult. You trusted me. That let me process everything I worked on in therapy, and I had some good conversations with my mom and dad."

"That's great. I'm so proud of you—that can't have been easy." She was amazing, this woman.

She grinned, a beaming smile that filled every corner of my chest. "Thank you. It sucked, honestly, but it also feels really good."

We laughed lightly together. "I bet it does. And so..."

She swallowed and reached up to run a hand through my hair, sliding her fingernails along my scalp. I only barely held in a groan.

"And so they want to come visit sometime and get to know you. I'll have to go back here and there but..." She cleared her throat, and her earnest gaze held mine. "But I'm home. For good."

A second later, we sealed the moment with a long-awaited kiss. There was no way to tell her how glad I was for this news, but I would show her with every press of my lips now and for the rest of our lives.

But first...

I pulled back and cupped her cheeks, leaving one more soft kiss on her perfect mouth. She smiled at me, but a confused expression took over as I dropped to one knee.

"Juniper, sit."

Junie sat next to me, her happy pant the soundtrack to this moment. I pulled out the ring and held it up, taking one of Winnie's hands in mine.

"This ring—"

We both broke off in a laugh when Junie lifted her paw for Winnie to take, so now I held one of her hands, and she held Junie's paw in her free one.

"You were saying?" Winnie said, pure joy radiating off her as she looked down at me and Juniper.

"This ring was my mother's. She wore it for the twenty-two years she and my dad were married. Will you marry me and wear *this* ring and be my wife for the rest of our lives?"

Tears slipped down her face, but she was still smiling. "Aren't we already married?"

I laughed because she was chuckling.

"Yes, we are. But I want to do it again. In front of our friends and family. I want everyone to know you chose me because you wanted to. That we wanted this for our own reasons, because we love each other and we want to grow that love for the rest of our days."

She sobered then, releasing Junie's paw and urging me to my feet.

"I have never wanted anything more."

CHAPTER FORTY-TWO

Winnie

Tristan slipped the ring on my finger, and we were kissing again, the dream of a life with this man sealed in our embrace.

Juniper's whine finally broke through the elation-fueled haze we'd been adoring each other in, and I dropped to a knee to give her a hug. "I know, you've been so patient! I'm so happy to see you, sweet girl."

I crooned at this angel dog while Tristan hauled my bags inside, somehow wrangling them all at once.

"I hope you don't mind that I brought more of my stuff," I said, not actually doubting but realizing just how much we hadn't talked about.

He understood, though. I could tell he did, even though it'd been hard. Juniper and I followed him inside and shut the door. The house looked largely the same—cozy and spotless, lived in and comfortable.

Tristan emerged from down the hallway empty-handed. "I'm glad you brought more. I moved my clothes back into half the closet in our bedroom, but—"

His words cut off when he saw my grin.

"What? What's that smile for, not that I'm not happy to see it." He ran his thumb over the curve of my cheek.

"Our bedroom. It's kind of surreal."

He stepped closer, crowding into my space like he couldn't help himself. "If it's too much too soon, say the word, but I figured there was no point in delaying getting settled together this time."

Wrapping my arms around his shoulders, I rose on my toes and kissed him. "We're married and we just also got engaged. I'm not sure what else we'd need to make it official."

His smile lit up his eyes, and he stole another kiss. "Then let's get your stuff put away, and you can tell me everything you want to catch me up. And after that, I'll give you a tour of your new house."

"My new house? You do remember I lived here for a few months before I left, right?"

He linked our fingers and pulled me with him to the couch.

"I most certainly do." Before he sat, he leaned in and whispered in my ear. "I'm just trying to find an excuse to get you to that bedroom I mentioned."

I chuckled, a thrill of anticipation racing through me, but then I straightened my face and said with as much gravity as I could muster, "Well, let me tell you, Tristan... I'm a sure thing."

He laughed and hugged me to him, the memory of his line on our first official date linking the past moment to our present and calming the rampant need for each other a touch.

When we settled on the couch, I told him everything. Every painful detail and conversation I hadn't shared over the last few weeks, I recounted as faithfully as I could remember now. The ever-present ache that'd taken up residence in my chest while I'd been away had eased the moment I saw him, but now as I rehashed the conversations with my parents and the updates from Jeremy's lawyer, I didn't feel so anxious.

"It sounds like you accomplished a lot—not only in the talks with your parents but in finding a new farm manager and interested buyer."

He squeezed my hand, the curve of his lips filling me with a giddy feeling I couldn't quite get a handle on.

"I did. I don't know when they'll end up releasing Jer, if at all, or when they'll do a trial, but I'll need to go back for that."

The judge had refused to release him on bail initially since he was deemed a flight risk based on their assessment, and his lawyer seemed to think serving time before the trial might allow him to plead out on time served and information on Calvin.

While Jeremy claimed to have no knowledge of Calvin's entanglement with a drug ring, Calvin had provided enough evidence to call Jeremy's statements into question. It'd been heartbreaking, but at least the truth was out there now. And Calvin was going away for a nice long time, so that was progress, too.

"I'll go with you. If you want."

I sat up and turned to face him. We'd been snuggled together, my back to his chest, but this merited face-to-face focus.

"I do. I already know I do. And I hope you won't doubt that because of how I left this last time."

He ducked his head and pressed his forehead to mine. "I believe you, and I won't doubt. You can always tell me what you need and I'll give it to you."

My heart glowed with the fire and pleasure of his words, and the knowledge we were going to have many more nights like this. More time together, just being next to each other, talking about big and small things, Juniper's snores nearby.

"Right now, all I need is you," I said, inching closer.

His eyes lit with anticipation and love. "Perfect. Just so happens I need you, too."

EPILOGUE

Four months later...
Tristan

I paced around my living room, staunchly avoiding any eye contact with the other restless men in the room.

"You're not actually worried she's going to bail, are you?" Kenny asked, arms crossed and leaning casually as he pleased against my kitchen counter.

Beast grumbled at him in what I assumed was annoyance, giving perfect voice to my own thoughts.

"What he said."

Kenny shook his head. "That woman loves you. I'm also fairly certain I can hear her in your bedroom. So I'm feeling confident for you." He patted my shoulder, then sort of jostled me.

I exhaled a sharp gust, frustration and nerves expelled. "Thanks, man. I'm just ready to do this. It feels like I've been waiting forever."

Kenny's grin stretched wide. "That is so adorable and also completely stupid since you've been married for six months already."

My unamused glare didn't appear to penetrate his thick skull, but thankfully, Adam came to the rescue.

"Your unending faith in Oak is noted, as is your confidence in Winnie, but right now, let's let the man feel his feelings without being harassed about it, yeah?" Adam took Kenny by the shoulders and steered him toward the door. "Why don't you go see if Bruce and West got everyone seated?"

I tipped my chin to Adam as he guided Kenny away. Maybe I shouldn't have been so anxious, but there was no denying it. I wanted to see Winnie and marry her. For real this time. With all the love between us out on the table, even stronger and steadier than it ever had been.

"I haven't seen her in almost two days," I grumbled, as though it explained my antsy behavior.

Beast looked at his watch and eyed me, right as Bruce came through the door.

"We got our cue, gentlemen." Bruce turned to me and held me by the shoulders. "I'm so happy for you and so glad to stand with you today."

We hugged, and then one by one, these men who'd become brothers wrought from blood and sweat and tears came and did the same. Kenny, then Beast, then Adam, then Dorian, then Wilder popped in, and Cookie, and West, who'd made it in late last night and would leave again tonight.

Friends who felt more and more like family filled the wooden chairs set in the yard. And Winnie's parents were there, too, supporting her—us—with their presence.

"Thank you all for being here. And for being with me through all of it."

My service. My growth. The process of becoming a man over the last few decades and for those local, for the ride that had been the last year of moving here to Silverton and establishing a home and then finding the love of my life.

"Honor's ours," Adam said, all of us standing in a small circle, the moment heightened with emotion.

"Alright, boys, break it up. It's time for the first look, and then we're getting this show on the road." Jess gestured for us to move as the bridesmaids came down the hallway.

My pulse spiked. Just another few minutes and I'd see her. She was right there. *Right there.*

"You ladies look gorgeous, may I just say?"

Kenny, of course.

"Why, thank you, Kenny," Elise Cordero said, raising a flirty brow at him.

"Oh, you are welcome, milady." He held out his arm, and they exited the house. They were walking together, and though we'd ribbed him about how much he seemed to like her, he broke the news that she was not on the market.

Cookie followed them out, returning to his usher duties for any latecomers.

"Ready?" Jo asked Adam, then flashed a smile at me. "Good luck, though you won't need it."

I nodded, accepting that. I didn't need luck at this point. I only needed Winnie.

"Yes." Adam's throat bobbed, his eyes sliding over Jo and then bouncing away. "Let's do it."

Arm in arm, they left. Nikki and Bruce had already come together and slipped out, as had Wilder, who would escort Jess.

"Come on, Saint Daddy, let's go." Jess winked at me as Wilder coughed.

"You really shouldn't call me that, Pop," Wilder said.

"Ah, but you're the daddy of Saint Security *and* daddy to the best baby on earth." And then she looked over her shoulder at Dove and widened her eyes and mouthed, "And *Daddy.*"

Wilder laughed loudly and was saying something about writing her up as they left.

Beast watched them go, his face no more readable than usual, and he nodded to Catherine, who nervously approached him.

"Having a nice day?" she asked, her voice soft and sweet.

I was surprised they'd partnered Beast and Catherine, but apparently, Winnie had made certain she was comfortable. Catherine had agreed to meet Beast and do the rehearsal, and if she felt too awkward with the giant grumbler, she'd tell Winn. I guessed Beast must've been on his best behavior and he'd reportedly said something—with complete sentences, so the word has it—that put Catherine at ease.

"Yes, and you?" Beast said, exiting with Catherine.

I wished Kenny or Adam or even Bruce were here so I could elbow them and we could share amazed glances. But good for him—making an effort to be more civil to people instead of treating everyone like they were on his naughty list.

"I'm West. Sorry I wasn't able to be at the rehearsal," Ryan West said, his debonair smile instantly charming Dove, the only remaining bridesmaid, who returned his smile with a grin of her own.

"Dove Jensen. Glad you made it." She took West's proffered arm and they left.

Dorian had already made himself scarce. He'd agreed to come, but I'd made clear that I'd love for him to stand up with me if he wanted, but that I wouldn't mind if he preferred not to. His preference, as predicted, had been to stand in the back.

West looked back and raised his brows at me—one small flash to calm my nerves.

Then the bedroom door opened.

And my heart beat in my throat, fingers tingling, because there she was in the dim hallway, and then closer, and *she's the most beautiful thing I've ever seen.*

I'd had the thought a thousand times by now, but here, in her long white dress and her hair pulled away from her face and cascading down her back, her shoulders and neck bare save a small necklace her mother had given her to wear, she was an absolute vision.

"Hey, there, husband," she said, a nervous smile on her lovely face.

Her words unstuck me and I rushed to her. "You're so beautiful, Winn. So beautiful. I've missed you so much."

We slotted together in a hug, and I breathed in the sweet scent of her perfume and the essence that was just her clinging to her skin.

"I missed you, too. I don't think I ever want to spend another night apart." She pulled back and caught my eye. "Think that's possible?"

We grinned at each other, happiness and anticipation practically swallowing me whole.

"I'll do my best."

She nodded. "I know."

I wanted to kiss her and make love to her and live until

we were a hundred. I wanted this moment to stretch on forever and I needed it to end so we could start the rest of our lives.

"I have loved you since your first email, at least in some way, and I've been in love with you for a long time now."

"Since January?" she asked, already knowing the truth since we'd exchanged these secrets between ourselves more than once now.

Shaking my head slowly, I drew her hands up to place a kiss on her knuckles.

"Quite a while before that, if I'd been honest with myself. But definitely from that day. And every day after has only grown that love and shown me how little I knew of love. I had no idea it could be this big and wide and challenging and life-giving. I am so blessed to call you my wife, and I couldn't be happier to marry you again today."

A watery laugh escaped, and she swiped under one eye. "Okay, you have to stop because I don't think Dove is going to appreciate all her hard work getting ruined before we walk down the aisle."

She leaned in, her chin raised, and I pressed a soft kiss to her lips, careful not to get carried away and cause any damage to the lipstick.

"I am so glad you wrote back to that silly fifteen-year-old. I'm so glad you let me keep writing and that you let me in bit by bit. I am so, *so* happy to be your wife and wear your ring and know we're making our home together, that we're choosing each other over and over again."

After another minute of soaking in this moment in ways we hadn't gotten to do, wouldn't have known how to do the first time, she hooked her arm in mine and we walked out into the blazing sunshine together.

Arm in arm, we processed down the aisle flanked by

friends and family and the wildflowers growing in twining, delirious little patches all over the yard toward the rest of our lives—choosing each other and choosing this journey together.

Thank you for reading Tristan and Winnie's love story! I hope you absolutely loved these two sweethearts! Keep reading for a little bonus epilogue, and don't miss Adam and Jo in Inspired By You.

BONUS EPILOGUE

Adam

I wasn't a man who rushed. I ran ten minutes early by nature and training, so running late made my neck itch. But so did this whole situation—my finding out a secret no one else knew about a woman I shouldn't have been spending time alone with.

It was that simple. Jo Malcom belonged with a man like my brother, Ethan. She belonged with someone who could give her everything she deserved and who wasn't too jaded or wary to love her.

That man was decidedly not me.

Still, I found myself rushing to get to her house after every possible mishap befell me, every frustration battered my resolve to leave early, and finally, I walked out of my house five minutes until our time to meet.

I hadn't meant to run longer and harder than I normally did, but maybe I needed the release of energy before I met her again. Or maybe I'd just had a frustrating few days on the job—dead-end leads with an issue we'd been having, frustrating interactions with my grumpiest coworker, and concerns over my quietest.

In any case, after a bit of mental prep on the drive to her tiny second-floor apartment situated above the Scoop storefront, I knocked on her door and braced for it.

She opened the door, smiling broadly, almost wildly, with a glint of such excitement it nearly knocked me off my feet.

"Hello there, friend. Ready to help me craft my next hero?"

The joy and anticipation and that very clear annunciation of *friend* set me at ease as I entered at her gesture inside. "Anything for you, Josie Wade."

Thanks again for reading! Don't miss Adam and Jo (or should I say Josie?) in Inspired By You.

Veterans of Silver Ridge Series

Small Town Veteran Romance

Love Undercover

Romantic suspense light

Back to Silver Ridge Series

Almost Perfect, Book 1

Almost Real, Book 2

Almost Sure, Book 3

Almost Home, Book 4

Almost True, Book 5

Almost Ready, Book 6

The Silver Ridge Resort Series

Unexpected Love at Silver Ridge, Book 1

Second Chance at Silver Ridge, Book 2

Patrolling for Love at Silver Ridge, Book 3

Fire and Ice at Silver Ridge, Book 4

Soldiers Overseas Romances

Sweet Military Romance

The Rambler Battalion Series

Sweet Military Romance

AUTHOR'S NOTE AND ACKNOWLEDGMENTS

Thank you for reading Safe With You! I am so happy to have Tristan and Winnie's story on the page. They've been calling to me for a while now!

Thank you, as always, to my husband and family, and especially my husband for answering questions about tiny military details to keep it real (looking at you, breacher!).

Thank you to Zee Monodee for seeing the joy in this one, and for helping to develop Winnie's people pleasing ARC into the self-actualized place she gets to. Thanks to Amanda Cuff for fixing my commas and finding errors, and thank you to Jamie McGillen for her fastidious final read.

Thank you to my amazing beta readers Amanda and Genny. I so appreciate your engagement with the characters, your sensitive feedback, and your willingness to tell me when something's just not working. This book is absolutely better thanks to your insights.

Thank you to my Facebook group for putting up with my constant requests for help naming Junie, and to my best friend Laura Z for coming in with the winner. I love Juniper/Junie and I love you!

Thank you to Suzan, my amazing alpha ARC reader, and to the many other amazing bookstagrammers and ARC readers who so generously give their time to read and post about the books. Specifically, thanks to Debbie, Toni, Rachel, Elise, Joanna, Cathi, Abby, Angeline, Judith, Hannah, Becky, Madeline, and many more!

And finally, many thanks to *you*. It may sound trite, but I won't ever neglect to say thank you because I truly am honored you've spent your time reading my book.

Now, time to get another veteran settled down ;)

ABOUT THE AUTHOR

Claire Cain lives to eat and drink her way around the globe with her traveling soldier and three kids, but is perhaps even happier hunkered down at home in a pair of sweatpants and slippers using any free moment she has to read and cook. Or talk—she really likes to talk. She has become an expert at packing too many dishes in too few cabinets and making houses into homes from Utah to Germany and many places in between. She's a proud Army wife and is frankly just really happy to be here.

You can also join Claire's facebook reader group for exclusive content and fun: https://www.facebook.com/groups/clairecain/

Website: http://www.clairecainwriter.com

E-mail: Claire@ClaireCainWriter.com

Newsletter sign-up for new releases, exclusives, and freebies, including a free book:

http://www.clairecainwriter.com/newsletter

amazon.com/author/clairecain

bookbub.com/authors/claire-cain

instagram.com/clairecainwriter

facebook.com/clairecainwriter

goodreads.com/clairecainwriter

pinterest.com/clairecainwriter

www.ingramcontent.com/pod-product-compliance
Lightning Source LLC
Chambersburg PA
CBHW050741190726
48285CB00005B/1484